WILLIAM GOLDING

A Moving Target

faber and faber

LONDON · BOSTON

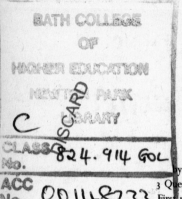
First published in 1982
by Faber and Faber Limited
3 Queen Square London WC1N 3AU
First published in this edition 1984
Reprinted 1988
Filmset by
Wilmaset Birkenhead Merseyside
Printed in Great Britain by
Richard Clay Ltd Bungay Suffolk
All rights reserved

British Library Cataloguing in Publication Data

Golding, William
A moving target
I. Title
824'.914   PR 6013.035

ISBN 0-571-13359-2

Contents

Preface

Five of the pieces included here began as lectures. I say 'began', since over a quarter of a century they have evolved in a curious way which may be worth describing. When you get down to it, what an audience wants to hear from a novelist is how he writes. Since how he writes is in intimate association with what he is and how he lives the novelist finds himself in danger of being his own raw material. If he tries to veer away he is informed politely—or it is discreetly suggested—that other areas are the preserve of specialists and that he had better stick to his own. Readers will remember how Mr Pickwick, a man capable of largeness of mind, made the mistake of veering from his own subject—the Origin of the Hampstead Ponds—to the allied but specialized Theory of Tittlebats and how that roused the scholarly wrath of Mr Blotton who knew tittlebats from A to Z. This is what—they suggest—might happen to the novelist if he strays. This is humiliating to anyone who feels that he might have more than one area of expertise, as it might be a corner of numismatics, music for the crumhorn or the life of St Barnabas of Cappadoccia. Or am I more than usually uninformed, and reporting on an experience uniquely my own? For when I am invited to lecture, after the first approach—'anything you like'—there is always the follow-up—'what our members, brothers, sisters, contributors, alumni, students, would really like is to have you talk about your own work.' I have always tried to resist this and have always given way in the end so that at last I find myself talking about myself with the grossest liberality. This leads to nothing but self-disgust. That disgust is partly responsible for the wide gaps of time that have separated, differentiated and altered these lectures. The earliest ones I gave were purely and simply to make money and free myself from the business of teaching, which I did not like. I took a load of typescript round American campuses, gave the same lecture time after time and ended by knowing it by heart like a part in a play. I could stand aside from myself on the podium and watch myself wooing the audience, being at once shamelessly timid and modestly boastful. I found myself dislikeable and concentrated on the thought of the money. Nevertheless, the lectures altered. Each audience received a very slightly modified version, and indeed, since my mass of typescript contained more than one lecture they tended to transfuse into each other. Years later, I found myself doing the same thing in Europe, not for money, but as a duty—*trade follows the flag*—and perhaps partly to find out whether in fact I *did* know anything, even about myself. What then is a lecture? Is it the last stage? Was there a happier conflation somewhere down the line? The question has been made more complex by the invention of cheap and portable tape-recorders. Since that day the lecturer's sins have followed him like furies. It was bad enough when—as once happened to me—a student had left a concealed tape-recorder running under the chair where I was talking off-the-record, as I thought. He did not bother even to listen as I spoke but turned up as I was leaving, reached under the chair and collected his loot. But a deadlier ploy is that of preserving the lecture with a view to comparing it with later versions. I have seen a member of my audience with a tape running and his earphone plugged in, nodding and smiling as he heard me repeat word for word what I had said somewhere else. It was disconcerting, to say the least. Indeed, I have seen two members of my audience prick up their ears and nod, smiling at each other because though they had no tape they remembered what was coming next.

For there are two sorts of lecture that deserve different names. There is that given by a scholar and teacher to his students. He will eschew—I think 'eschew' is the word—all flamboyance, all emotion, all dramatic shape. He will, as he lectures on tittlebats, hold in contempt anything but an austere eye kept on the business in hand. His not to woo; his only to inform. Then there is the other sort which is, to tell the truth, a show, a performance, a drama. The podium in this case is a stage, nothing but, with a one-man-show in progress. The root of the difference is confused. It is based perhaps in the temperament of the lecturer, his sense of what is fit, his intellectual approach both to aesthetics and ethics. I cannot help feeling, uneasily, that there is a shamelessness about the second sort. For my lectures *have* been performances, all rushed up out of that same mass of paper for an occasion. Truth is single, but so is an occasion!

If now I publish a version it is partly in the hope that to fix the form permanently will be cathartic and discharge me of *this* stuff at least; and if I ever lecture again I shall have to find new material or talk about someone else. On the other hand this may be my lot: in which case I have left the podium, or stage, for good.

A group of these articles consists of book reviews. Here too there has been not so much alteration as adjustment and addition to the previously published versions. Editors generally specify the number of words they require in a review; and I generally find that I have written about twice as many as he has space for. In this book I have restored some of the reviews to the length they were before I cut them to conform with editorial requirement. The article *My First Book* appeared as one of a series by writers in their specialist journal and perhaps this shows in a matter-of-fact approach.

Another group is composed of straight travel articles written for travel magazines. These remain as they were originally published. But the pair *Egypt from my Inside* and *Egypt from my Outside* stand apart from the others. The first was published in a travel magazine as a travel article without any travel. The second followed as a kind of meditation on an actual journey. They are a 'before and after'. The second one makes little sense without the first. So I hereby apologize to the rare book collector who has a copy of *The Hot Gates*, since he will now have paid twice for the same essay. But there was nothing else to be done, except perhaps include an explanation nearly as long as the first of the two essays.

PLACES

Wiltshire

from *Venture*, September–December 1966

There was once a Wiltshire gardener who was given a piece of land to clear. He worked at his accustomed pace—the slow pace of the true countryman, which can be kept up all day and accomplish absolutely nothing. But the land belonged to the vicar, who kept an eye on him and urged him on. At last he had finished and the vicar congratulated him.

'You have done well, my man,' he said, 'with God's help.'

The gardener spat on his spade.

'You should have seen this place, Vicar,' he said, 'when God had it to Hisself.'

It is a long time since God had Wiltshire to Himself. For the last five thousand years, we Wiltshiremen have plodded on, and He, we must suppose, has always added His invisible assistance—though of late years, in view of some of our activities, it may not have been so readily granted. Certainly, when He was alone here, the place was very different. The central structure of chalk down was covered with heather and scrub, and the valleys choked with trees, undergrowth and swamp. Since then, man's slow tread and slow work have changed everything. We have no untouched nature. What we call 'nature' in this country is something so lived-in, so brushed and combed, that it is hardly to be distinguished from a

3

garden or park. Five thousand years of grazing has carpeted our downs with a short and perfect turf. Even the roots of the original flora have rotted away, and we can restore the natural vegetation to the mind's eye only by an elaborate pollen analysis. The rivers are cleared of weeds, and cultivation stretches to the edge of either bank. Some people think that our small patches of forest are remaining portions of unspoiled nature, but they deceive themselves. Savernake Forest, for example, has been tended by woodsmen for eight hundred years. It is a beautiful forest, of course, but not a natural one. It is divided geometrically by rides and planted avenues. Trees that fall do not rot; they are cut up and carted away for firewood. Even the clumps of trees that stand so elegantly here and there on the downs are the work of eighteenth century landscape artists.

The elm trees that seem so natural a backing to a grey village church are not indigenous. They were brought here by the Romans eighteen hundred years ago, so that they might train their vines on them according to the precepts of Virgil. The vines did not take, but the elms remained. So did that most decorative bird, the pheasant, which they brought with them to strut ornamentally in the courtyards of their villas. So did Roman blood, since the legions occupied the land for more than three centuries. Roman blood was mongrel enough, especially that of legions raised in every part of the empire. We—Celt, Roman, Saxon, Danish, Norman—are even more mongrel than they were. To be English—and more specifically, Wiltshire—is to speak English and be used to English ways, nothing more.

What, then, makes Wiltshire different from anywhere else? Why do I, who could live anywhere, choose to go on living here? I believe the answer is that Wiltshire has a particularly ancient and mysterious history that has left its mark in every corner. Almost every question we ask about that history goes unanswered, and tantalizes. The Romans seem modern, compared with the nameless tribes, nations, empires, that rose and fell here before Claudius Caesar conquered the land. It is evident that Stonehenge and Avebury were centres of wide influence and that those who designed them controlled a vast labour force. There must have been a kingdom here, but no one knows the king's name or even what language his people spoke. Silbury Hill may be his grave or cenotaph—perhaps literally his pyramid—but no one knows. If we ever find his body it will be burnt fragments of bone in an earthern pot, and we shall be little wiser than before. Of course there are names attached to places, but they only tantalize again: Wayland's Smithy and Wansdyke refer not to men but gods. The whole land is seamed and furrowed with ditches, erupts with grassy forts and is scattered with the mounds of enigmatic graves.

I do not wish to exaggerate my interest in prehistory. Everyone has heard of Stonehenge; yet it is true that only after you have spent a liftime in Wiltshire do you come to some sense of the richness of event, the subtlety of change and the astonishing age of everything. I could show you a school that was founded only a hundred years ago yet has on its grounds a mound said to be the grave of Merlin.

I could take you to a certain old house, and I believe you would exclaim at its gabled quaintness. You might be sorry to see how a road only a few centuries old lies between it and a river; and how a still more modern road has severed the house from its garden and thrown it back on itself to brood on the encroachment behind a high wall. But then I should tell you what no tourist would have the time to discover: there is another road, that runs at right angles to the others, though it is invisible. It comes up from the river and goes straight under the foundations of the old house. It is the track along which the stone was hauled from Wales—perhaps about 1400 BC, when nameless people were *re*building Stonehenge. This is antiquity on a time scale to compete with Egypt.

Or I could show you the remains of the castle that William the Conqueror built at Old Sarum—inside an Iron Age fort that is inside a Bronze Age one. I could give you a drink in the inn outside the fort, which is still called the Old Castle Inn, though the castle itself was abandoned in the sixteenth century. The Romans built a town near the fort, but it vanished until only the other day, when Salisbury dug drains for a new housing estate and rediscovered Sorbiodunum.

I could take you to Grovely Wood, to a spot known only to three or four people, where you can pick Roman coins out of the mould if you care to take the trouble. In the middle of that wood is a block of sandstone that must have come a long way—and not surprisingly, since it is all that is left above ground of a Roman temple. Yet perhaps the temple has left something behind that is even more enduring than sandstone; for once a year, the young people of the nearby parish go to the woods to have fun and gather green boughs, and come back in procession shouting 'Grovely! Grovely! Grovely!' Nobody knows why, or what 'Grovely' means; but if they had a voice, I think the burnt bones in the buried pots could tell us.

I must be careful not to make Wiltshire sound like a graveyard; yet if I am to explain my own relationship with the county I must . dwell on its antiquity. For me the land had the wrinkled complexity and austere beauty of an ancient face. Certainly it has other beauty too—a width of sky over the downs, a glitter of water, green escarpments, lush water meadows, buildings that seem to grow naturally out of the earth itself. There are the flowers too. Some of them are very rare; and I know one medieval house where you have to be a friend of the family before they will let you into a small wood to see a flower that grows nowhere else in the whole world. It is a beautiful flower as well as a unique one; and alas, I must neither name nor describe it, since I have given my word not to.

We have our wild orchids; and since in this last century we have become aware belatedly of how precious a heritage our flowers are, when the rare ones flower, volunteers stand guard over them. It is an amiable characteristic of the English, this love of flowers; and it is not without significance that we fought our bloodiest dynastic war under the banner of the white or red rose. So my Wiltshire life is, and has been, flowery. I remember the acres of bluebells that look like woodland lakes, anemones and cowslips, wild daffodils, the white daises of a cathedral close, or banks of purple loosestrife hanging over and almost eclipsing the dazzle of a river. Wiltshire has no more flowers than any other part of England; but it is in Wiltshire that I have seen them—buttercups and scabious on the short downland turf, harebells so delicate the weight of a bee will break them, purple orchids that seem to have a private access to the darkness under the mould.

Its history and its flowers seem insufficient reason for living in Wiltshire, and I do not think they can attract tourists. Tourists will not see what I see, for it is invisible. They will not clamber through the woods to find an orchid or a ruin. They will see Stonehenge in daylight with a guide, not at midnight with clouds scudding across a full moon. They will see Salisbury Close and perhaps admire it. They cannot enter every house in turn, or know the astonishing history of each, or the ghost stories that are never written down. They will find us mild, and the country mild. We are not exotic or grand. We have no Yosemite, no Grand Canyon. We have kingfishers, not cardinals; sparrows, not birds of paradise. The airfields and army camps spread. The base at Porton denies it has anything to do with germ warfare——so often that nobody believes it.

I cannot help it if tourists are cheated by travel photographs into thinking that Wiltshire is nothing but greenery, whitewash and thatch, grey stone churches, trout streams and downs and ancient monuments. Wiltshire is a place where most people live because they have to, like all people everywhere. If you ever see morris dancing here, it will be performed by eccentric doctors, university lecturers, solicitors. The few genuine country people left find the dancing incomprehensible and funny. No photograph will reveal the defects we share with you in your own hometown——the bunched telephone wires, road signs, advertisements. It will concentrate on the quaint. It will have discovered someone who can pass for a countryman and will have posed him outside a carefully selected pub, on a fake settle, with a mug of beer in his hand. When the photograph is of whitewashed cottages, the caption will not tell you that these cottages have been taken over by generals, writers, actors and the like, while the villagers live in the housing estates that are more sanitary but wholly unphotogenic.

The most abiding reason why I have lived in Wiltshire for half a century is the simplest of all. Twenty-seven years ago I was walking along a road near my home. I came on an American G.I. He had walked out of his camp to get away from the unbearable closeness of his buddies. He stood under a green bough and looked across the open fields to the downs. His hands were in his pockets and his shoulders were hunched. A fine perpetual drizzle fell through the trees so that the downs were no more than a grey shadow; and if a slight breeze veered toward us it brought an almost imperceptible dampness to lie close on the skin. We fell into talk, and I found that he was desperate to get back to the Bronx. This desperation—and anyone who has fought in a war will recognize it—was so strong that he was nearly sick, hunched glumly, and swallowing now and then. It would not have taken much to add tears to the dampness on his cheeks. He described Wiltshire briefly and pungently, and I forgave him at once. For I too was on leave and had just crossed the dangerous Atlantic from New York, my heart like

> —a singing bird
> Whose nest is in a water'd shoot.

I remembered very well my own desperate longing, and how the thought of Wiltshire when I was in New York had set me swallowing hard and spitting at Manhattan like a cat. Now I was expecting on the morrow to go off to some damned place—no matter how interesting or famous—some *damned* place or other; but for the moment I was in grey, drizzly Wiltshire, and at home.

An Affection for Cathedrals

from *Holiday* magazine, December 1965

Among the virtues and vices that make up the British character, we have one vice, at least, that Americans ought to view with sympathy. For they appear to be the only people who share it with us. I mean our worship of the antique. I do not refer to beauty or even historical association. I refer to age, to a quantity of years. Provided a public man is old enough, we forgive him any folly. Provided a building is old enough, we discount ugliness, discomfort, dirt, and employ a special government department to shore it up. All the religious revolutions of the last five hundred years have affected only the top half of our minds, and left us with a little of the medieval attitude towards relics deep in our British unconscious. This is the most harmless thing left there; but still, it conditions our aesthetic attitudes.

For what is a work of art? Is it the form or the substance? 'Both,' we feel, when we think about it at all, 'but if we must choose, give us the substance.'

There was much outcry when our National Gallery began to clean the dirt of centuries off the old masters. We had got used to being able to catch no more than a glimpse of the original, and to viewing great art, as it were, on a dark and foggy night. Perhaps we felt the Master had said, 'It looks rather gaudy now——but wait for five hundred years till it's really dirty and then you'll be able to enjoy it properly.'

Stone that has mouldered out of shape is left just so. We do not believe that a reconstruction, a filling of the old form with new material, would result in anything genuine. We prefer a lump of the original stone, against which we lean a notice saying: 'Such a work of art as this is irreplaceable. Please do not touch.' On the other hand, one of the most beautiful churches in my part of the country, for which we have to thank an eccentric nobleman of the nineteenth century, is an accurate reproduction of an eleventh century church in the south of France. Yet no one goes to see it; as if we ought to be moved, not by repeated performances of a symphony, but only by the first, with the composer conducting.

A ludicrous belief, you will agree; and yet I must admit, against all sense and reason, that I share it. The truth is, we have a primitive belief that virtue, force, power—what the anthropologist might call *mana*—lie in the original stones and nowhere else. Yet we must know these stones; they must be part of daily life so that we may have adjusted some sensor to the correct wavelength for reception, as you might adjust your eyes to a dim light.

Our old churches are full of this power. I do not refer to their specifically religious function or influence. There is a whole range of other feelings that have, so to speak, coagulated around them. These feelings are worth analysing and the analysis might help us to understand ourselves. I think particularly of the two English cathedrals I know well—Winchester and Salisbury. I can hold models of them each in my head, weighing them against each other. Let me give Winchester every advantage I can think of.

Winchester has had three cathedrals on the same site; and probably a pagan temple before that, since there is a sacred and pre-Christian well in the crypt. Even the present building, begun in the eleventh century, is the accretion of at least four hundred years of construction and four styles of architecture. The city was once England's capital; so the cathedral is stocked with the graves of kings, queens, cardinals and archbishops—a most distinguished crowd who contribute historical perspective. In a desire—which we British understand if no one else does—to share a roof with these top people, hundreds of commoners and minor nobilities have crowded in and got themselves buried in the less fashionable parts of the building. Here, the very stones speak to you in English or Latin or Greek. What they have to say varies from the pathetic to the mildly funny. What precisely is implied by the inscription to Davis Williams D.C.L.? All we are told of him is that

IN THIS CATHEDRAL

HIS POWERFUL AND MELODIOUS VOICE

WAS SINGULARLY IMPRESSIVE.

But I must confess that my favourite is a Royal Navy inscription, stiff-upperlipped, a masterpiece of understatement to

WILLIAM CARMICHAEL FORREST

1ST LIEUTENANT H.M.S. DOTEREL

WHO LOST HIS LIFE BY THE ACCIDENTAL

EXPLOSION OF THE SHIP'S MAGAZINE

AND CONSEQUENT FOUNDERING

OF THE SHIP.

To saunter and read these is a quiet pleasure. One does not need much scholarship to feel the pathos in the memorial of those children

IN ORIENTALI INDIA HEU! LONGE

A PARENTIBUS SEPULTARUM.

You may find your lips twitching at the quotation thought apt for Jane Austen, our demure satirist of English life:

'SHE OPENETH HER MOUTH WITH WISDOM;

AND IN HER TONGUE IS THE LAW OF KINDNESS.'

Doctor Johnson gave it as his opinon that in a lapidary inscription, no man is on oath, but one feels that Miss Austen might have been better accommodated with some other quotation from the Scriptures.

For a Winchester man, might *mana* reside in the statuary? Winchester is crowded with statues. Like the inscriptions, some of them are funny. Those marble parliamentarians, those gesticulating statesmen of the eighteenth century seem to have nothing to do with religion or death. Are they perhaps persons who stepped inside to shelter from sudden rain and had so gross an ignorance of the nature of the place that they harangued the high altar; and were struck so, justly, as an example to those who come after? Sometimes the dust of commoners has taken a revenge and lies on those aristocratic noses to make clowns or masks of them, so that a whole splendid monument seems to hold up nothing but the face of zany. Time has taken an even neater revenge on my favourite Winchester statue. He is a seventeenth century nobleman, just about to set out on a stroll or enter some drawing room. You can see every hair of his wig, every thread of his lace, see even the pattern woven into his silk coat—see, still, the narcissistic smugness written in every line of his complacent face. Below him is the inscription which was to proclaim his lineage and his virtues. But here is the joke: you cannot read a word of it. Some statues carry modern, explanatory notices; but no one has cared to tamper with the anonymity of this alabaster gentleman. There is a gleeful conspiracy to keep him in the state to which the decay of monuments has called him.

Of course, not all Winchester statues are laughable. At the east end is a tiny bronze statue of William Walker, raised by public subscription. He was a diver; and at the beginning of this century when the building was in danger of collapsing into its own soggy foundations, he worked daily for six years, in slime and stinking darkness, until he had underpinned the walls and made the cathedral safe. Winchester thinks highly of him.

Then there is a figure in its own chantry—a small room or chapel where it was intended that mass should be said in perpetuity for the owner's soul. The whole thing looks like a gigantic four-poster; and the figure lies there in bed, apparently asleep. No expense has been spared. The figure is not only carved but enamelled and deceives the eye, as do the waxworks of Madame Tussaud. Even the cardinal's red hat is exact, though stone. To the thoughtful eye, this is not a Christian tomb at all. It resembles an Egyptian one, with a figure provided as an eternal home for the *ka*, the life spirit. Indeed, the apparent security of the figure is no more than a desperate attempt to cheat death, a last throw made by a man who had some considerable acquaintance with sin. This is the tomb of Henry Beaufort, a political churchman, chancellor of England, and so on, whose deathbed in 1447 was one of the most terrible recorded. He tried, in his delirium, to bribe death to pass him by. Shakespeare makes articulate what lies behind the calm figure and the cardinal's hat:

> If thou be'st death, I'll give thee England's treasure,
> Enough to purchase such another island,
> If thou wilt let me live—

It is an eerie tomb; and not all its huddling as near as possible to the shrine of Saint Swithin can keep me comfortable if I stand in that part of the cathedral. If this is *mana*—and I do not think it is—I can do without it. Not the tomb of William Rufus, placed with kingly indifference to the convenience of others, on the centre line of the building so that processions have to divide around it; not those blue-and-gilt coffers with their loads of ecclesiastical and royal bones placed on the surround of the sanctuary; indeed not even Winchester City with its Round Table, its ancient school and holy well can give me what I get from more familiar stones in Salisbury.

I am not the only one who feels so. A few days ago I walked in Winchester Cathedral behind two people from Salisbury. The cathedrals are only twenty-five miles apart and Winchester is the richer. But these ladies from Salisbury did not find it so. Somewhere on the downland road that links the two cities, they had passed an invisible barrier and found themselves outside their own diocese. Winchester, they felt—Winchester, once England's capital—was provincial. What were cardinals and Kings to put against Poore, Longespee, Herbert and Hooker? The stones of Winchester were the wrong shape and the wrong sort. I had begun to eavesdrop in a spirit of kindly amusement, but I found myself to my astonishment agreeing with them. I had come, as I often do, to admire Winchester and be affectionate to it; and it took these ladies to bring me to my senses. I knew I had always felt as they did but had never had the self-awareness to admit it. Winchester *is* made of the wrong stone. It is the wrong shape. It stands on a slope, and it has no spire.

Driving home across the downs, I was now prepared for the

invisible barrier, and heard a distinct 'Ping!' as I passed through it. The barrier was the exact point where Salisbury and Winchester influences were balanced. Like a space probe passing from moon's gravity to earth's gravity I was now hurrying faster and faster towards my own experiences of *mana*. I do not live in the close; but I was going home, and I was going home to the cathedral.

Fifteen miles away you can feel the cathedral begin to pull. It seems ageless as the landscape. You sense that the rivers run towards it, the valleys opening out, each to frame the spike of the spire. As for the roads, where else should they lead? Even today, though motor traffic is imposing a new pattern on the old one, you can see how the tracks make deeply for the spire and draw together at the ancient bridge just outside the close. It has been a long, steady work, this influencing of the landscape, this engraving and rubbing out, this adjusting and twitching of a whole country into place. And *mana*, however subtle, however indefinable, has at least one quality that aligns it with other forces: it varies inversely as the square of the distance. Fifteen miles away it begins to pull; but stand close to the walls and you feel you might click against them like a nail to a magnet.

A critic may bring up the sane, sad theory that you feel this way because the cathedral has become part of your life, and that *mana* is no more than familiarity. Of course there is something in this. Your mind becomes stocked with memories enough to fill the huge building itself. There are vistas you remember as a graded series of pictures, because you first walked there when you clung to your mother's hand. A particular Salisbury monument comes to my mind in three sizes; one when I looked up to it, one when I saw it at eye level, and one, alas, when I stand and look down. There have been the great occasions, celebrations of victory, when orchestras have played and massed choirs sung. There are grotesque memories too—one of a flooded cathedral with a punt moving solemnly up the nave. There are memories of inexpressible beauty: a floodlit cathedral, a magic cathedral under the full moon; a bonewhite spire against the smoke from burning Dunkirk, with the lightning conductors glittering like emeralds; a rose-coloured cathedral, yet washed from below with the reflected whiteness of a million open daisies. There are memories of the cathedral when it seemed no more impressive than a barn. It is a splendid instrument for meteorology to play on, and never looks the same two days running. Yet meteorology is not *mana*.

Does it lie in our statues? We have not so many as Winchester since we have never been so central to affairs. What statues we have are mostly imperfect. The left wing of religion is always knocking our cathedrals about and the right wing makes them over-elaborate. The left wing, the iconoclasts of the seventeenth century, have left their trade-mark in the painted glass—or rather in the absence of it. What enraged them was a face; and sometimes you can see a saint in a window with plain glass where his face used to be. This must have been tremendous fun of course—think of breaking things and being virtuous into the bargain! You can see *their* like any day of the week in a newsreel, turning over cars and breaking shopwindows. One inconoclast was so famous he even got the nickname 'Blue Dicky' for his skill in smashing painted glass with a pike, going from window to window, and as the chronicler says, 'rattling down their glassy bones'.

But there has been another specialist at work in Salisbury. He is nameless and timeless, but you can identify him by his individual psychosis. He cannot see a stone projection without wanting to break it off. Why, in Athens, in the year 415 BC, he was up all night, bashing away at—but that is another story and too indelicate for an essay on cathedrals. In a church he has to be content with noses. It is no good when you walk round Salisbury cathedral and look at our maimed figures to think of a slow decay. Stone noses don't fall off, particularly when an effigy lies on its back and its nose points at the vaulting. Each of these breakages represents an episode, a moment of time. It was darkish, I believe, and the cathedral as nearly deserted as may be, when the little man stole out of the shadows with his hammer. Bash! Clitter clatter! and he is away over the downs, fingering the stung place on his cheek where a minute fragment of Bishop Poore hit him, but giggling and jerking with a possibly sexual excitement which dies down gradually so that he broods on the great days in Italy and Greece, and that wonderful *young* time he had in Egypt, when statues were statues and you had to use a sledgehammer. He left our cathedral with hardly a nose in the place.

Yet he did not injure the building as much as indifference has injured it. In the eighteenth century the fabric was wholly neglected. Anyone who took his religion seriously was dismissed as an 'enthusiast', as damning a label as 'communist' is today. Significantly enough, the cross on the top of our spire was replaced by a useful weather-cock in that century; a mechanism, perhaps, by which the venal and indifferent canons regulated their affairs. If you read the statutes of the cathedral you will find that, during the eighteenth century, not one addition was made. Round about 1760, however, the canons got people to build houses in the close, and gave them a 199-year lease for nothing but the condition that when the lease expired the houses should become cathedral property. Today, these leases are running out and the exquisite houses reverting to the chapter. It was a superbly long-sighted stroke of business that makes Wall Street look like a kindergarten. But these same canons so neglected the cathedral structure that during a storm of about the same date as the leases, the great west window bellied like a sail in the wind, then burst.

Even so, it is arguable that restoration has done more harm to Salisbury Cathedral than indifference. In the late eighteenth century there came a man called James Wyatt. He swept away monuments or altered their position. We had chantries—Beauchamp and Hungerford—clapped like earmuffs on each side of the Lady Chapel. He took them away and re-erected them, one in a public park where children have kicked it to bits, the other in the grounds of a laundry. He pushed the old choir screen into a side chapel. He tore down and threw away the acres of painted glass that the iconoclasts had not reached, and filled the windows with clear glass that lets the daylight in; as if inviting anyone who should pray in the cathedral to do so with eyes open, lest he should be led astray by some sense of awe and mystery, and the feeling that a church is a different sort of place from anywhere else. Wyatt opened vistas in the vast interior as though the building were a gentleman's estate. He was part of the Gothic revival, which was neither Gothic nor a revival but a misunderstanding of a church's function and a misreading of history. The only good thing he did was to reveal the bones of the building itself. Salisbury Cathedral is unique in England because it was built all in one style, like Blenheim or the Crystal Palace.

Round about the year 1200, Bishop Poore was standing on a hill overlooking the confluence of the local rivers, according to legend, when the mother of Jesus appeared to him, told him to shoot an arrow and build her a church where the arrow fell. The arrow flew more than a mile and fell in the middle of a swamp. There, with complete indifference to such things as health, foundations, access and general practicability, the cathedral was built. Eighty years later, with a technological gamble which makes space travel seem child's play, the builders erected the highest spire in the country on top of it, thousands of tons of lead and iron and wood and stone. Yet the whole building still stands. It leans. It totters. It bends. But it still stands; and Wyatt stripped the building to the point where we can see the members of that ancient engineering as clearly as they may be seen in a bridge; so that a model of the cathedral, however small, is a pretty, even an exquisite thing. I have heard rumour that there is in fact a weight-bearing stratum in the swamp; but if there is, and the thing does not float by some miracle, the builders could not have known about it. So it stands, a perpetual delight, a perpetual wonder, with the whole of our little body politic shrugged into shape about it.

Perhaps the wonder is not so visible inside. There, you may be more conscious of the bending pillars, of Wyatt's daylight emptiness in which the soaring stone is too naked, too austere. Yet a Gothic cathedral is never quite without the quirkish and personal. The noseless bishops and knights on their tomb slabs preserve a timeless dignity; but a hundred feet above them squint the faces in which the medieval stonecutter recorded his opinion of the boss. It was never a flattering opinion, but always full of life, always contemporary, with the mordant immediacy of a political cartoon. Tourists seldom examine these faces because they have not the time; and some of these cartoons are nearly inaccessible. But if you have the hardihood to use your binoculars, it is astonishing how the faces leap down. You are looking straight at the life of seven hundred years ago, the life of the tavern and street, the sweaty, brawling, cruelly good-humoured life that later congregated on the Left Bank or in Greenwich Village; and still later was to be debauched finally by television and mass sales into respectability. You can look straight at the work of artists who would never be knighted or win an international prize. In these carvings is the integrity of an art that did not know temptation.

The tourists walk through. Conducted parties group to listen. Sightseers wander. At moments when there is no other noise, you hear always the showering sound of heels on stone. This slow drift goes on all day. If one of the daily services is in progress, part of the building is cut off symbolically by ropes of red silk stretched between pillars. Far off, inside the rope, the choir sings, or you hear the echoing versicles said, not sung, to a congregation of three or four in a dim side chapel. When the major services are held, such visitors as do not wish to take part but are only there to see what the inside of a cathedral looks like, stand grouped under the west windows, with wary vergers to see they don't turn their backs on the high altar. At these times you may see such richness and ritual as the church has retained or renewed from medieval times: gold crosses, candles, a robed choir, priests in glittering copes, bishops and deans in mitres. There will be processions: but in general they will reach the altar by the shortest route. For though the ambulatory is still there, its stones worn by the feet of ancient pomp, the church has rid itself of all that; and there is a perpetual wing of the church that regards even the lighting of one candle as a step toward the fires of Smithfield. When your meditation has got as far as that, you may turn back to the thought of Bishop Poore and his shining faith, with relief. Yes. Let Winchester keep its mixed architecture, its King Alfred, King William Rufus and Saint Swithin. Even though we have only Saint Osmund, a junior saint of whom next to nothing is known, and whose canonization was so much in debate it took centuries of diplomacy at Rome to get him recognized, nevertheless our building is a miracle of faith.

Yet this may have nothing to do with *mana*. A few years ago, when shapeless stones from Salisbury spire were piled on the cloisters, their replacements already in position four hundred feet overhead, you could have seen me stand and regard them with a strange and slightly sheepish, even furtive respect. They were just stone, you might say, that was all. They were not art, they ·were not architecture. They were a formless substance but I could not take my eyes off them. Did I not say we British prefer the substance if we must choose? The historian of religion might mutter about the stones that they were 'relics by contact'. But contact with what? It was *mana*, indescribable, unaccountable, indefinable, impossible *mana*. I think somewhat wryly how I stood the other day in the nave of Salisbury Cathedral, near a local cleric. He watched, with a kind of benevolent suspicion, as I held my hand close to a pillar, then moved it forward and back, like a man trying to find out if he has switched on the bars of an electric fire; but suspicion seemed to be winning over benevolence—so I went away.

Through the Dutch Waterways

from *Holiday* magazine, January 1962

My old boat, the *Wild Rose,* is technically a converted Whitstable oyster smack. She has a sort of eccentric inelegance and ought to be in a maritime museum, for she was built in 1896. My wife and I, with our children David and Judith, planned a trip in her through the canals of Holland and across the old Zuider Zee. We took my friend Viv with us, partly because we like him, partly because he knew a little about Holland and partly because he is the only man I know who can keep the *Wild Rose*'s ancient auxiliary engine running.

We started at Flushing—an ancient port, clinging to, rambling along, and at one point piercing the ancient sea-wall, the dike that surrounds the island of Walcheren. We moved in through two locks, and then into a yacht basin, and at once some Dutch characteristics commended themselves to our notice. Except in show places like Cowes, a yachtsman expects the smell of decaying wood, slime, weed, mud, rusted and insecure ladders, and stanchions which once had a use but now are nothing but paint-threatening hazards. But the yacht basin at Flushing was an oblong of still water with a neat, cemented edge, and a wooden gangway leading round it. At each berth there were piles driven into the bottom, enamelled white, their iron caps picked out in vivid orange. There was no notice forbidding the dumping of rubbish in the water; and there was no rubbish either. There was no rubbish anywhere, unless you count my ancient boat; for the basin was crowded with Dutch craft, eccentric in build, but charming—and all more glossily enamelled than the piles.

We were to find that this is a Dutch habit, and sometimes a mania. When you cannot think what else to do with something in Holland, you give it a coat of paint. Out of any ten Dutchmen you see, as they go about their business, at least one will be covering an object with bright paint—a fence, or a post, or a gate, or a stone, or a hole in the road—anything that has a paint-holding surface.

We had barely realized our status as a slumship in these spotless surroundings when we saw a number of tradesmen waiting for us on the gangway. They took our orders politely, with neither truculence nor subservience. Then they rode off on bicycles. Out of our ten typical Dutchmen, at least three will be riding bicycles. They came back quickly, with goods of moderate price and high standard; and I have always found this to be the case in Holland, whether it be car rental at the Hook, boat rental at Rotterdam, theatre tickets in Amsterdam, a haircut in Groningen, lunch in Enkhuizen or a bunch of flowers in Utrecht. A Dutchman trades fairly, asking a fair price and giving a fair service, and the same cannot be said of Europe as a whole. In Holland a sucker is safe, though frowned on with a sort of tut-tutting compassion.

We stocked up, spent a quiet night and then moved out into the canal that divides Walcheren in two. In the centre of Flushing we came to a bridge and had to wait while it was opened for us. Perhaps because we were in the mood to enjoy anything, the bridge, flooded with traffic and neat and powerful in construction, seemed to us wholly charming. As we approached, the red-and-white bars descended to cut off the traffic, and the middle span lifted. It was a stripped mechanism, functional, with long arms that seemed to need no effort to raise a weight of many tons. Yet the whole was so exactly balanced that there was a dream quality of ease in the movement. Nothing of the whole mechanism but had a use and was confined to it; and yet the occasion, the smooth water, the silent bridge, the calmly controlled traffic, combined to make what I can only call the poetry of order. As we moved through, we exclaimed and nodded to one another. The bridge was so modern, we said, it had the delicate elegance you see in a high-speed plane or racing car. It was the Dutch equivalent of achievements in that engineering world which produced jet aircraft and atomic submarines, the world of streamlining and calculations to the nth. This is not mere tourist country, we said—even their bridges are the newest in the world!

Viv put his head out of the hatch.

'This dam' engine won't run much longer.'

'Never mind,' said Ann. 'Enjoy yourself. Look at that bridge. Whatever will they think of next?'

Viv wiped his forehead with a wad of waste, and peered aft.

'*That* bridge?'

He gave a short, cynical engineer's laugh and disappeared again.

The bridge sank into place behind us and we turned to look forward at the most typical sight in Holland. The canal that would take us across the island lay like a sword-blade, shining and drawn to a point. There were trees looking at us over the bank, clouds and blue sky mirrored, a towpath, and miles away, a huddle of buildings that looked quaint even at that distance.

There was something shining in the air over the houses. At first we thought it might be an airliner catching the sun. But since when have airliners been made of gold and hung motionless? My wife said it was a captive balloon, and the children decided it was a flying saucer. Yet this single gleaming point of light in the soft, blue sky seemed to be causing no distraction. Dutchmen passed along the towpath on their inevitable bicycles, and they were as phlegmatic as ever. Whatever was gleaming there, in a local suspension of the law of gravity, was causing no panic. But could anything in Holland cause a panic? Would not the day of judgement find them doing no more than insuring that the dikes were holding and all accounts in order? With one of those flashes of common sense which come late in such situations, I got out the binoculars and focused them on the gleam.

The huddle of quaint houses was a town—Middelburg, in the centre of the island. The gleam suspended over it was a golden crown; and with the binoculars I could see that this topped a fantastic, not to say frivolous, tower. This, then, is the scene which repeats itself all over Holland—a canal leading to a huddle of houses, with a golden crown hanging over them. Sometimes you see the gleam first, then gradually make out the tower or spire hardening into sight below it. All spires in Holland, apart from the crowns, have an air of modest fantasy. This one at Middelburg rose up first as a tower with tall, lancet windows. The tower supported a bulbous structure, topped at last by the golden crown. The whole thing looked like a graceful piece from some antique chess set.

Viv appeared once more in the hatch.

'You'd better cut the motor.'

'Can't we even go slow ahead?'

'Not unless you want to blow up. What d'you think these blue fumes are?'

There was indeed a faint haze of gasoline round the afterend of the boat. David dropped his book, ran for'ard and hoisted our tattered brown staysail as I switched off. There was the faintest breath of wind to give us way, but so little that the ripples from our bow were moving up and down against the bank before our stern had passed them. Viv sat down on the deck. Ann turned over on the catwalk in the sun, said 'Mmmm!' and went to sleep again.

Holland is a huge country. I say this in the full knowledge that I am stating an apparent paradox. I have flown across Holland in a few minutes. I have driven a car from one end to the other in a single day. But for all that, I declare Holland to be a huge, ample country, full of silences and vast airs. Moving stealthily towards the gold crown over Middelburg, we knew that the right speed for a visitor to Holland is the speed of a slow boat. That way you get the feel of the country into your blood. How else to appreciate the most remarkable quality of geographical Holland, its wide, wide light? The sky seems always not moist, but soft, as though water were hung in it like scent in a girl's hair. The softness conditions the light. We saw no hard shadows, only defined luminosities.

How strange that the Dutch, these foursquare, practical people, these sailors, farmers and engineers, should live in a pastel country that seems woven of light itself! The water-heart of Holland is a scatter of islands—mudpats, if you like—lying at the mouths of the great rivers of northern Europe. They are part of a plain that stretches from the Pennines of England to the Urals in Russia. To be out-of-doors in the water-heart of Holland is like being at sea. Uninterrupted sky comes right down to a horizon that is close at hand at every point of the compass. Whenever we went below, dazzled by this abundance of light, we descended into a darkness that drove us on deck again, into the bland, enormous air, where the fluffy white clouds rode high, and the gold crown sparked nearer. This happened wherever we went. The pastel earth seems to swing like a basket from a balloon of sky.

Halfway to Middleburg we met what must have been almost our only example of Dutch rubbish. We drew alongside a pair of wooden objects floating in the water and found they were castoff clogs. What unusual Dutchman had been so carefree as to fling them into the sparkling water? We felt this was so unlikely that there must have been an accident; and indeed the clogs, floating soles upward, looked for all the world as though a drowned Dutchman were hanging from them, his feet on the surface and his head brushing the bottom. But there was no Dutchman, of course. If there had been, he would have been rescued, neatly and methodically, and fined for causing a disturbance. So the ownerless clogs drifted astern, turning their toes apart slowly.

The Dutch call these wooden boots *klompen*, which is exactly what they are. For presently we passed another Dutchman busy being typical. He was repairing an inch or two of canal bank that had got out of place. He wore bright yellow *klompen* and whenever he moved they went 'Klomp! klomp! over the stones.

Out of our ten Dutchmen we have not many left. One, we said, would be painting something, three riding bicycles—and now we found that another two would be repairing an earthwork. All over Holland all the time, armies are at work repairing earthworks to keep the sea out, or to keep a canal in. In Friesland I have seen them busy in a field in high summer, cutting back the long grass to insure that a mere runnel of water went where it was wanted, and more important still, did not go where it was not wanted.

We docked with surprising neatness in Middleburg, under sail only. David and Judith got the dinghy into the water and sailed it. Viv emerged from the engine room.

'I think she may last a few hours longer now. Next time may I bring my own engine? Ah—Middleburg! Come with me.'

He led us away through the cobbled streets with an expression of deep purpose and stopped at last in front of an antique shop.

'Yes. It's still there. See?'

There was the usual display in the window—every sort of disused article from copper warming-pans, through nineteenth-century jewellery, to some not very inspiring prints.

'See what?'

'Your bridge.'

It was our lovely bridge at Flushing, accurate in every detail, even to the red and white bars that regulated traffic. But *this* bridge was made of wood, and the picture had been made in the seventeenth century.

'They were building that sort of bridge when Newton was writing his *Principia*. It's a design even older than your engine.'

I can hardly describe the revolutionary effect of this discovery on our ideas about Holland. What we had taken, in our innocence, as a triumph of technology, we now saw to be an old Dutch custom. In this country, men have always worked sensibly with things, always made a bank as wide at it need be, and no more, given the span of a bridge the exact thickness it required. That print saved us from making the common tourist's mistake. We were not to be deceived by the fairy-tale charm of the houses, their quaint gables and profuse ornamentation, into thinking that this was a doll's country. The houses were the homes of commercial giants of the seventeenth century, and those imposing buildings backing on to the inner canal, decorated as if for some eternal party, were warehouses that had held the riches of the world.

Yet this love of decoration is a strange quirk in the Dutchman's character. Wherever you go you find even the cottages are not thought properly dressed until they have been set with patterns of different-coloured brick, or plaster moulding. More important buildings—town halls, guildhalls and churches—sometimes break out into sheer fantasy. The result is usually pleasant to see; and perhaps this is reason enough for a practical people.

We strolled back to the *Wild Rose* for supper and an early bed. After we woke next morning we lay for a while enjoying the sight of the roundels of sunlight that fell through the ports and lay so still on the bulkhead and the deck. Nothing is so still as a canal; this is its great charm for sailors. But presently the air became anything but still. We realized it was a Sunday morning, bell-ridden and earnest. The bells shook clouds of pigeons out of every tower into the sunlight, under the gold crown.

We got up to look around us, and now we saw the sight that is featured on posters all over the world. You remember the Dutch girls, smiling out of a flower field, and wearing those white-winged caps? Here in Middleburg we saw droves of ladies pacing through the streets in what is usually described by foreigners as the Dutch National Costume. Now this was not a show put on for tourists. For one thing there are few tourists in Middleburg on a Sunday morning; and for another thing what these ladies wore was not National Costume. These costumes are religious, and the expert can tell by looking at them whether a lady is a Catholic or Lutheran. Nor do the ladies smile as in the posters. They are not attracting tourists. They are going to chapel or church in their Sunday-go-to-meeting clothes.

The costume varies a good deal in different parts of Holland. In Walcheren the ladies wear thick shoes, black skirts, embroidered aprons, bodices and shawls, and white-winged caps. Just beside the ear is placed a curious ornament, and a Dutchman who did not fear to gossip on a Sunday morning told me that its shape proclaims quite clearly which church the lady is going to. Sometimes her ears will be hidden by gold plates like a horse's blinkers; and sometimes she will wear beside them an arrangement of gold wires and springs like antennae. Perhaps the blinkers are to keep the eyes from straying, but if so, as far as I could see they were strictly unnecessary. These ladies were uniformly devout and serious.

The costumes—and we must face this squarely—are of an astonishing ugliness. They are quaint, yes. Whether she be an ancient lady tottering down a cobbled sidestreet under the booming bells, or a child of sixteen who spent her Saturday on the beach in a swimsuit, no female, positively none, can go unregarded in these garments. But to look is not necessarily to admire. Even the men who accompany them, in embroidered waistcoats, velvet jackets and trousers, with gold chains across their stomachs and buttons of coral or topaz—even the men are decorative. They made me remember nineteenth-century illustrations in books by Verne or Twain. They had just that air of floppy inelegance. The women—but there. Even the prettiest girl can make nothing of the Dutch 'National Costume'.

But I must stress that these costumes are *real*. They are not dressing up. They are a part of belief. And since I am on the subject, perhaps I had better add a warning to the tourist. In another Dutch town—I am not going to say which, because the memory still makes me uncomfortable—we went ashore on a Sunday morning, dressed with the innocent eccentricity that goes with sailing. Our women wore slacks. I thought they looked charming, but the older Dutch ladies thought them scandalous. In a square where the fluttering leaves of plane trees sifted the sunlight, we fell in with a flock of Dutch ladies in 'National Costume', who hissed at us like a flock of geese.

It is not my business to remind you how the Dutch have fought for their religion, suffered and died for it. But I bid the tourist to beware on Sunday morning in Holland. He may give offence when it is the last thing he has in mind, or would willingly do.

We stayed in Middleburg for a day or two, then moved on across the island to the north side, and the town of Veere. Then we climbed a vast tower and saw Walcheren spread out below us, and understood something of its nature. Like the other mudpats, it is a pie dish, set in shallow water and resting on the bottom of the sea. If you breached the enormous retaining wall the pie dish would sink, so to speak. Lie in a field, and though you lie among flowers and grass and trees, and are inspected by meditative cattle, you are still below the level of the North Sea.

Veere was quainter than Middleburg. It is an ancient fishing village, with a castle that hangs on the side of the dike like a disused wasp's nest. The town hall is as fantasticated as a wedding cake. Along the quayside the old houses have magnificent doors, painted every colour, and ripe for a museum. But Veere was not yet dead—it has died since—for the little harbour was full of fishing vessels. The prospect of its doom depressed us, so we went through the lock and out into the arm of sea water that lies between three islands—roughly speaking—into the East Scheldt.

England has a lot in common with China. In both countries, customs which at first sight seem downright silly often have a deep layer of good sense tucked away somewhere. Being an Englishman, and understanding this, I did not expect the buoys to mark a precise line between deep water and shallow. I expected, as in England, to feel my way fifty or a hundred yards beyond them. When we passed a buoy, and my son who was heaving the lead remarked that we had about three inches of water to spare, I snorted and carried on. Ten seconds later we were hard and fast aground with the tide falling away from us.

So there we were, under an August sun, watching miles of sand appear, and knowing that we must wait till next day for water. Viv and I, the adult males of the party, decided to walk ashore to one of the islands and buy some grease for the stern-gland which was leaking a bit. We walked over sand, and a mile of almost impossible bog, to the island—one of the Bevelands, which name I take to mean 'Cow country'. We climbed the inevitable dike, picked our way down to the bottom of another pie dish, and walked through farmland which might have been a thousand miles from the sea.

We found a fat, jolly man who kept a garage, laughed a lot and taught us the Dutch for propeller—'SSSSCCChhrrruuufff!' He took us to a bar which was full of more fat, jolly men, all looking exactly alike. When they found that we had crossed the bog they got jollier and jollier, and taught us what the bog was called. It was the 'blubber'. This word rang through the bar, and as they said it they laughed till they shook and the bar shook and probably the island shook too. They produced English coins of the eighteenth century, and musket balls turned up by the plough, and a skull. Then we had to drink from each of the curiously shaped bottles behind the bar.

We soon found ourselves quite able to converse with them as they laughed and we laughed and the skull sat on the bar counter and grinned as if it knew a thing or two. Then just when we were preparing to leave, we found that they proposed to drive us back across the island to a place where the blubber was more negotiable. We all piled into a car which groaned and sagged, and we set off singing a Dutch song. Under the dike we had a last drink with them of whatever it was, shook hands, embraced and swore eternal friendship. In the light of the hot, full moon we could see how the tears glistened down their cheeks—or was it sweat? We slid down the outside of the dike to cries of encouragement and caution. We crossed the blubber taking strides of fifty yards at a time, we cantered through pools and gullies—and there was *Wild Rose* sitting quietly in the middle of miles of moon-bleached sand. So we stood under her stern and sang a Christmas carol until the rest of the crew emerged and threw things.

One of the facts we had grasped from our friends in the bar was that our projected journey by canal to Amsterdam would have to be postponed. It would take us all summer, they said. We should be lucky to make it in a couple of months. They suggested we should all meet there at Christmas. How they laughed! '*Wij wensen u prettige feestdagen!*' A merry Christmas! Far better to go out to sea again, and make for Ijmuiden, where we could find the great North Sea Canal.

So next morning we sailed out between Walcheren and Beveland. You cannot go that way now. We passed between the unjoined ends of a new dike which will cut off all this water, and the machines were dumping earth in the gap as we passed through it. Today, Veere is indeed a museum piece. We bashed a choppy sea and then the wind changed and we fled away up that flat, diked coast, watching the sand yachts on the beach outspeeding us at more than thirty knots, and we were glad when we made the calm waters of Ijmuiden.

Ijmuiden is an artificial harbour on the coast, and you look out of it into the canal. The Walcheren Canal is a blood vessel, but the North Sea Canal is an artery. It is so wide that with an east or west wind the water can be quite choppy. Perhaps on account of a slight change in the weather, the whole atmosphere seemed to be different here. Things were busier, and brisker. Of course the character of the traffic had changed too. Here were the big ocean-going steamers, an unending procession of them, so that now we were dwarfed, and on sufferance. For this canal links the sea and Amsterdam. We began to be thankful whenever we saw a boat of more or less our own size. There were a few Dutch yachts, but they were not being leisurely. Like us, they were trying to get this bit of the journey over. Yet when the wind fell and the water smoothed out, there was a certain charm about the canal. There were strings of barges, ferries, fishing boats bound for the banks, there were even some of those snake-like barges which carry oil and go all over Europe, but only seem at home within spitting distance of a windmill. What a curious and delightful life the families lead aboard them! We passed close by one, clean and gleaming with paint. The mate and his wife and child were living in neat accommodations in the bow. They had sash windows and pot plants. The captain and his family lived in a larger house at the stern, with sash windows and pot plants. They had a front window too, with the ship's wheel in it. The captain was on the wrong side of the wheel to make a signal, so he grunted to his wife, who reached out a hand from where she was cooking and sounded the hooter. The children were playing all over the boat.

If I were not what I am, I would like to be a Dutch bargeman, turning out of the North Sea Canal into a side canal and picking my way between green fields.

'Good morning,' we answered to the mate and his wife as we slid past: and then, further down the street, so to speak, we greeted the captain and his wife, and the children who were half-hidden by potted geraniums put out to air. We got our replies, and altered course to avoid a liner.

As we approached Amsterdam the traffic thickened, for this is the meeting place of a whole net of canals. We were hard put to it not to be nervous of these sliding ships with their thumping screws. It was like being in the port of London, or off Manhattan. The pace was urgent, the pace of Big Business, not the farmer's tread. It was impressive, and perhaps beautiful in a smoky way. Indeed, still prepared to admire, we cried out at all the splendour of a great building which dominates the water front of Amsterdam, only to find out as we came close that it was the Central Station: although why we should not admire a railway station is difficult to explain.

We tied up among the litter of craft beside the ferry which

crosses the river from the Central Station and went ashore for a meal. We proposed to be exotic. Dutch life is shot with influences and memories almost, of the Far East. Dutch cooking is heavy and not very adventurous, except in the big international restaurants in Amsterdam, so we proposed to see what Indonesia had taught them. We found a place in the Leidsestraat where they do the most famous Eastern meal of all. This is *rijsttafel*, to which only gargantuan eaters can do justice. We put ourselves in the waiter's hands and could hardly believe what we got. There was a great quantity of steamed rice as a foundation; and then about twenty dishes each more unusual than the last. We had bits of pork, skewered and cooked in thick sauce, a dish something like the Turkish *Shish Kebab* but more elaborate; we had meat in black sauce and eggs in red sauce. There was meat in coconut milk, cucumber sticks in vinegar, bean sprouts in pastry—there was, in fact, more than we could eat and more than we knew how to eat. In the end we made piles of mixed food on a foundation of rice and literally dug in. There was also a small plate of *sambals*—ferocious peppers, the tiniest taste of which is enough for any palate. Most people leave Amsterdam with a hazy recollection of picture galleries and diamonds. But I remember a steaming pyramid of Indonesian food which took over an hour to eat, and left me as tight as a drum.

Sleepily we clambered aboard. Sleepily we passed under a stupendous overpass and locked out of the canal into the old Zuider Zee.

I had better explain. The old Zuider Zee is a shallow stretch of water measuring about forty miles across and fifty miles in length. It is a real sea. The Dutch won a famous victory on it, with ships of the line, broadsides and all the rest. It is comparable in extent with the English Channel at the eastern end, and it is a challenge, almost a temptation, to the Dutch. As we set out to the north-east, in the direction of the island of Marken, we did not realize that we were sailing over villages and farms already dotted in on the charts. The Dutch propose to reclaim the lot, and when they have done so there will be a perceptible change in the shape of the map of Europe. For the name Zuider Zee is out. The Dutch have rechristened it 'Ijsselmeer' and are cutting it up into 'polders'. At least one polder is made already, a stretch of farmland twenty miles each way. Others are projected, to fill in the rest of the sea.

Travelling by car it is possible to miss the effect of these polders altogether, but stepping *down* from a boat into fields, sitting under a tree, watching the black and white Friesland cattle knee-deep in the lush grass, hearing the charm of birds from a patch of woodland, it can come over you with astonishing force that you are literally sitting on the bottom of the sea, and that is where the Dutch have lived and will live, from generation to generation.

What are they like, the engineers who conceive such a thing? Do they ever dream over a chart, put down a pencil point and think, 'Here we shall plant a beech tree and my grandson will climb it'? Do they ever visualize the actuality of the street corner, at present lying forty feet under water? Certainly, as we moved out from Amsterdam into the Ijsselmeer my own head was full of phantoms. I have listened hard enough for the drowned bells of Lyonnesse off the tip of Cornwall or the Breton coast. But this was listening to the future—an easier thing to do. So we went sailing like a balloon through the streets and woods, the churches and hospitals of tomorrow.

We did not wish to cross to Friesland immediately because a pattern was forming in our minds and there were nearer things to see. The dike at Walcheren was killing Veere. What was being killed by the polders of the Ijsselmeer? We made for the island of Marken, which is only ten miles from Amsterdam and was once as remote as the Americas. It was famous for the costume of its women and a certain boorishness. But when we got there, the dikes were reaching out. Though we could still sail round it, Marken was getting ready to be a part of the mainland. Today, you can drive there in a car.

After a night of backing and filling in the Zuider Zee we came to Hoorn, farther up the coast. Sliding into the harbour in the shadow of a curious tower which looks as though it has been cut in half down the middle, we made fast by a cobbled street. We were so early that we went ashore for breakfast, since the *rijsttafel* had settled nicely. We went through streets where the houses leaned against each other at every angle, as though they had given up. In the central square that is dominated by a statue we found a restaurant.

Dutch breakfast is even bigger than English breakfast. We each got a plate covered with slices of sausage of varying size and thickness, and another plate covered with slices of various cheeses. Then there were rolls, butter, jam—they begin the day well in Holland. At another table a commercial traveller was spreading cream cheese on a piece of firmer cheese and eating the mixture like bread and butter. He saw our appalled curiosity and bowed.

'Is good so.'

Then he added a touch of jam to the cream cheese, perhaps in a spirit of bravado. He was certainly fat enough already. He talked to us with his mouth full.

'You will like Hoorn. Is a good place for visitors. You have seen the statue? There, outside the window!'

He gulped.

'And the museum—there is much strangeness in Hoorn for you.'

'Do you know the town well?'

'I was born here. Once Hoorn is like Amsterdam. But not now. Now is not good for business, for trade, for ships. Is good for tourists.'

He finished his coffee, paid his bill, said goodbye and waddled away across the square.

Hoorn is a piece of real earth. There is a perceptible rise in each street as you approach the square. Ages ago it must have been an island while the rest of the country was still under water. Thus Hoorn has a history as long as any place in Holland, and a long pride to go with it. Was this not the birthplace of Coen, who founded Batavia? Is not his statue in the square to prove it? Once Hoorn was a home port for East Indiamen, but now we shared the port with nothing bigger than a few barges. The town has only a swarm of memories. I saw sights in the back streets that I saw nowhere else in Holland—houses whose paint was peeling, and grass appearing between cobbles. There was an indefinable odour of listlessness. Soon no one will come to Hoorn but tourists; and when that happens to a place, it dies at the very moment they give it a new prosperity. Hoorn, gateway to the Far East, is forty miles from the sea.

We sailed up the coast from Hoorn to Enkuizen, where the men in the fishing boats asserted perhaps a little too sturdily that they would always be able to reach the open sea. We passed on to Metemblik and saw a lighthouse that will one day be out of sight of open water. We had acquired a new sense of change and fatality. Two sides of the Dutch character are at war with each other. The Dutch are great farmers and great sailors. But every time they create a new farm they destroy an old fishing ground. My own sentiment is for water, but the Dutch are more logical. There is much more sea than land; if anything must lose, let it be the sea.

We sailed across to Staveren in Friesland and entered canals again. Friesland, famous for cattle, impressed us most by its barns. These are vast structures with the farmhouses built into one end. They ride in the lush countryside like ships and the foliage of trees breaks against their tall sides like spray. We dawdled in winding canals not much wider than our boat, through an Arcadian country, a land of woods and shallow lakes, and sunshine and flowers. Each little town is a knot of canals filled with small boats of every description. It is a place in which to waste time, to refuse to move, to be indifferent to everything but the birds perched in the rigging, the waterlilies in the side canals, the sun sleeping in a green glade.

And then it was time to think about home.

We returned to the Ijsselmeer and came to our last, perhaps most impressive, vision of Holland. We stood north from Staveren and presently there appeared a stain on the horizon, a stain that hardened, lifted. It looked like a cliff but it was man-made: the Afsluitdyk, the Enclosing Dam. It cuts off the whole of the Ijsselmeer from the open sea, a bank in the sea that is eighteen miles long. There are small harbours of refuge inside it, probably built for the ships that worked on the original construction, but now very convenient for small boats. So we were able to moor, and climb on the bank.

It is stupendous. There is a motorway across it and sheep crop the short turf where so many Germans died in the retreating army. There is an observation tower too, built at the point where the breach was finally closed. There are sluices at either end a hundred yards wide. As the tide falls, the captive waters of the Ijsselmeer run through them and as the tide rises, the sluices close. The rivers of

Holland bring in new water all the time. Nature is harnessed to defeat herself. Hoorn was once a salt-water port; but now the waters of the Ijsselmeer are fresh.

There is a lock at the west end of the Afsluitdyk, but the day was a Sunday; and by a mixture of business and piety only too familiar to an Englishman, the lock was closed on Sundays. So we waited there for the morrow, the Texel and the long haul home.

There was an old Dutchman beside us in his small yacht, who taught us more about the truth of the country than anyone else. He was a very distinguished old man, the equivalent of a judge of the supreme court. When he discovered how much we liked Holland, he expanded. He told us of the awful fix the Dutch were in, with the Ijsselmeer and the project for Port Europe. Both schemes were running out of money.

'But,' said he thoughtfully, 'it is more sensible than making H-bombs, don't you think?'

I looked at the fresh waters of the Ijsselmeer.

'Haven't you done enough,' I said. 'Can't you stop for a moment?'

'While there is still land to be reclaimed? My dear sir! We have a proverb. "God made the world, but the Dutch made Holland." '

And you feel that this is true. You feel it in the opening of a bridge or a lock, in the rich, cultivated earth of a polder, in the sight of a factory, looming like a ship over the level land. Is not this how men should live, making their country and keeping it? On the map of the world Holland is a very small country: but in every way save mere extent of miles it is a very great country indeed.

Delphi

from *Holiday* magazine, August 1967

We set off for Delphi from Athens that morning. The reason we had the road to ourselves was visibly running down the windows of the car, and invisibly buffeting us, so that we slewed sometimes through the puddles on the broken tarmac. Three of us were novelists and the fourth my wife, who yields to no novelist in eloquence. But we were more and more silent as the rain poured down. Though we might have taken comfort in the fact that we were not on horseback, wrapped in sodden cloaks or stumping through the mud with sandals and a stick, we were soft people who liked sunlight, and Greece was grey and wet and windy. The winding road past Cithaeron, where Oedipus was exposed as a baby (poor Oedipus if it was raining), was dangerous with mud. And halfway up, the rain was joined by mist. The road to Delphi has always been dangerous, but never more than now.

It was evening as we began the last thirty or so miles through the mountains. Of all Greek regions, this one has the aptest name—and the most forbidding—Sterea Hellas, which may be translated as Barren Greece. Here what you see is never soft or human, but always gaunt and remote, a land fit for eagles. Where the mountains are accessible for pasturing, the lambs and kids are always guarded lest birds of prey swoop on them. What villages there are, are either the centres of small valleys where a few olives grow, or airy places hung on the sides of cliffs—with, you would think, little reason for being where they are and no resources to fill the pockets and stomachs of the inhabitants.

I felt all this harshness as we rolled and slid on our way, though I could see little of it. To take my mind off the road, I shut my eyes and thought of Delphi, the place we were travelling to see. It is right, perhaps, that one's first approach to Delphi should emphasize remoteness and inconvenience, because here, in the great days of the place, men came on sufferance. The glimpses we were getting were of the skirts of Parnassus—not so much a mountain as a mountain range, and all sacred to Apollo. No good road crosses it. It lies at the hard heart of Barren Greece, dividing the east from the west. At the southern end of the range, Delphi lies right against the face of the mountain.

Yet, I thought to myself, Apollo was only a kind of front man at Delphi. Greek religion came in layers, each age superimposed on an obscurer and more savage one. The layers existed together, since nothing is as conservative as religion. Dig down, and just below the surface you come on human sacrifice and, at the bottom, traces of cannibalism. Also, everywhere, you come on the fact that the religion of primitive Greece was a woman's religion, worship of the Great Mother, the Earth Mother. The male gods came in later, between 2,000 and 1,000 BC. They were energetic and brash, but men knew, uneasily, what was the ancient goddess's due. At Delphi, though Apollo was officially in charge, the oracle was given by a village woman, the Pythia; and she was said to be thrown into a trance by a vapour that rose out of the Earth Mother, a cleft in the earth. Apollo had taken over the oracle. Men said he found a snake there and killed it. What the women said is not recorded. They may have smiled discreetly, knowing in their bones what recent archaeology has revealed as fact—that small clay statuettes of the Earth Mother found in this part of the world date as far back as ten thousand years before Apollo was even heard of.

When Zeus wanted to find the centre of his new estate, the earth, he let a dove fly from either hand, at opposite points of the rim, and they met at Delphi. He was right, in a way. Whichever road you use to reach Delphi, you reach at last a place beyond which you cannot go. You find yourself, you find Delphi, leaning up against the marble knees of Mount Parnassus, as though listening for some communication from the mysterious heart of the earth. It is a locked door. Any advance must be on another plane, an emotional one, a spiritual one.

The silence in the car had lasted half an hour. Peter, who was driving, cleared his throat. 'What's everybody thinking about?'

'Delphi. I was busy believing the legends.'

But Peter knows the classics by heart. 'Let's face it,' he said, 'Delphi became famous in the same way that restaurants, theatres and spas have done—under the immediate patronage of royalty.'

I thought about that as we negotiated a snake-like descent of hysterical complexity. Croesus, King of Lydia, was a man of a thoroughly scientific turn of mind. When he came to the throne he looked for a reliable source of information about the future—wisely, since he proposed to be a conqueror, a notoriously tricky profession.

He decided to conduct an experiment. He sent the same question to every oracle, instructing his messengers to wait until a certain hour of a certain day before they asked it. At the appointed time he shut himself away, and with his own royal hands cut up and cooked a lamb and a tortoise in a bronze pot. The question the messengers asked the oracles at that very moment was: 'What is Croesus, King of Lydia, doing *now*?'

Most of the oracles came out of the test badly, but Delphi performed the apparently impossible. Its answer was clear:

> The smell has come to my sense
> of a hard-shelled tortoise
>   Boiling and bubbling with lamb's
>   flesh in a bronze pot

This convinced Croesus, and he adopted the oracle. Lydia was rich in gold, and the presents he sent were of fabulous magnificence: 117 gold ingots each nine inches wide, three inches thick and eighteen inches long; mixing bowls, casks, sprinklers, basins, all of gold or silver; a gold statue of a woman four and a half feet high; necklaces and girdles for the Pythia; a golden lion that weighed nearly a quarter of a ton. There was no wealth anywhere like it, outside the tomb of an Egyptian pharaoh.

Croesus also sent the reason for it all—the next, the crucial question. His empire bordered on the vast empire of Persia, and he wanted to know whether to declare war on Persia.

'*If Croesus declares war*,' said the oracle with finality, '*he will overthrow an empire.*'

So Croesus promptly invaded Persia and was defeated. His next message to Apollo was reproachful. But the priests of the oracle waved it aside, saying: '*The god said you would overthrow an empire and so you did. You overthrew your own.*'

I spoke my thought aloud. 'Apollo doesn't come out of the Croesus business very well.'

'Ah, said Peter, 'you think of him as a gentleman. He wasn't. He played the lyre, not cricket. Seduction, rape, blind animosity or arbitrary favouritism—you misunderstand the nature of the gods.'

We were silent again. I thought, this time, of the gods, and felt a kind of desire to placate them. It would be like them to burst one of our tyres, or to carve a piece out of the road on the edge of a precipice. But it was a comforting thought in our grinding, skidding car, that in time the gods had suffered more than the men. The old, thunderously selfish answers from the oracles took on a note of querulousness. An ethical tinge appeared in them, as if the gods had been listening to the playwrights and philosophers, or had even got religion. But at last, like an administration on its final legs, listlessly patching things up but unable to achieve the radical change necessary, the gods tottered towards their end. Long before Christianity was born, Delphi was in decay.

We were there at last. We slid around a corner, and ancient Delphi lay above us and below. There was no moon, but even in the starlight we could see the ascending levels of ruins, foundations, walls, heaps of stones and broken columns.

We stopped for a few moments to look. The ruins climbed up away from us until at the top they lay against a sheer cliff. Below us were more ruins, then the darkness of the valley. The air was still, and the only sound was the dashing of water from the Spring of

Castalia, where once the enquirers purified themselves before asking their questions. The cliffs at the top were the Phaedriades, and even in that starlight they seemed to justify their ancient name—Shining Rocks. Silence added to the remoteness and austerity of this locked door into the earth. Then we moved on into the modern village of Delphi, perhaps a quarter of a mile beyond the ruins, where the hotels are good.

When we looked out in the morning, the Greek weather had played a fantastic trick. The sun was shining. A large air had opened over the mountains. We could see down to the Gulf of Corinth, and across it to the mountains of the Peloponnese. Ancient Delphi shone as brightly as the Phaedriades.

We went out quickly, and when the inhabitants of the village saw us coming, they smiled with amusement and pleasure. We were the first swallows of the tourist season. As we approached, each shop opened as by magic, to put out its pots and pans, carpets, rugs and shawls and peasant costumes, until the street looked like a bank of exotic flowers. But sadly, when you have seen one tourist shop in Greece, you have seen the lot. There is some centralizing system by which they are all supplied with the same objects. Everywhere you can buy the gold death-mask of Agamemnon, Nestor's gold cup, Leda seduced by Zeus in the likeness of a swan, goatskin bags, worked leather, and pictures of overpowering inartistry. We passed on.

That morning ancient Delphi, with its steep ascent between broken stones, looked mild and friendly. Everywhere there were trees and flowering shrubs, and crimson anemones hung from the crevices. Outside the museum, the attendants were sunning themselves.

The cobbled ascent of ancient Delphi zigzags between the enigmatic piles of stone. An expert or a local guide can identify these piles for you; and you will find yourself intently observing the base of a wall, or half a dozen paving slabs, and nodding wisely. When you turn away, you will at once forget what the guide said. Far better to wander at your own pace, absorbing the atmosphere, letting the minute observations accumulate, which are what you will remember of Delphi—those flowers, perhaps; the worn capital of a fallen column; the soil plainly loaded with fragments of worked stone or chips of pottery. Then there are those sights that explain themselves—an open-air theatre; a megalithic wall in which the stones, never rectangular but always hexagonal, pentagonal, triangular, are fitted as neatly as a jigsaw puzzle in order to defeat earthquakes; a massive stadium where the footholds for the runners are still clear to see on the starting line.

We stopped by a rather plain, square building.

'It's the treasury of Athens,' said Peter. 'This place was so sacred that all the cities of Greece used it as a kind of bank.'

'It seems in good repair.'

'Rebuilt,' said Peter. 'The stones were scattered all the way down the slope—a thousand feet—right down to the river.'

He pointed up to the Temple of Apollo, where the Pythia gave the oracle, and went on, 'Geologists say there could never have been a cleft in these rocks or a vapour that came out. They say the woman chewed laurel leaves and raved because she was suffering from slight cyanide poisoning.'

I willed myself to take on the difficult role of professional believer: 'Then why were the oracles often so good, so prescient?'

'The priests. Men. So many people came to them from all over the world that they had a complete intelligence system. Pythia mouthed; then the priests decided what she had said, and gave you the official version a day or two later.'

'They were remarkable men,' I said. 'One imagines them so clearly. They were educated, sophisticated, a bit donnish, perhaps. Fretful men of good will who regarded the woman, with her staring eyes and twisted mouth, with a kind of sad compassion. They knew so much more about the world than she did—except for that one dubious, dark quality that might have something in it, for all one's professional disbelief.'

'Exactly so,' said my wife. 'One can almost hear them speaking. "But don't you *see*, dear man? If we say she meant that, it'll mean one of these dreary little wars again." So with the best will in the world they would adjust the oracle.'

'And they could be bribed too,' said Peter

We moved on up the winding path, but more and more slowly.

The sun was so hot now, the light so bright. At the top we found the stadium, scooped out of the crest of a hill that lies against the Phaedriades. It was a bath of heat. From here, if you stand on the edge, you can see a prospect of mountain and valley that is unrivalled even in Greece. It was, I thought, so like a Greek god to choose for himself and his oracle, not the most convenient place nor the most suitable commercially, but the most beautiful. Perhaps for Apollo, beauty and convenience were the same thing. Certainly here, with the Gulf of Corinth blazing like a peacock's tail, with the Shining Rocks, the trees and flowers, and the worn structures of broken marble, one could feel that peace for which the priests of the oracle were so concerned.

'Last time I was here,' I said to my wife, 'the season was in full swing. I heard all the major languages of Europe. There were huge parties, each addressed by its appropriate guide. I thought then that out-of-season was the right time to come. But now I am afraid I shall never understand Delphi.'

'The trouble is,' said she, 'Delphi has become nothing but archaeology.'

'It died long before,' said Peter. 'Do you know the story of the last oracle given here? Julian the Apostate wanted to restore the worship of the old gods when the rest of the world was already Christian. So the authorities fished out a Pythia and went through the ritual as best they could, though it was half forgotten. She went into a trance all right, and some sort of voice spoke through her:

> Tell ye the king: the carven hall is
>   fallen in decay,
> Apollo hath no chapel left, no
>   prophesying bay,
> No talking spring. The stream is dry
>   that had so much to say.

That was the end.'

We were silent, all thinking, I believe, of our favourite Greek village, the name of which shall not appear in print. There the muleteers and donkey drivers wake you at dawn, clatttering in with loads of fish and vegetables, and strange cries. All day, children tumble in the streets or play around the drums of ancient and unexcavated columns. At night, in moon-drenched corners, the grandmothers—the *yayas*—gather, black patches against the white dust, to talk and laugh and sing in cracked voices that seem as old as the place itself. Men wear sprigs of green behind the left ear, and sometimes dance by themselves in the cafés to the sound of the bouzouki and the zither. The poorest village in Greece is never without argument and song and laughter, but in Delphi there is nothing but the broken stones on which we foreigners come to sit and be lectured. It is beautiful and dead.

'I think,' said Peter, 'we are beginning to feel flat. It's time we went down to the museum.'

In the museum we looked at the bronze charioteer. This is the great treasure of Delphi. It is simple and austere, formalized by the robes. The face has a secure, a timeless calm. It illustrates, perhaps, the maxim carved on the west front of the Temple of Apollo: 'Nothing in excess.' It seems so far removed from the dark Pythian inspiration, one wonders how the Greeks ever brought the two together. Like everything else at Delphi, it arouses curiosity and questions that cannot be answered. The door of the earth is locked.

That evening we were still silent. I think it was a silence of disappointment, not with the beautiful dead place but with ourselves. We had expected, with tireless, human optimism, to come to some terms with the riddle of Delphi, yet found nothing. Even when we left, driving back as the light of sunset was still bright on the Shining Rocks, it was with a sense that other, more perceptive people might well discover what we had come for and failed to find. For the oracles given here altered the shape of history. Any oracle consulted both by Alexander the Great *and* Socrates must be taken seriously. In this bland place, so splendidly organized now for tourists, was wrought something of the way in which we live. For all of us, the question continued to nag—a historical question, a philosophical question, perhaps even a religious question. We shall go there again.

Egypt from My Inside

from *The Hot Gates*

When I was seven, I wanted to write a play about Ancient Egypt—not the Egypt of the Badarian predynasts, or of Ptolemy and Julius Caesar, or of General Gordon; but the Egypt of mystery, of the pyramids and the Valley of the Kings. Halfway through the first page of my scrawl, I was struck by the thought that these characters ought to speak in Ancient Egyptian, a language with which I was unacquainted at the time. I abandoned my play therefore and started to learn hieroglyphics; so that I cannot now remember when those sideways-standing figures, those neat and pregnant symbols were not obscurely familiar to me. My inward connection with Egypt has been deep for more than a generation. When my mother took me to London, I nagged and bullied her to the British Museum; and if I think of London now, that museum, with the rich Egyptian collections is at the heart of it.

I do not wish to claim that my interest has been one of exact scholarship or painstaking science. The work of scholars and scientists has brought up massive information which denies the mystery. They are all children of Herodotus, the first Egyptologist. It is entertaining to meditate on Herodotus in Egypt. He was the first, for example, to point out the peculiarly dense quality of the Egyptian cranium, and he brought forward statistical evidence for it. He inspected an ancient battlefield and tried Egyptian skulls against

44

those of their opponents as a child might strike one pebble on another. He found that in every case, the Egyptian skulls were the more durable; a fact he attributed to their habit of shaving the head and exposing it to a nearly vertical sun. Later, the guides showed him some statues of women with their hands lying on the ground before them. They told him these were women who failed to preserve the virtue of a princess, and had their hands cut off as punishment. There the matter might have ended had Herodotus been a decent, credulous tourist. But he insisted on examining the statues for himself. He found that the statues were wooden, that their hands had been pegged on, and in course of time had dropped off. The legend died with a whimper. It was a meeting between two opposite psychic worlds—perhaps even a meeting between two ages. It was common sense and experiment at odds with vivid imagination and intellectual sloth.

I salute the Herodotean method grudgingly and am wary of it. It is a lever which controls limitless power, but a power in which I am not much interested. The method has begotten that lame giant we call civilization as Frankenstein created his monster. It has forgotten that there is a difference between a puzzle and a mystery. It is pedestrian, terrible and comic. Because it both bores and frightens me, I laugh at it, and find my image of it in a half-witted countryman and the way he made a discovery. He stood there with his beer, describing his first day-trip to London. He dropped statement after statement into the ruminative silence. He told how a nice young lady spoke to him in the street. Very friendly she was. She took him to her flat, where she gave him a meal and such a strong drink that he missed his last train. Then—would you believe it?—she gave him half her bed; and such was her social perception and delicacy that she didn't wear a nightie, because he had no pyjamas. In the morning, this kind young lady gave him his breakfast, and a warm hug at the door —.

At which point in his story, he stopped suddenly, took the mug of beer from his lips and cried, with a mixture of astonishment and conviction: 'Eh! If oi'd played moi cards roightly, I could 'ave 'ad that wench!'

In dialectical terms, this is an example of the change of quantity into quality, the laborious collection of information which may eventuate in a new theory of the whole. Those to whom the method is their only tool are as dull as they are laborious. They will decide, for example, that a statistical survey of the desiccated bodies of predynastic savages in desert sand, leads them to believe they have discovered the source of the Egyptian conviction that the body would be resurrected and therefore must be embalmed. This is an interesting theory, and relevant, I suppose, to the lurching progress of human society. It gives to desiccated flesh a kind of material dejection, as if it were the body of a dog. What it is not relevant to, is the child, looking down on dry skin and bone, and hearing for the first time a brassy yet silent voice inwardly proclaiming: *That is a dead body; and in course of time that is what you will become.*

I must admit that the Egyptians themselves were partly to blame. They did not always deal with mystery. They declined whenever possible from high art and preoccupation with first and last things into a daylight banality. The ponderous self-advertisement of their pharaohs, the greed of their tomb robbers, the cruelty of their punishments, the dullness of their apothegms, are understandable and recognizable in modern terms. How at home we feel with the foetid Victorianism of some of the trinkets that littered the tomb of Tutankhamen! We recognize as almost contemporary, the dull portraits of stupid burgers with their stupid wives. It is the sort of thing we might very well do ourselves. It is not much worse than the average advertisement or the average television programme. It means no more either. Even on a higher level than this, the level of supreme craftsmanship, the Egyptians are likely to present us with an art we can see round, accept as a notable statement of the transience of life and no more. Look at the gold face mask of Tutankhamen. It is beautiful, but there is weakness in the beauty. It is the face of a poor boy, sensitive perhaps and idealized, but vulnerable. It looks at us, and for all the marvellous trappings of royalty, we see that death is a final defeat. The gold shapes no more than the sad lyricism of Herrick:

> Fair daffodils, we weep to see
> You haste away so soon.

It was not by this I was caught as a child. Indeed, in those days the
boy still lay undiscovered in his tomb. Certainly I was attracted—as
who is not?—by the time-stopping quality of the place and the
climate. I delighted in the copper chisel, left in a quarry five
thousand years ago but still untarnished and shiny in that dry air. I
found poignant immediacy in a schoolmaster's correction of a
copybook text. That classic story, the prints of the last feet to leave
the tomb still visible on the floor in a scattering of sand, shut time up
like a concertina. Yet though I learnt as much as I could of the
language and the script, memorized king lists and all the enneads of
the gods, these things remained peripheral. I must go back down the
years, remember what it was like, and find out what I was after.

There is a museum dusk and hush. It is a winter night and visitors
are few or none. I have had my nose to a showcase for two hours. I
have listed and drawn every object there, every bead, vase, fragment,
every amulet, every figure. I have pored over the blue faience Eye of
Osiris until that impersonal stare has made me feel as still and
remote as a star. The *Ded*, that tree trunk for which the method will
one day find a Freudian explanation, seems to me a veritable Tree of
Life. I know about symbols without knowing what I know. I
understand that neither their meaning nor their effect can be
described, since a symbol is that which has an indescribable effect
and meaning. I have never heard of levels of meaning, but I
experience them. In my notebook, the scarab, the ankh, the steps,
the ladder, the *thet*, are drawn with a care that goes near to love.

It seems to me, as I lean over the case, that I might get
somewhere—as if I, or someone, at least, might break through a
crust, an obscuration into a kind of knowledge. That feeling makes
me hold my breath—turns my fascination into a kind of desperate
struggle, an attempt to achieve a one-pointedness of the will. Yet
what am I after? What am I trying to discover? For it is not merely a
question of symbols. As I back away, I know there is something else
beyond the glass of another showcase which is vital to
me—something, a language perhaps, a script of which these beads,
figures, amulets, are no more than the alphabet. Man himself is
present here, timelessly frozen and intimidating, an eternal question
mark. Let no one say there is nothing to a mummy but bones and

skin. Reason tells us one thing; but a mummy speaks to a child with a directness that reason cannot qualify. The mummy lies behind glass, and not a visitor passes without stopping to look sideways with an awed and almost furtive glance. He commands attention without movement or speech. He is a brown thing, bound in brown bandages, some of which have flaked away, to show parchment, a knot of bone, and dust. He is at the point where time devours its own tail and no longer means anything. If he has information for the passer-by, it is not to be defined and not to be escaped. His stiff fingers, each showing a single nailed point—except for the right index which has dropped a joint among the bandages—are laid on a quivering nerve of the human animal, which no education, no reason, no faith, can entirely still. If children are not hurried past by their parents, they look, and ask urgent questions. Then comes the crunch, and parents fight a rear-guard action with the example of cut hair and nails and a reminder of heaven. But he is more immediate than heaven; and after a child has studied the gaunt effigy and the silent wooden box with its staring eyes, there is nothing more to be said—no defence against the new half-knowledge that will lend to a grandfather clock or a tall cupboard a subsidiary suggestion their makers never intended.

The mummy lies there, then; and we cannot feel in our bones that it is just a thing, nor that it is indifferent. The hollow eye-sockets with their horn-like lids drawn a little apart, the stick-thin neck, the broken cheek that allows us a glimpse of the roots of teeth, have a kind of still terror about them. It is eternally urgent, as inevitably to be inspected as air is to be breathed. So as I leave my showcase—and the only sound is a door shutting where an attendant prepares to turn the hush into a vigil—I keep the showcase between me and him, then circle, facing him always, till I stand where I can see the naked bones of his head. He excites, moves, disgusts, absorbs. He is a dead body but on permissive show behind glass. So I stand, watching him; and I do not credit him with my humanity. I do something far more mysterious and perhaps dangerous. I credit myself with his. He is part of the whole man, of what we are. There is awe and terror about us, ugliness, pathos, and this finality which we cannot believe is indifference, but more like a preoccupation.

We are so mysterious ourselves. Else, why was I so desperate, so frightened and so determined? Why did my will produce the next step and reveal to me my own complexity? For one day, when I was about ten, and leaning over a showcase as usual, I found a man at my side. He said 'Excuse me, sonny.' He moved me away from the case and opened it with a key. I watched him with respect for he was a curator. He was one with my heroes, Schliemann, Pitt-Rivers and Flinders Petrie, men I believed in touch with levels and explanations that would have surprised them had they known. In some sense, this curator had the hot sand, the molten sun of Egypt lying in his turn-ups. I felt his tweedy jacket had been windblown on a dozen sites. He was big. Was he not what I wanted to become? His face was a little fat, and reddened. There was a ring of sandy curls round the baldness of his head. He was a cheerful man, as I soon discovered, whistling in the hush as if it were not sacred, but so habitual as to be unnoticed. He hummed sometimes to himself, as he arranged the amulets in a pattern which pleased him better. He took notice of me, questioned me, and soon found out that I was as learned an Egyptologist as I could well be, considering my age. At last he asked me—who desired nothing better—if I would like to give him a hand with some work he had to do. We went together through a museum I already felt to be more personally mine, I in the shorts, jersey, socks and shoes of an English schoolboy, he in his tweedy jacket and baggy flannels. We passed out of the Egyptian department, through the hall devoted to relics of the Industrial Revolution, through another hall full of stuffed animals, and up wide, marble stairs to the geological department. One corner of the room had been partitioned off from the rest. There was no ceiling to this part, as I discovered when the curator opened the door with another key and I followed him in. It was a makeshift division in what had once been a room of a splendid and princely house.

But it was a division full of significance. There were rows of green filing cabinets, with papers sticking out of the drawers. There were shelves of books, proceedings of learned societies, and other expensive volumes that I had heard of but could not afford. Lying open on a desk was the British Museum facsimile of the Book of the Dead in all its rich colour. Wherever I looked, things added up into an image of the life I guessed at but had not known, the world of the wise men, the archaeologists. There was a diorite vase, surely from the depths of the Step Pyramid: there was a Greek dish, from Alexandria, perhaps, but most scandalously misused, since I saw a fat roll of cigarette ash in it, and a curl of half-burnt paper. There were predynastic flint knives, and in one corner of the room a broken, sandstone altar, its scooped out channels waiting patiently for blood.

But all these, which I took in at a glance, were nothing to the main exhibits. A sarcophagus, tilted like a packing case, leaned against the left-hand wall. The lid leaned against the wall alongside it, inner surface revealing a white painting of Nut, the Sky Goddess. I could see how the lid had been anthropomorphized, indicating by its curves the swelling of hips and chest, the neat hair, the feet. But the painted face was hidden in shadow, and stared away from us at the wall. Nor did I try long to see the face, because the lid and the box were no more than a preliminary. Before me, only a foot or two away on a trestle table, head back, arms crossed, lay a wrapped and bandaged mummy.

There was a new kind of atmosphere, some different quality in the space between me and it, because no glass kept me away. Glass multiplies space, and things in glass cases have an illogical quality of remoteness. I was not prepared for this difference; and I was not prepared for the curator's casual habitual approach. He stood on the other side of the mummy, hands resting on the table and looked at me cheerfully.

'You can give me hand with this, if you like.'

I could have shaken my head, but I nodded, for my fate was on me. I guess that my eyes were big, and my mouth pinched a little. Yet at the same time there was an excitement in me that was either a part of, or at war with——I am not certain which——my awe and natural distaste for the object. If I have to define my state of mind I should say it consisted in a rapid oscillation between unusual extremes; and this oscillation made me a little unsteady on my feet, a little unsure of the length of my legs; and like a ground bass to all this turmoil was the knowledge that by my approach, by my complicity, by the touch which must surely take place of my hand on the dead,

dry skin, I was storing up a terrible succession of endless dark nights
for myself.

But he had commenced without waiting for more than a nod
from me. He was untying the long bandages that harnessed in the
first shroud. As they came free, he handed them to me and told me
to roll them up and put them on the side table. He hefted the thing
itself and it turned on the table like another piece of wood. It was
much harder inside the bandages and shrouds than you might
suppose, turning with a sort of dull knock. He took off the outer
shroud a large oblong of linen, now dark brown, which we folded,
the two of us, as you might fold a bedsheet—he, holding one end for
a moment with his chin. I knew what we should look for next. Each
limb, each digit, was wrapped separately, and the amulets to ensure
eternal security and happiness were hidden among the bandages.
Presently they appeared one by one as we took the bandages
away—little shapes of blue faience. It seemed to me in my wider
oscillation, my swifter transition from hot to cold, that they were
still warm from the hands of the embalmer/priest who was the last to
touch them three thousand years ago, and who was surely standing
with us now, whenever now was. But our operations had their own
inevitability; and at last I laid my compelled, my quivering and
sacrilegious hand on the thing in itself, experienced beyond
all Kantian question, the bone, and its binding of thick, leathery
skin.

The curator glanced at his wristwatch and whistled, but with
astonishment, this time.

'I've kept you late, sonny. You'd better go straight away.
Apologize to your parents for me. You can come back tomorrow, if
you like.'

I left him standing alone or partly alone, where I knew I should
never dare to stand myself. The face of the sarcophagus was still
hidden against the wall, but the curator was smiling at me out of his
round, red face, under a fringe of curly hair. He waved one hand, and
there was a hank of browning bandage in it, above a brightly lit and
eternally uncheerful grin. I hurried away through the deserted
museum with my contaminated hands to the dark streets and the
long trek home. There I told my parents and my brother in excited

detail about what had happened, was cross questioned, and finally prepared for the terrors of bed.

Now it is important to realize that I remembered and still remember everything in vivid and luminous detail. It became the event of my life; and before I returned to the museum, I talked the thing over passionately, with my parents and myself. I suffered the terrors of bed. I wrote an essay describing the episode when I went to school, and got extravagant praise for it. I brooded constantly about the lid of the sarcophagus with its hidden face. Yet it is important to realize that none of the episode happened at all. From the moment when I stood by the showcase, brooding and desperate, wishing, as singlemindedly as the hero of a fairy tale, till the time when I ran helter-skelter down the museum steps, I was somewhere; and I still do not know where that was. There was no curator with a red, smiling face. There was no mummy, and no sarcophagus. There was a partitioned corner of the geological room, but it contained rolls of maps, not bandages. I looked at the place in daylight and knew myself to be a liar, though I do not think now that a liar is exactly what I was. It was the childish equivalent of the Lost Weekend, the indulgence behind which was my unchildish learning, and my overwhelming need to come to terms with the Egyptian thing. The whole self-supplying episode is a brilliant part of the Egypt from my inside; stands with all the other pictures, the black and gold figures at the final entrance to Tutankhamen's tomb, the Hall of Pillars at Karnak, and all the vignettes, fantastic, obscure, meaningful, that illustrate the Book of the Dead.

But the episode resolved nothing, only made the need bleaker and more urgent. I took my desperation down from the daylight of the geological department and the rolls of maps, and stood once more by the showcase in the Egyptian room, where there was a mummy and no curator to open the lid and rearrange the amulets. All day I wandered, brooding and drawing. As night fell I knew there was still one thing to do. For the face that did not exist on the lid of the sarcophagus that did not exist had been turned to the wall and I had never seen it. But there was a 'real' sarcophagus in the Egyptian collection. It stood on its feet behind glass by the wall. It looked across the room. It was nearly seven feet tall; and however I moved about the room among the showcases it gazed fixedly over my head.

There is nothing quite so real as the eyes of a primitive carving. Everything else may be rough-hewn, approximate or formalized. Indeed, the eyes may be formalized too, but if so, all they exaggerate is the stare. I know that it is necessary to meet that stare, eye to eye. It is a portrait of the man himself as his friends thought he should be—purified, secure, wise. It is the face prepared to penetrate mysteries, to stand pure and unfrightened in the hall where the forty-two judges ask their questions of the dead man, and the god weighs his heart against a feather. It is the face prepared to go down and through, in darkness. I too can go down and through, I can revisit the man with his red face and fringe of hair. I can comprehend and control the silent mummy by meeting those eyes, and understanding them, outstaring them. I go to the opposite wall, though it means being near the wrecked, dead thing. I get one foot on the valve of a radiator and lift myself perhaps eight or nine inches into the air but it is not enough. The mummiform sarcophagus with its carved and painted face still stares over my head as if there were a picture above me on the blank wall. I get down from the radiator and carry a chair from the door, but carefully; for who knows what might move, at a sudden noise? I am trembling, and every now and then, this trembling is interrupted by a kind of convulsive shudder. My teeth are gripped and I am at my apex. I put the chair soundlessly by the wall and climb up, then turn to look across the nearer, bandaged thing to the massive, upright figure. I am at eye-level with the awful, the pure face before its judges; but it does not see me nor a picture on the wall. Those formalized black and white oblongs focus where parallel lines meet. They outstare infinity in eternity. The wood is rounded as in life, but not my life, insecure, vulnerable. It dwells with a darkness that is its light. It will not look at me, so, frightened yet desperate, I try to force the eyes into mine; but know that if the eyes focused or I could understand the focus, I should know what it knows; and I should be dead. On my chair I search for the unattainable focus of its vision in growing fear, until there is nothing but shadows round and under the staring oblongs which have detached themselves and swim unsupported. I scramble down, go quickly and silently away through the halls where the Chinese idols and the eyeslitted suits of armour are friendly, normal things; and outside the revolving doors there are red buses, and wintry-breathing people, and cars.

It will be observed that I do not understand these transactions; which is as much as to say that though I can describe the quality of living I do not understand the nature of this being alive. We are near the heart of my Egypt. It is to be at once alive and dead; to suggest mysteries with no solution, to mix the strange, the gruesome and the beautiful; to use all the resources of life to ensure that this leftover from living and its container shall stand outside change and bring the wheel to a full stop.

'The Egyptians', we are assured, 'were a laughter- and life-loving people. They were earthy. We meet them only in their coffins and get their lives out of proportion.' It may be so; yet for all their life- and laughter-love, that *is* where we meet them. That is what they made of themselves and I cannot see how we are to escape it. Whatever the Egyptians intended, they brought life and death together in the most tangible way possible. Their funerary rituals, their tombs and grave goods, their portrait statues on which no human eye was supposed to rest, their gloomy corridors irradiated with paint, their bones, skin and preservatives—these are not just a *memento mori*. They are a *memento vivere* as well. I recognize in their relics, through the medium of archaeology and art, my own mournful staring into the darkness, my own savage grasp on life. I have said how familiar to me their bad art is. When a shoddy ship model confronts me, with the scale all wrong and the figures no more lifelike than a clothespeg, I am at home in daylight; for it is the sort of model I might make myself. But their great art, I cannot understand, only wonder at a wordless communication. It is not merely the size, the weight, the skill, the integrity. It is the ponderous movement forward on one line which is none the less a floating motionlessness. It is the vision. Beyond the reach of the dull method, of statistical investigation, it is the thumbprint of a mystery.

We are not, for all our knowledge, in a much different position from the Egyptian one. Our medicine is better, our art, probably not so good; and we suffer from a dangerous pride in our ant-like persistence in building a pyramid of information. It is entertaining information for the most part, but it does not answer any of the questions the Egyptians asked themselves before us. And we have a blinding pride that was foreign to them. We discount the possibility of the potentialities of the human spirit which may operate by other means in other modes to other ends. For if we or the Egyptians confine ourselves to the accepted potential, the limits are plain to see. For them perhaps, it was those four pillars, the arms and legs of Nut, the Sky Goddess, beyond which investigation was useless. For us, the limit is where the receding galaxies move with the speed of light beyond all possibility of physical investigation. Yet in their effect on us and in their relationship to those other guessed-at qualities of the human spirit, they are the same limits.

Well. Most of us today are children of Herodotus. But though I admire the Greeks I am not one of them, nor one of their intellectual children. I cannot believe as the sillier of my ancestors did, that the measurements of the great pyramid give us the date of the next war, nor that pounded mummy flesh makes a medicine, yet my link with the Egyptians is deep and sure. I do not believe them either wise or foolish. I am, in fact, an Ancient Egyptian, with all their unreason, spiritual pragmatism and capacity for ambiguous and even contradictory belief. And if you protest on the evidence of statistical enquiry they were not like that, I can only answer in the jargon of my generation, that for me they have projected that image.

Egypt from My Outside

University of Kent at Canterbury, February, 1977

Since the age of seven and perhaps before that, I have had a personal preoccupation with Ancient Egypt as if through its *objets*, history, literature, its imagery and mythology there was something important to be learned that was personal to me and could be got nowhere else. Through poverty, the necessity of doing a job in one place and family commitments, I was never able to go to Egypt itself and it remained the imagined place of half a lifetime. During the Second World War, when asked by the Admiralty where I would wish to serve I replied 'the Mediterranean' and at once found myself in the Arctic. I wrote an essay on my relationship with this imagined country and called it *Egypt from My Inside*. But it was not until the winter of 1976 that my wife and I realized if we did not go at once it might well be too late. We drove off, therefore, in a battered Daimler, I taking an elaborate journal with me. Somewhere at the back of my mind was the feeling that Egypt itself would provide sounding examples of that language which the imaginary Land Of The Nile had seemed always on the point of whispering in my ear. If the imaginary land whispered, how loudly the real place would shout!

Is this a travelogue, then—should it be illustrated in colour? The great Egyptian voyage, the one we all take in some form or other, was not up or down the Nile, but across it, from the land of the living where the sun rose to where it set in the land of the dead. Some kind of acquaintance with that east-west voyage was the reason for our own one from north to south.

The journal that I took with me is one I have added to, volume after volume, for a dozen years. It is one of those refill pads with holes at the side of the page so that when it is full you can clip it into a file. Years of travel have led me to this choice. The pad is pliable and will go in any luggage, stuffed in. The main problem is to find always a good place to rest it in a good light. The trick with a journal is immediacy. Of course there's nowhere near enough time to record everything that happens; but it is astonishing what memories can be reclaimed by a few notes, in total recall—only those notes must be made quickly. There's a constant battle going on between tiredness, abundance and a natural desire to write well, to be, shall I say, vivid and eloquent. Sometimes, if I wake early, even before first light, I get up and do the journal. Which day is that, then, you may ask? Things do get a bit mixed. Or sometimes, when stuck, as for example on a ship, bored to distraction as I am by sea travel, there are many hours to spare and an entry in the journal can widen into an essay, more or less. Then another crowded day may have next to nothing in it except a name and address, the time of an invitation to dinner, and a single sentence that I fondly suppose to be an epigram worth retaining. Sometimes I record ideas for writing but they seldom come to anything. At home my journal might have a record of what is happening in the water garden, or the local scandal. I'm trying to explain what a ragbag of a thing my journal is. If you sow through all that a steady record of my dreams—a record on which some of my psychological or psychiatrical friends seem eager to lay their hands—you can see that its constituents vary from something with a touch of Jennifer's Diary about it to the inside of a blood pudding. I am interested also, to find myself justifying the wide spacing of my novels by the thought that all the time I am writing these millions of words, even though most of them are useless and few meant for permanence. I feel guilty if I miss a day and that seldom, or almost never happens, sick or well, rain or shine. The only other component was suggested by a very old friend of mine. He accused me one day—at least I felt it as an accusation—accused me of being more interested in things and places and ideas than in people. This may very well be true. After that I began to include what you might call character sketches in the journal, beginning with one of my very old friends. I ought to add that the only person who has read what I hope are the more entertaining bits is my wife, not at her insistence but at mine, since pushed out of sight in any writer, no matter how austere a front he presents to others, is the desire for someone to read what he has written.

So we drove off to escape the English winter, from the warm sun of Wiltshire in January down to Venice where it was snowing. We went by car ferry through two ghastly storms to Alexandria where the temperature hovered round freezing. We found ourselves out of imagination but into reality at once. Yet that same reality was also a fantasy. We found ourselves in a cataclysmic social complexity where by reason of the language and the script we were inarticulate and illiterate, knew neither the laws, nor customs nor habits of thought. We were lost at once and might have sunk without trace. At once we found deceit, lying, broken promises, cheating, indifference and an atmosphere which veered hour by hour from sloth to hysteria. At least that was how it seemed; for tourism in the Middle East is organized wholly round the package tour. We, an old man and his wife in a battered car, were fair game. There was civil war in the Lebanon, unrest in Lybia. Alexandria and Cairo were crammed with wealthy refugees—not the sort you see on television but those who got out of the place while the going was good, with all their wealth about them. There were sixteen thousand tourist beds in Egypt with thirty-two thousand tourists in them if not more.

I quote:

> Unwilling to drive in Alexandria unless we had to, we taxied to the tombs which of course aren't Egyptian at all but Roman. They had an oddly theosophical touch—what you might call Blavatski in Latin. But at least the trip got us out of the freezing hotel and the tombs were warmer. When we came out there was a crowd, all arguing as to where we should go next; we knew the Graeco-Roman Museum was open, having passed it

that morning, but the crowd knew it was shut and they won. Tired already, demoralized and realizing that we were going to be a source of income to anyone in sight we let the taxi driver sweep us off to some sight or other. He flashed us past what must have been Pompey's Pillar into a traffic jam of trams, taxis, trucks, donkeys, cars, camels, mules, wagons, calèches, small boys pushing hand barrows—he ran us into such a packed randomness, such violent immobility that even he, clearly a master of brutal noise and speed, gave up and drove sideways into the slummiest alleys where both he and the pedestrians seemed to agree their lives weren't worth living. He decanted us at a gallery of propaganda pictures in the Quaitbai Fort. These were pictures of the Glories of Egyptian Naval History in which we British figured extensively but not as Jolly Tars or Sons of Neptune or Hearts of Oak but as convenient objects for deeds of Egyptian daring. Our taxi driver came with us and rubbed in the moral by pointing now and then to some heroic Egyptian figure and saying 'Egyptian', then to some victim cowering and pleading for his life and saying 'Inglees'. It was the sort of experience which calls on whatever reserves one happens to have of objectivity, perspective and those high-sounding qualities with which the powerless are wont to console themselves.

However, we were stuck in Alexandria until we could bribe our way into some hotel in Cairo. While waiting therefore we summoned up what courage we had left and determined to drive ourselves out in our own car come what might. We went east along the coast in the direction of Aboukir Bay and Rosetta where the stone was found. We saw a bit of the delta—saw that famous black earth of the valley at last—and on the shore came on one of King Farouk's palaces. We drove for at least a mile through its gardens. There were whimsical bridges and pavilions and the palace itself was a megalomaniac's daydream. However, a strong argument for kings, emperors and all that lot is that they operate like a space race. Granted the illogicality of spending all that money on moonwalks—I don't grant it—we have the results and could not have got them any other way. Kings and NASA operate like nature with her broadcast of ten thousand seeds or a million spores for one plant. Without idiotic wastefulness we should not have all our palaces and gardens and tiny jewelled fragments of the moon for our enjoyment.

In Egypt you learn rapidly what privilege is and you get on its side as quickly as you can and stay there. We persuaded our hotel manager to wangle us a room in Cairo. He did a lot of phoning and provided us with a paper as evidence of the booking. So greatly daring we drove off from Alexandria in the direction of Cairo. We were already wary of information, dismissive of promises and reliant on bribery. This change in outlook was demonstrated when after a hundred miles of desert we came down through trees and saw three huge triangles cutting their shape out of the sky.

'Look, Ann,' I cried in true travel book—or at least article—style, 'the pyramids!'

But she had seen too many things that were not what they seemed.

'Well', she said cautiously, 'they're the right shape.'

Of course our piece of paper from Alexandria meant nothing. We weren't booked in anywhere. We had the whole job of finding a hotel to do all over again. We ended up in a strange kind of restaurant with a bed or two and a large swimming pool about half a mile from the pyramids. The swimming pool had not been cleaned for years I should think. It was full of a kind of green jelly. While we were sitting by it and drinking coffee, a Czechoslovakian Package Tour arrived by the hundreds. Instantly they saw the pool they leapt in with cries of delight. Black slime worked up through the jelly as they disturbed it. If there is any bilharzia in Czechoslovakia that is where it began.

As we now had one of the few beds in this odd place we drove off up to the pyramids by way of an approach road which is not pictured in archaeological journals nor in travel brochures. It is lined with booths, cab ranks, shops and impossibly sleazy hotels. It ends at the sort of pavilion which was built, I suppose, for Edwardian visitors, from which sewage is seeping down the hillside towards the major sign we British have left in the area, a nine-hole golf course. We were already suffering from Gippy Tummy or whatever name you choose for it among the many, and this did not improve our powers of enjoyment or perception. However, we picked our way through the parked cars, the crowds of the package tours, the camels and horses and buses and touts and police. We touched the great pyramid with outstretched fingers. It seemed the natural thing to do. It seemed an instinct—*I am touching the Great Pyramid!*

I had wondered if I should find anything new to say about the Great Pyramid on my first visit. All I could find at first was to admit the difference between the photographs and the thing standing over me, a ponderosity in keeping with the savage desert, but all hanging over a dim green valley of canals, houses and trees, with the occasional minaret. My second thought was that at least fifty per cent of the people who see the pyramids for the first time do so while wondering how long they can hold out against diarrhoea. Here Napoleon told his soldiers that forty centuries of history gazed down on them. I wonder how he felt. He suffered from piles in later life. If he didn't take them to Egypt I should think that was where he got them. We strolled about on that first day. We were pestered a bit but not too much, all things considered. The only things that climb the pyramids now are boys and goats. The goats are black and dotted in silhouette on the lower courses. Realization did come a bit gradually; but then suddenly we were happy to be there and marvelling at the buff, off-white, ochre, brown and grey stones that reared up round us. They do indeed have to be seen to be believed. One's respect grows too for the archaeologists and other tomb robbers who have actually coped intellectually where they could with these ungraspable buildings, climbing up and down, suffocating, crawling under lintels, worming their way along tunnels, trying to get knitting needles or visiting cards between the stones—blasting unsuccessfully to open them, like that caliph who thought they held treasure. Anyone who looked to accomplish anything round there had to think big.

We met two friends from the ship—Americans who worked in Cairo. We went to dinner with them then took off in the dark for the *son et lumière* of the pyramids. The show wasn't at all bad. Of course it romanticized Egypt like the travel posters, of course it was nationalistic and warmly optimistic, full of misinformation; and of course it steered its way like a trick cyclist so as to offend no tourist nation, but within those limits it did what could be done. The Sphynx, no longer enigmatic, had the principal speaking part. The whole thing swept along and was like——was like what? It was like Dvořák's *New World Symphony*, Walt Disney's *Fantasia*. It was the meeting of tourists with their expectations. Now this pyramid lit up, now that, now a door here, now an angle there——now a voice drifted in from half a mile away in the desert, now from startlingly near at hand——it was a necessary vulgarity and most enjoyable. Only the scene stealer, a wild dog from the western horizon of sand, *Anpu*, *Anubis*, despite all the protestations of life and triumph ran and trotted and snuffled in the good old way from tomb to tomb through darkness and light, the unanswerable intruder. There was a young couple near us with two children who were a nuisance but must be recorded as they were part of the occasion; as was also an incredible Norseman who for whatever reason had supposed the *son et lumière* of the pyramids would be under cover! He had come without a top coat or blanket and froze solid. His teeth chattered so that you might have thought that somewhere or other in the schmaltzy music there was a Spanish dancer. A story (credited to the Lebanese refugees) is going round that Nasser once saw this *son et lumière* and was deeply moved by it. He strode forward and said to the Sphynx 'I'm boss round here. I'll do anything for you.' The Sphynx replied, 'Get me an exit visa.'

Next day after breakfast we drove back to the pyramids. From anywhere in the city, even if you can't see them they are difficult to miss. After all, it seems that most of the people in history have been to them, or——one's thoughts tremble on the edge of lunacy——have *wanted* to see them, and this gives them a kind of gravitational attraction. What nonsense! But we found them, gravity or no.

It was profoundly satisfying, after suitable medication, to sit and look or to stroll. After a bit we drove off to the right, round the Great Pyramid and past the others of Chephren and Mycerinos. The whole place is exciting in a way that is not dark or morbid, or mysterious even. It is a barren landscape with shapes, and brilliant sun, and exhilarating from the colours and masses and the juxtapositioning of sand and stones. Ann made a point when she said that she appreciated the pyramids as a texture which would surely vanish if the size were to be reduced. It is useless therefore to make a model of the pyramids! Their texture carved in dense stone is yet full of light and energy, of details not quite repeated but all, as it were, alluding to the Platonic Idea of symmetrically piled oblongs. We watched some young men climb the south-east edge of the Great Pyramid. When they reached the top they were fifty feet higher than the spire of Salisbury cathedral. When I blinked down at my feet, looking away from the too bright sky, the tiny black ants working there seemed as big as the men and as capable of building one of these objects. Chephren's pyramid is smaller but seems graceful in a different way from the Great Pyramid—perhaps because some of the limestone capping is still in place. As for the Pyramid of Mycerinos, though it's a monster like the others, the scale makes one ready to cry out, 'What a delicate little thing!'

Nevertheless, beyond the pyramids there is an old British Army Camp. I think it must have been a telecommunications centre; and here the time-stopping quality of Egypt was evident. Thirty years after we British left there is no sign of decay. Even the notices left pinned to the doors of the wooden huts are not browned but white, with the lettering as legible as ever it was. You might think the conversations of the officers' mess were still hanging in the dustless air.

Our American friends arrived, Mr and Mrs B. They went straight to the kiosk on the hacked-out plain of rock and bought four tickets for entry to the Great Pyramid. It was the crunch. I do not suffer acutely from claustrophobia, but have enough to make long, narrow places faintly intimidating. For sixty years I had felt how awful yet how necessary it would be to enter the Great Pyramid—that ascending passage, less in diameter than the height of a man and perhaps—I could not remember—thirty yards long—should I be able to take it? In the past few days I had built up an even stronger resistance to entry, feeling that we had troubles enough, with Traveller's Tummy and always the risk of finding we had no bed. Now, to my apprehensive bewilderment I found myself with the other three on a kind of conveyor belt activated by Mr B. It was power of command. Glumly I followed the others. We climbed a few huge courses where parties of tourists were sitting like starlings on telephone wires. I adjusted the electronic flash on my camera and came on the other three being shown the *descending well*, an escape route perhaps of men left in the pyramid, if that ever happened. It was as likely to be the way by which the pyramid was robbed, in extremest antiquity.

Then there was the ascending passage, brightly lit but oh my God, *fifty* yards long—or was it a mile? It was brightly lit though and had two wooden handrails on either side of wooden steps.

Sixty years' brooding flew out of the window. My conjectures, my assumptions of darkness and crawling, of confinement and fear were all groundless. I had omitted one thing. The ascent is steep and a little fatiguing. But—admirable engineers that they were!—to a man standing upright because the passage slopes, its working height is not its diameter but a diagonal. The diameter was enlarged in the same measure, effectually, as the tunnel was sloped! As I plodded up the steps, my head more or less between my knees, I felt no claustrophobia at all. Then we came to the great gallery and my imagination boggled because the huge roof stones must have needed strengthening at some time—but what time? Massive angle-irons have been driven between them to clutch them and hold them safe. But when? You are in a place of such age that all you can say is that the angle-irons must be no older than the opening of the pyramid in modern history—a few hundred years? They are rusty with the damp of expirations from millions of passing people. Yet the air seemed fresh for it was still morning outside. All the same it makes a man doubly thoughtful to look up, see how the roofing blocks have been squeezed out of line by pressure and reflect that some day the lot must cave in, even in the Great Pyramid. Here the light is bright too. Railed steps override the strange 'benches' on either side of the gallery. You could see the 'pawl marks' easily enough as well as those angle-ironed blocks of the encorbelling that supports the dreadful weight of stone. At the top of the gallery we ducked into the tomb chamber, empty but for the broken stone sarcophagus, and the black gaping holes that were the inwards ends of the two 'air vents'. I personally was incapable of realizing where I was. There was a dignified 'Sheik of the pyramid' in residence who started to tell us all about it. So I blew the occasion and took flash photographs and felt a fool. I knew intellectually where I was but was astonished by nothing so much as the ease of our penetration, or alternatively my own bravery. We came away and found the descent even easier than the ascent. I would sooner climb two hundred feet in a pyramid than twenty feet up a mast. There was a minute or two of discomfort when we had to wait in the ascending passage, crushed against the wall while a tour party squirmed past us. At that time the ascending passage was full of flesh and breath and *squeeze* and guides shouting to people to keep moving. But then the last fat woman of the tour was past, groaning and breathless. We were free. We clambered down to the end of the ascending passage where some young Italians were playing pop music on a cassette. We came out, the four of us without a word said, and made off for a drink.

I break away from the object of our travel to condense the difficulties that occupy thousands of words in my journal. We were finding the business of living, of getting accommodation, of seeing about visa-extensions and insurance for the car taking more and more of our time. These are the trials from which a package tour would have exempted us though I still think there were many compensations. All the same, in the chaos of Cairo it seemed we might be about to founder without getting any further. We used a Shepeard's guide, not to show us the Glory That Was Egypt but to thread for us the maze of bureaucracy between the stranger and possession of *car-visa*! In one office to which he took me, there were fourteen young men sitting at desks beyond the guichet like an adult education course. Each had to initial our bit of paper; and this is because all these young men were graduates. Sadat, whom we came to admire when we grasped the size of the job he had taken on himself, had promised every graduate a job; and this gloomy parade was one result of it. It was ironic that we might be forced to retreat through ignorance of custom and through sheer mental and physical exhaustion. This was not the Egypt of the museums I had haunted. This was a country inhabited by thirty-eight million Arabs, indifferent, amiable, hysterical. We wanted to get on up the Nile but were always mentally herded back to Cairo by horror stories. I quote:

Today we have been in Egypt for three weeks and spent most of them in the desperate business of getting beds and food and information—the food bad, the beds hard, the information misleading. The fact is, tourism is geared to the groups and we are odd people out. We are tired. The weather is about what it would be in February in England or a little colder. Where have all the flowers gone? We can only stay in this hotel for one more night. We can't batten on the B's. Ann woke this morning and said, 'I'm tired.' I have just been detected talking to myself. I said out loud, 'A proper hill billy buster.' I wonder what that means or gives away in meta-phonetics? If I don't watch out this expedition is going to collapse. Ann has just had a sponge-down in the beastly bath. It's becoming like dressing for dinner in the jungle. I don't think anyone else baths here except the American who does nothing else. He is seven foot tall and we call him behind his back the Elongated American. He croaks on about how unwise we would be to drive up country. We'd be murdered, robbed, raped, starved and run out of Kleenex. He apparently owns an island off Cape Cod and is so rich he is used to boring the pants off people. Talking of pants I must get round to changing mine but it's such an effort.

Next day.

Happy, happy pair! And what extraordinarily generous, life- and laughter-loving friends the good God continues to provide us with! B has met up with a prof of English Studies in the Utopian University! He is on his knees begging us to accept the hospitality of an archaeological institute at Luxor where we shall be loved, cherished, shown everything—what a moving, tear-jerking thought it is, an island of Western civilization! Ann, asked by me now what I should add, said, 'Nothing.' Then, 'Who's it written for?' I said a bit too instantly. 'Us.' 'Well,' she said, 'send us good wishes then, we need them.' So I do. I hope when you reread this you will feel the full weight of your newly restored personalities behind it. God bless you, dear old people, what fun you had though you didn't know it at the time! The skies have brightened, courtesy of the All-Utopian Foundation.

We meet Professor R at the B's tomorrow, I having, spontaneously, and come to think of it, without telling the B's, invited him there.

So cautioned on all sides by Cairene expatriates all of whom regard a drive up the Nile as a penetration into darkest Africa, we left at five o'clock in the morning. Once out of Cairo the slight blemish of dust and perhaps fog that sometimes dims the city was replaced by diamond-clear air. Luxor is four hundred miles from Cairo and as we did not know what state the roads would be in, or where petrol would be found we had prepared to take two days over it. But caution proved unnecessary. The road was good, through magnificently fertile country with the desert on the right. All the pyramids were ranged on its edge in display. They appeared one after the other, the Step, the Bent, some anonymous heaps and at last the pyramid of Meidum, looking, with its broken top, like the plinth for some statue of more than Egyptian grandeur. We got to El Minia absurdly early, so we drove on to Assiut. The place had an Hotel Lotus and we tried it. The lobby was fifty per cent occupied by a huge bed on which lay a man in dirty pyjamas. A woman, huge as the bed, her dirty face made up heavily, sat in a chair by it. With a sort of foolish momentum I asked for food but already wanted the way out. We were shoved into a room across the passage which contained nothing but one single bed. This was flattering in a way but the one loo in the hotel was filthy so we left, smiling brightly and shaking our heads. Nobody minded. I shouldn't think they mind much in Assiut. It was obviously going to be Luxor or bust. But we reasoned that a country like Egypt with a state of war on its hands would have at least one military road carefully looked after from one end of the country to the other. So it proved to be.

Our minds relieved we could afford to enjoy ourselves. The Nile Valley is wonderfully beautiful. The green of the fertility varies from new green grass through goose-turd green to turquoise. Where the black earth can be seen the crops are lovingly manicured, exquisite patterns of onions, cabbage, lettuce, corn, wheat, oil seed, rye, barley, millet, it may be, and square miles of sugar cane. Along the road there are no villages; or rather every village is a town bulging

with tens of thousands of people, people, people. The countryside
seems as full as the towns; and there we could see the results of
perhaps eight thousand years of co-operation. You could see the
brown and nearly naked fellahin, so like the paintings in all those
museums, working together as if by nature, hundreds of them
hoeing in a line and singing together, hundreds—a corvée
perhaps—clearing a ditch with ant-like method. Everything is
plumed with palm trees and acacias. Through it all the river at a kind
of High Tide, courtesy of the High Dam, glitteringly distributes
largesse and disease with imperial impartiality. Side canals reflect
everything, people, donkeys, camels, the occasional car dating to the
days between the world wars, trucks with a nasty habit of driving at
you to see if you are chicken and the occasional plundered wreckage
from a crash or an irreparable breakdown—and *people*! There is
nothing like it, they swarm, brown as ants or white-clad like their
cocoons, varying in facial colour from light brown to jet black—and
the cliffs of red or yellow sandstone swinging in here and there to
compress the valley and then pushing off practically out of sight so
that for half an hour or more you have a green horizon; and winter
warming up, February becoming at last quite postively un-English!
Windows down, we swept along over the good road. We learnt not
to stop unless nature insisted. To stop was to be swarmed over by
the ants with their clamour of *Baksheesh*, *Baksheesh* and starting was a
great difficulty. They said in Cairo that you don't stop after an
accident but drive on like hell because if you have killed anyone you
will be killed by the crowd. There is nowhere in Egypt where a
crowd takes more than ten seconds to assemble. We drove as
continually as possible and with great care through the bright day
and hot air. It dawned on me that no one need use any deduction
from archaeology to reconstruct a prehistoric village. We were
seeing them. Away from the road and the river and standing like
islands among the patterned fields were now and then closer clumps
of trees among which brown walls were visible—mud walls piled up
and leaning against each other. These were hamlets or perhaps
extended families, with no cars, bicycles or wagons, but donkeys, the
odd camel, and human feet. There were no hoardings, no wires, no
aerials. There were the trees, the people and animals and the brown

walls that grew up out of the material from which they had been made. They were an adequacy and rightness that like the brown and habile bodies of the men were exactly what they had always been. In a way, we were driving through Ancient Egypt.

We had thought it impossible to get lost, but we did. However, it was not so very serious and though we broke the behest of the Utopian Embassy and drove after dark we reached Luxor and our haven.

This institute is an impressive place. It is full of archaeologists and we shall spend a week with them. Some are British but most American. They are flatteringly eager to show us what is to be seen and, my goodness, Luxor is of course where it's at in Egyptological terms. Indeed, we have struck lucky. We have the additional luck to be here when they are entertaining an American VIP of such eminence the Egyptian government has provided him with a body-guard—a vast captain of police who looks at each newcomer searchingly if one is near the VIP, as if he were a dog and the visitor is threatening his bone. I don't want to reveal the VIP's name so shall refer to him and his wife as Gimel and Beth. As a kind of unconscious crusher, Gimel produced a list of his scholastic achievements when we sat down to dinner and they would give away his name if I specified them. They *were* a crusher and I felt like a black-beetle. We strolled after dinner. Luxor lies on the east bank of the Nile behind a fringe of trees. The corniche or riverside drive is loud with the clopclop of the horses pulling calèches and the whisper of *baksheesh*, *baksheesh*. There were huge sailing boats on the river, some of them with the kind of sheerlegs for masts that you see in tomb paintings. Right in Luxor is the temple and Karnak is only a few hundred yards away at the other end of a processional way lined with sphynxes.

I couldn't get to sleep for relief and too much seeing. So I got up at four o'clock to fill in my journal.

The temple here is a stone's throw away outside the window.

The Nile itself is no more than fifty yards away. I can realize none of these things. It is now half past four, near enough and as far as realizing where I am, that is, solidly in Egypt after more than sixty years of wanting to be there, I might as well be at home. The wall is whitewashed in front of me. I have touched it and told myself where it is and what is more that there is a library of twenty-seven thousand books on Egyptology beyond it but nothing means anything. We have been in Egypt for a month. What is the matter? I am seeing the outside of things when I want to see the inside. Do I know what I mean? Later today we are to undertake the voyage spread out like an unrolled papyrus from here, the lifeside by ferry to the deadside. Perhaps I don't mean anything really. I must have made an assumption somewhere that stone is to be seen into and through, that an image can have its meaning, if not wrenched from it and flung out in words at least absorbed by the mind or the emotions or bit of the human psyche relevant to that sort of transaction. I will be collected, observant and steady. Where I wish to stop and stand and stare I will do so. There *must* be some virtue in a thing seen in its proper place. I will isolate myself in fierceness and concentration. I will see what is there.

Next—no, the *same* morning after breakfast we set out on Luxor's voyage—that short and enigmatic journey across the river to the land of the dead. It is a journey shown with careful gravity in every tomb of any size and on what must have once been millions of papyri. The dead man took with him across the Nile all the possessions which we have since looted in such quantities and scattered throughout the museums of the earth. Now we were to make the trip alive—K, the director of the institute himself, I and Ann, Gimel and Beth and the vast captain of police flourishing his handgun. But on the far shore of the Nile we were not met by catafalques or hearses but taxis which took us noisily to the foot of the brown and yellow cliffs. K, determined that we should have a special treat, took us not the ordinary way into the Valley of the Tombs of the Kings but up the cliff, over a saddle of the mountain then down a threadlike path so that we should approach the valley from the desert. We toiled up, slipping in the loose shale, the Colossi of Memnon far behind us, the Ramessium of Ozymandias not quite so far, the temple of Queen Hat Shep Sut tucked under our left elbows, a temple already crawling with worm-like tour parties all following their leader as we were following ours. We were moving through the splendid photography of the coffee-table books, knowing pretty well what would appear on the next page. But an errant water wagtail from the Nile perched on a rock near us. Ann exclaimed, pointing. The police captain, who by now seemed to include us all in his awful care, flashed his handgun and cried, 'You want I shoot 'im?' It was a dangerous moment being so well protected. Now we could see down into the valley of the Kings, also full of worm tours crawling from tomb to tomb. Gimel drew alongside me. I was recognizing this path we were on. It was a faint, white thread on the first photograph of the valley I have ever seen, in the *British Museum Guide to the Egyptian Antiquities*, et cetera. That was when I was a child, small. It was a shot taken from down there of up here. I had said to myself—he said to himself—'one day I will walk there, alone, because it will be where they walked and I shall feel them.' Want to be somewhere long enough and when you get there you remember wanting to be there. Want as a child and as an old man you do not achieve an ambition. You remember a child wanting. Time is exact or place is exact, not both. The world *is* Heraclitian. You cannot bathe *once* in the same river.

Gimel said conversationally, 'You know I shouldn't have thought writing stories was a full time occupation for a man.'

We descended to the loud valley and went at once to something I had always wanted to see. It was the tomb of Seti I, huge, and everywhere painted in the remote, the inscrutable vocabulary of belief. There was an ancient zodiac on the ceiling, the stars all marked as red spots, the figures quite unlike those we have derived from Chaldaea. The tomb was lit by strip lighting, had wooden steps and handrails and the guided tours came through in every language but Ancient Egyptian or this riddle magic on the walls. Gimel had his guide book out and was reading from it aloud while the police captain, gun out, examined the walls for danger. Yet the illustrations of the journey of the dead, which was identified with, confused with the sun's journey through the sky—through the day then back through the serpent of the night—were mysteriously compelling. In the final great chamber Nut, the sky goddess, appeared twice, back-to-back; and suddenly you see, you *read* in that remote language that she is the sky at day and at night. There was a picture of the dead king in the presence of the High Gods; and this was not only beautiful but deeply moving. Gimel drew my attention to a couple of graffiti in the large niche right down at the deep end. I read that Januarius saw these marvels, and the other in Greek said that Antoninianus marvelled at all these wonderful things. Gimel compared my version with the guide book then nodded in agreement. It dawned on me that he had set me an O-level question in the classics. We came up out of the big tomb and went to the rest-house for a drink. I photographed the rest-house and that threadlike path on the mountain with a feeling of savage irony that I was not sure I understood. Then we taxied away from the entrance to the valley and had lunch in front of the Ramessium. The area round the temple, the *temenos* I suppose it should be called, is full of fragments, the wreckage of Ozymandias among them. He *is* impressive in decay and Shelley wrote like a sixth-form Marxist; but then he hadn't seen the wreck. Suddenly I saw my way. There was a broken scarab beetle on the ground in the grass and near it, Ozymandias's colossal foot, six feet long at least, four feet high and broken off at the ankle. I asked Gimel with a touch of servility to allow me to take a photograph of him. Benignly he agreed. I got him to stand on the foot, one leg behind the other, hand behind his back, as he surveyed the surroundings. He looked down, saw his new foot, smiled, grinned, laughed out loud then hung his head in mock shame. Why bother to use words when there's meta-language lying about in such quantities and of such size? Deliberately he posed so as to make the photograph one of a pompous bore who was always putting his foot in it. Suddenly we were all very good friends, exchanged telephone numbers, addresses, promised to write, to come and to stay. I don't suppose we shall ever see each other again.

So back to the Institute. The police captain that evening was heard grumbling that he'd guarded kings and presidents and they'd had the sense to stay in one place and not go climbing all over the mountains. The last I saw of him, he was sitting in the foyer, gun in hand, his feet in a bowl of warm water.

We spent a splendid week among the archaeologists and were restored to ourselves. We saw the Colossi of Memnon which in ruins are more impressive than most statuary when it is in mint condition. K, the director, took me to climb the mountain on the other side of the river. He is an active young man. At one moment near the top he stopped, turned round and said, 'My God, for a moment I thought that was your last gasp.' But from the top you could see fifty miles of the Nile between its two green strips and endless desert. We saw more paintings which were in tombs the Institute had specially unlocked for us—tombs that were very peaceful indeed. We became accustomed to eating a snack in a kind of broken-down farmhouse where the backs of the Colossi of Memnon were only one green field away from us. Somehow to have experienced them across a crop and from the wrong angle had a more daylight reality about it than the usual critical approach from in front.

Our last day in Luxor came. The next day after us a VIP was coming to Luxor who was so big a VIP that already the top three floors of the Winter Palace Hotel were taken over by his outriders. The VIP had expressed a wish to look over the Institute. When I said I wanted to go to the bank for some money, K, the director, said he'd come too. He'd been summoned to the presence of the Mr Big who was the forerunner of the VIP. When we got to the bank—but I quote from my journal:

K said he wouldn't come in. The bank manager is a huge Nubian who owing to a linguistic misunderstanding believes that K is a devotee of physical fitness. This meant that before K could cash a cheque he had to compete with the manager in doing press-ups on the office floor. He could stand that once a month but not more. He would see Mr Big then wait for me. When I came out with my money he reappeared and at first I thought he was crying but saw soon that he was laughing. He had been frisked twice—once on entering the elevator and once on leaving it. He had been passed from one aide to another and finally been led in to Mr Big in a room full of electronic equipment, with lights flashing and blipping all over the place. He was about to suggest some kind of programme to Mr Big when one of the lights went mad and a microphone voice said, 'Flashback to control, flashback to control, over.' Mr Big said, 'Pardon me,' flipped a switch and said, 'Control to flashback, control to flashback, I have you on band zee q seven. Over.' Whereat the microphone said, 'Flashback to control, flashback to control. Irwin. Those cigarettes. Do you wish kingsize or super?'

We tore ourselves away with determination. Restored as we were we had determined to go further and see if we could drive to Aswan where the two dams are and various curiosities. As we drove off, through country that seemed even more fertile than lower Egypt a deep personal truth forced itself on both of us. It was not just that live people had taken over from dead ones. It was that strangeness of climate, vegetation, civilization, culture, expectation were making it less and less possible to look straight at what we saw. The working boats on the Nile with their huge lateen sails were a lifetime's study in themselves. So was the canal system, come to that, or the railway system where the roofs of the carriages are more crowded than the inside and where it is alleged that until you fall off or are pushed off, you travel free. We had too much to look at and were going blind with too much seeing. Nor, except for the Institute, did we fit in anywhere. We were freaks with our car and our ignorances. But now, driving towards Aswan and less frightened—practically old Egyptian hands in fact—we had come to amend that first panicky reaction to Egyptian society. We had misread most actions. We decided the word 'Gypped' entered the English language as a synonym for 'cheated' because that was what our people in the forces, the police and administration made of the way the Egyptians treated them. For one thing, our countrymen were—and now we as tourists *are*—an occupying force. Then again, it is a matter of custom. Where everyone bribes, nobody bribes. Where everyone lies, in a strange way, everyone tells the truth. Where everyone cheats, everyone is honest. The language of experience in a strange country is every bit as enigmatic as tomb paintings. I have re-examined these statements that seem so paradoxical and find they are true. As we drove on towards Aswan between the layered bare walls of the desert, through a bursting, rioting fertility among the teeming black people—for now they were more Nubian than Egyptian—I began to be in the same degree as I ceased to be frightened, diffident. Women strode along, black, erect, the basalt faces uncovered, their robes of green and flame and gold, the huge water pot balanced on their heads. They were noble, statuesque and caryatid. Some of the men had a pharaonic grandeur about them. What relevance, I thought, have we to them, or they to our purpose? What connection is there between this steel creature I am driving and those dusty feet? What have those feet to do with the painted tombs?

We got to Aswan in the dark and found a room in the New Cataract Hotel. It is luxurious and not expensive as these things go. But the place was so beautiful we did little but tacitly enjoy the beauty without trying to look beyond it. We had had enough culture, it seemed, and at Aswan there are green islands in the river. We wandered on the island of Elephantine and lost ourselves in a Nubian village. We were conducted thence or led, if you like, as prizes thence, by two Nubian boys who were as black as a tar barrel. The toughest said that he was Muhammad Ali and (pointing to the smaller one) that was Mustapha Arafat. The two bashed any other boys who approached. They were worth every penny they cost. We had ourselves rowed from this island to the one that used to be called Kitchener's Island but is now Plantation. It has a tropical garden and we had promised ourselves more quiet enjoyment on the lines of a visit to Kew Gardens. But the moment we landed two Nubian gentlemen in full ethnic costume leapt out from their place of concealment and began to sing, the one meanwhile playing a gusli, the other beating a drum. We paid them to stop, which they did. The place was peaceful after that and it was a pleasure to examine plants rather than paintings. We had glasses of tea at a kiosk in the centre of the arboretum. Here the staff consisted of many Nubian waiters who kept making rough passes at a handsome Nubian lad who was clearly the Miranda of this enchanted island. He spent most of his time hiding in the bushes. We came back to our boat whereat the two Nubian gentlemen appeared again and again burst into song. I was so angry I pointed the camera at them. All that happened was that still singing, still sawing and beating, they moved rhythmically round into a better light. It was an exotic place.

To our surprise and I hope well-expressed pleasure, two of the young archaeologists from Luxor turned up by train and put us back on the proper cultural guidelines from which we had strayed so pleasantly. They showed us the tombs across the river where the painting was of great archaeological interest but varied in aesthetic quality from pedestrian to local yokel. Our young friends were very kind, he finding, she explaining, until we had seen most of everything from the unfinished obelisk to the famous inscriptions on the island further up the river under the Low Dam. My journal comes a bit short on culture at this point as if it were suffering from indigestion. Indeed, the entry for the evening after begins a bit moodily.

I am on the balcony of our hotel room on the eleventh floor. A donkey down there in the Nubian village is venting his immortal anguish, so much more expressive of ludicrous desire, pain and ambiguous ends than a dribbling nightingale! To make a proportion sum of it, he is, this donkey, to a cat on a roof top as a double bass is to a violin. Not that the village down there has any roofs in this rainless area. We look straight down into roofless domesticity. We have a view of the cataract, the twisted rocks, the low dam and the desert. We are here for five nights unless things go badly wrong. In this place never be sure of anything until it has happened and then let your refuge be incredulity. On our balcony this evening we can see that this is an area where electricity from the High Dam is not so much cheap as given away. Up river there is a village like a heap of spangles and beyond that the sky over the dam glows softly like a moonrise in temperate countries. Every courtyard has its light, every hotel glitters and even the desert is scattered with casual sparks as if all the Bedouin are wired for light as well as sound. Below us the Nubians reveal carelessly all the sanctities of home. And indeed why should they care? We are gods up here, cut off, not to be communicated with, given neither power nor responsibility and withering away as gods do when their worshippers desert them. In the middle of the village as night falls is a lighted patch, with robed gentlemen talking by some heaped fruit and a group of little girls like a spilt basket of flowers. There are other children larking about. I should like to know what goes on but cannot. It is not just the distance and height, it is not even the language. It is ten thousand things, few of them definable.

The entry breaks off there and resumes after dinner in what I cannot help feeling is a more cheerfully philosophical frame of mind.

Well. We have had dinner amid the thunder and shouting of the groups in a dozen languages. The wine was awful and when I saw the price I burst out laughing it was so exorbitant. The waiter snatched it away and brought, believe it or not, some stuff called Nefertiti. She was just drinkable. Now, on returning to the balcony it is odd to see what a difference an hour has made to the view. Every camel in the desert must be fitted with headlights. The donkey is still at it, but in mellower voice. Facing us in the south is an archaeological discovery of unique significance. It is the moon. She is filling towards her first quarter but not as in European latitudes, tilted on her beam ends. She lies there afloat on an even keel, her lotus'd stem and stern at equal height. She lies afloat in the deep blue waters over the earth, a veritable boat, voyaging from east to west across the Nile, as boat-like as ever a boat was, but—and perhaps Nefertiti had a hand in this—even rocking slightly. How should they *not* think of solar boats, those people of the wall paintings and pyramids when every month they saw a lunar one? This discovery will make headlines in the Quarterly.

But we were running out of steam. Next day we drove to the High Dam and then beyond into what we found was an army camp where a tank surveyed us with its gun, evilly. So we came back. We flew to Abu Simbel and were less impressed by that phoney advertisement of pharaonic machismo than by the skill of the Italian engineers who lifted it from the riverside to the top of the cliff. But we had seen too much. The nervous strain of trying to live in a country where we had by now perhaps a dozen words and could barely make out the script on the rare signposts; and, of all things, the strains of seeing which after a time burns out the eye so that it rests dully on what should fascinate was wrecking us. Thinking and seeing I suppose to be functions of each other; and in this old land so new to us day after day our eyes were dragged out of our heads by beauty and strangeness. Filled to overflowing, exhausted and reduced to a kind of hysterical tremulousness that the young, and perhaps the rather older than that, cannot understand, we had come to an end. We drove back to the Institute at Luxor, then to Cairo and our friends, then to Alexandria and to sea at last, on the way to Europe. It was then, on board ship with Ann still coughing from the dry air and my eyes half-blinded with strain, that I did try to consider what had happened, what the trip had meant to me and what the relationship was between prospect and actuality. The question resolved itself into one of trying to grasp beyond the records in my journal, with its irritations and complications, the few times I had really *looked* at the wall painting I had waited so long to see. Those times, I found in retrospect, were as complicated and as irritating and fascinating as the rest. I came to write as follows.

I ask myself how the traveller sees when he examines an Egyptian wall painting in a tomb rather than in a museum. The first thing to remember is that he does not see it in a tomb as the word is ordinarily used, at all. Oh yes, there are exceptions, some narrow, difficult tombs! There are tombs where the climb, chute, slide and scramble, the depth and heat add up to such difficulty that only a determined interest in what you have come to see can battle with, and sometimes ward off, claustrophobia. But generally the traveller sees a wall painting in a commodious kind of wine cellar which is reached by a tall corridor. In the more famous examples the corridor is divided down the centre for two-way traffic. The strip lighting is whitish-blue, from mercury vapour lamps I suppose. In the remoter places the lighting varies. In one, the guardian crawled down in front of us. He dragged a smoky hurricane lamp behind him. In

some——and this was interesting in itself——an Egyptian sat outside
the entrance to the tomb itself, caught the sunlight in a mirror and
shot it down the corridor to a second Egyptian who deflected it
round a corner to a third Egyptian whose duty was to catch what
light was left and direct it where the traveller wished to fix his gaze.
All three men tried to keep their mirrors still, but they had to
breathe, their hearts had to beat, the sun himself and the earth under
us were all the time changing their relative positions. The rocks
expanded or contracted in the varying heat; and whatever all this
amounted to was not only caught and transmitted by the mirrors but
by the nature of optics, each mirror, as in an old-fashioned
galvanometer, doubled the movement. Add to this the generous
desire of the third Egyptian to be helpful and keep the mirror
impossibly still and it is clear why the last reflection cast over the
wall fluttered and quivered like a butterfly at a window. Under those
wildly vibrating wings appeared those portions of the painting that
the archaeologists had assured the guardians would be of most
interest——appeared and disappeared, stayed for a shuddering second
or so then gave flittering way to another section. Turn to the man
holding the mirror, he and you dim enough figures recognizable only
by the random side-effects of this elaborate system, and he will smile
agreeably, bow, moving his hands and the mirror so that the
butterfly dashes wildly from the floor to the roof then back again,
perches on your boots it may be and jazzes back up the wall to cover
as much as illuminate a cow and cowherd, a handful of
hieroglyphics, two women walking in step, one hand to the forehead
one to the sky, the ritual tears falling for a grief that is no longer
anywhere to be felt; and the butterfly flits over a god with a bird's
head; and you are lost from all chance of feeling and perception,
because the life of the light, the butterfly, you have come to
understand by way of the bow and the pleasant smile is the
functional end of this chain of service that leads back to open air and
the sun. You become aware of nerves and blood and bone and life
and men, not painted on a wall, not fixing up neon lights and
changing bulbs but here turned into a kind of machinery, the
third-world equivalent of the anglepoise light on your desk at home,
a thing that shines a light where you want it. You concentrate again

on the butterfly at the wall. Probably the artist used mirrors, for the Ancient Egptians had them. They had silver too, and apprentices to hold the silvered plates of copper, or slaves, perhaps. The owner of the tomb will have seen it just so then, many times before he died, eating and drinking with his family at the picnic while the slaves shone the likeness of a butterfly over the painted likenesses of a live man and his hopes and his property. But I was not used to slaves and could not ignore them. That long, angular arm of light, quivering with nerves and the beating of hearts was a service I had never found the trick of accepting without a kind of shame; though God knows there is hard enough work in à mine or power station and I switch on a light without thinking twice about it! So the traveller (to cloak him with a little impersonality) will aim his camera at the dancing butterfly and either catch it as deftly as he can, or use the flash, explode the whole place with an eyeblink of light that leaves green images floating in darkness. He moves out of the tomb wondering what equation he can make between the money in his pocket and the service of the mirror-holders. He thinks to himself that at least he will be able to examine his photograph when he gets home and finds out what was really there.

What was really there! Does that mean anything? Consider.

In the major tombs with mercury vapour lamps which are on the circuits of the package tours you can stare at the murals as long as you like, though your feet will be trodden on and your back nudged every minute or two. Between the tours you *can* wander; but this time the light is wrong, because in the traveller's mind the anglepoise of service or the hurricane lamp have been a necessary part of seeing, like the experimenter being part of the experiment. The light is too steady, too matter-of-modern-fact. Though Pharaoh Seti was a god and indeed *the* god on earth he could not command the sun either to stand still or perch quietly at the fingertip of its own reflection. Every thing is perverse. For here and there the tombs are invaded—a good word—by daylight and the effect is to make them seem smashed and sordid and trivial. Some of the remoter tombs are so complicated with shafts and tunnels they are dangerous. There, where you enter from sunlight to what seems like total darkness you bump into the guardian, who is well named in these cases, for he has gone ahead and stationed himself before a deadly gulf and so prevented you from falling down a hundred feet or more and thus putting the tomb to its original purpose. So you blink slowly into seeing with your own torch or it may be the guardian's paraffin lamp or perhaps a demented butterfly all over again; and as the now familiar pattern of gods and men, demons, property, joy and feasting, death and resurrection pass before you you wonder once more how much *your* life is worth. Add them all together, these efforts to see, experience, understand—I found myself thinking the only way was the natural one, that is to die and to be mummified—a thought so crazy I wondered whether the sun had carried more clout than I thought.

The truth is I carried the wrong equipment with me—naiveté, credulity and that kind of monstrous egotism implicit in a man thinking he might see more than others would. What we had needed on our voyage was something that I at least had always had in short supply, common sense, organizational ability, a methodical examination of the literature, decision in choice of subject, method of examination, judicious apprisal, above all a steady eye and a steady belief—a heavy, heavy burden for those not so equipped by nature.

Only in one way could I say I had seen what I came to see. The beauty was a bonus, the realization of the being of contemporary men a rebuke. But there *was* a vocabulary, a resource of images and these were images of power—not power in the political/social sense but acting directly on the man who beholds them. How should they not? They rose up in the minds of people so like us we might as well call them ourselves. Whoever examines that vocabulary whether it be painted or graven, or made of metal or clay or faience, is looking at his own interior language at some level or other. But to allow that language to carry out its business of transmutation in the less overt, less obvious regions of the mind would require the sort of self-abandonment and long absorption that no traveller can afford to give. If he could ponder these images of his own range the result might well be dangerous. For it is a mixed language, intended to be secret as indeed it is; but so is the language of insanity and some of the language is malevolent and insane, though some is of great consolation and power. I do not mean hieroglyphic inscriptions but the wild, severe and multitudinous mythology. Sometimes in our travels among the tombs, and more and more often as we came away from them, a verse from the psalms kept running through my head. 'Day unto day uttereth speech and night unto night sheweth knowledge.' If you go to the Greek you find that the word for 'uttereth' is not 'uttereth' at all but 'belches' or 'vomits'. That is what day does to day. The knowledge that night shows to night may be some traffic in the unconscious only to be expressed in that beautiful, wise, malevolent and insane language of the wall paintings. I cannot indeed pretend to have seen what night does to night though I may guess at some of it. Perhaps it was in the insolent expectation of some such experience that I went to Egypt. Yet I believe that life is central to the cosmos and that there are some times for some people when the deeps of that cosmos like the deeps of our minds open out.

Men are prisoners of their metaphors. Nevertheless, to speak by the method, so much sun had been emptied over us it was with a ringing head and weary eyes that I had ended by seeing what day had to say unto day. We had bathed in natural beauty. We had seen outrageous wealth and privilege. We had seen a child of fourteen, heavily pregnant and labouring through the sand after her decrepit master. Instead of voyaging to a country and enjoying it I had added unutterable complication and confusion to a simplistic picture. We had heard the hiss of *Baksheesh! Baksheesh!* no longer as a prayer but as a demand and even as a threat. They whisper, 'We crowd in on you with our importunity because our shamelessness is your shamelessness. Give us our share!' I think of the laziness and the amiability, the hysteria and slaving work, the ancient history guarded with tanks and radar and anti-aircraft guns, the desert silence and then the hawk screaming down with talons out to kill. I remember the awful purity of Old Kingdom Art, the Coney Island of Abu Simbel, the drunks and phoneys, friends, archaeologists and artists, the guides and guardians, the river endlessly varied and the same with its smiling glitter and thousand diseases. It is too much. A man moving somewhat eccentrically in Egypt ought to have learnt a lesson from it all. Perhaps the lesson was the quaintness of going to a country of forty million live Egyptians and expecting to confine your attention to the work of half a million dead ones. It has become a vast annexe to life and will make leaving it all the more difficult—life, I mean. Which is perhaps why the Ancient Egyptians tried to take so much of it with them.

Gaia Lives, OK?

Grand Design: The Earth From Above, by Georg Gerster

from *Guardian*, September 1976

In the history of Perception, man's literal 'point of view' like so many other aspects of life has altered with accelerating rapidity during the last few generations. It was only late in the eighteenth century that he could gaze down from a point in the air above the earth's surface with a, so to say, mapping eye. Even in the nineteenth century this was so unfamiliar an experience that Edgar Allan Poe could describe how the earth appeared from a balloon in a way that simply is not accurate. He supposed the horizon to remain always at eye level so that as he rose the earth appeared to curve in the centre like a deeper and deeper cup. In fact the eye as it rises accepts an increasing depression of the horizon. Even the sea navigator after a long passage during which his eye has become habituated to an horizon which really *is* more or less at eye level may find himself accepting any land which appears as at eye level too so that he and his ship seem to be sliding into harbour down hill. The pilot of a plane finds that if he wishes to fly level he must aim at a point higher and higher above the horizon the higher he is flying. He is on the way to seeing the earth as a sphere though he never gets there. Even balloonists twenty miles up and it would seem on the fringes of space must stay in the atmosphere not just physically but psycologically too. There remains the sense of attachment however delicate, the feeling that 'what goes

up must come down' in the normal operation of gravity. These are
no more than advanced states of man's ancient outlook, whether
from tree or hill or mountain—the sidelong glance at a prospect.

Nevertheless, allied to photography the experience of the
stratosphere became accessible to everyone. If the whole round of
earth did not appear, still great cantles of it, whole countries and
whole shapes not to be inspected before now except on maps
became visible. This might have made some change in general
sensibility. To know intellectually that the Mediterranean lies to the
south of England and on the other side of France is not the same
thing as seeing the dark line of water beyond Marseilles in a
photograph taken over Hampshire. But the possible change in
sensibility was to be overwhelmed by the last and greatest expansion
of the human 'point of view'.

Mr Gerster in his present entertaining but expensive volume has
cornered the middle station in the process. He appears to live
neither on the surface of the earth nor in outer space, but in the air
apparently at heights varying from a few hundred feet to about ten
miles. His material is the ruglike stuff that slides by under the wing
of the plane. He has gathered together aerial views of the marks
made on the earth by man's repetitious activities—his farming, his
mining, his forestry, his road or city building. The eye of the camera
lifts for a wide view or swoops in for a detail. The patterns have
interest and some charm. They surprise and occasionally appal. They
are puzzles, some of them not to be solved except by reference to the
letter press. I speak here of pattern for the material itself, its quality
and value, being the earth, is not in question. So a field in the Mato
Grosso makes a good, if uninspired, abstract painting. The island
town of Mexcaltitlan in its lagoon is a piece of modern jewellery, but
not a masterpiece of modern jewellery. Irrigation systems
photographed in black and white only too often resemble the sheafs
of abandoned canvases one sees stacked against the wall in the
studios of aspiring but unsuccessful artists. The lasting memories of
this book must be of the natural features of the earth rather than our
trivial alterations to her skin. For in that respect the coral insects
have had more effect than we have. We see the mountain Jebel Musa
thrust up under a sprinkling of snow and the sight is beyond

description. Here is a hint of the limitations of the whole collection. Mr Gerster has gone high but not high enough.

Our growing knowledge both of the microscopic and the *macro*scopic nature of the earth is not just a satisfaction to a handful of scientists. In both directions it is bringing about a change in sensibility. It is an enhancement to life. We can see crystals in smears of mud at one end of the scale and glimpse the subterranean birth of oceans at the other. Those who think of the world as a lifeless lump would do well to watch out. Only the other day something must have irritated her and with a *moue*, it may be, she wrecked cities from China to the Philippines and blew out the side of a huge mountain in Equador. She must be obeyed. Her mind must reside, I think, in those networks of white fire among the clouds. For if we find electrical discharges coexistent with consciousness, why should we not find consciousness coexistent with electrical discharges? If we ourselves experience a spark of awareness as we cook puddings in our skulls what are we to make of auroras or tropical storms? Dare we guess at the mind that may be staring out at us from the unimaginable violence of the sun; and so on out to the glitter of the farthest star? As children sense first a breast, then an eye, then a face, a whole person, a whole family, so we may be growing up out of our lonely egotism. We can see our mother. Beyond the eye level the next order of significance, of acquaintance, is seen not from the jet plane or the balloon but from the satellite. It is from pictures taken out there in a side-stepping of gravity that we may sense the *pathos* which surely is not fallacious. Since the demise of the tetrahedral theory no one has been able to conceive a pattern in the distribution of hydrosphere and lithosphere and now we might well guess that the very patternlessness is the signature of life and individuality. Arabia and the Horn of Africa are seen to be thrust apart as by striving hands.

Surely, eyes more capable than ours of receiving the range of universal radiation may well see her, this creature of argent and azure, to have robes of green and gold streamed a million miles from her by the solar wind as she dances round Helios in the joy of light.

IDEAS

Surge and Thunder

from the *Spectator*, 14 September 1962

I opened Mr Fitzgerald's new translation of the *Odyssey* (*The Odyssey*, by Homer. Translated by Robert Fitzgerald.) with a foreboding which was not lifted when I saw that he had given each book a catchy little title: 'A Goddess Intervenes', 'The Lord of the Western Approaches', 'A Gathering of Shades', 'The Beggar at the Manor', and so on. This seemed to me to portend a transmutation rather than a translation and to some extent I was right. But Mr Fitzgerald has laboured the Biblical stint of seven years over his book. This devotion brings its reward and his verses have economy, speed and excitement.

> 'Dear friends, no need for stealth: here's a young weaver
> Singing a pretty song to set the air
> A-tingle on these lawns and paven courts.
> Goddess she is, or lady. Shall we greet her?'
> So, reassured, they all cried out together,
> And she came swiftly to the shining doors
> To call them in.

There is a splendid rowdiness about some of the speeches:

> Old Silverbow
> Apollo, if he shot clean through Telemakhos
> In hall today, what luck!

A poet himself, unlike Sir Thomas Browne, Mr Fitzgerald may be excused for thinking he knows exactly what songs the Sirens sang, even though Homer was not so fully acquainted with them:

> This way, Oh turn your bows,
> Akhaia's glory,
> As all the world allows—
> Moor and be merry.
> Sweet coupled airs we sing.
> No lonely seafarer
> Holds clear of entering
> Our green mirror.

The green mirror is forgivable in return for 'Sweet coupled airs we sing,' as a paraphrase of ἵνα νῶϊ τέρην ὄπ' ἀκούσῃς. Then again, the natural descriptions are vivid.

> —nearby
> A cave of dusky light is hidden
> For those immortal girls, the Naiades.
> Within are wine-bowls hollowed in the rock
> And amphorai; bees bring their honey here;
> And there are looms of stone, great looms, whereon
> The weaving nymphs make tissues, richly dyed
> As the deep sea is; and clear springs in the cavern
> Flow forever.

In brief, then, all is eminently readable, enjoyable, highly legible in this sumptuous production, and might be thought to do everything we ask for.

But what *do* we ask for? According to the publishers, we modern readers demand 'living diction, clarity and swiftness', and certainly in this *Odyssey* we get all three. Nevertheless, with Greek slipping more and more out of the education of anyone but the specialist, it may be worth asking how near Homer such a version takes us. For the publishers' claim is based on a false assumption: that there is an ignorant public who, when they find the *Odyssey* on the railway station, between *Bombshell for a Blonde* and *Death Takes a Tycoon* may happen to choose the first of the three without any knowledge that it is more than just another book. But people are not as ignorant as that. The appeal of a translated *Odyssey* will always be to people who want information as much as, if not more than, entertainment, and who know that they are reading a book as remarkable in its way as the Bible.

Homer made concessions to his audience, and Mr Fitzgerald makes them to his readers, but they are never the same ones. He condenses in the interests of speed, he is colloquial in the interests of living diction, he changes his translation of stock phrases or lines in the interests of variety. A simple example is the *'O moi ego'* which Odysseus uses in moments of stress. This is a phrase, colourless as 'Aye me': but Mr Fitzgerald makes of it in one place, 'Who in thunder?', and in another, 'O damned confusion!' These are liberal beginnings to speeches where the eloquence is never pejorative. Transmutation, paraphrase, is one thing, translation is another. The present version may be a more fascinating one than, say, Caulfield's hexameters—and how bad some of *those* were!—but it is less like Homer. The colourless epithets and stock phrases, the repetitions, *are* Homer whether we like it or not; and an attempt to get round them, however much it may startle the groundlings, is nothing more than a falsification of the original.

But, of course, Mr Fitzgerald has taken on a job which has become more difficult even in the last generation. Every age, they say, gets the translation of Homer that it deserves. It is a wry comment on our own age that we have been presented with evidence which underlines the impossibility of any accurate translation whatsoever. A translation is a book, and Homer is the most unliterary of authors. The work of Aristarchus, of Bentley, of Wolf, of a thousand others, is insignificant beside Milman Parry's demonstration, during the 'thirties of this century, that Homeric poetry exemplifies nothing but oral composition. To the veriest amateur of the language, this was a revelation. All the epithets, phrases, repetitions, even the contradictions, fell into place. They were not evidences of incompetence, or carelessness, or even naivety. They were the oral techniques, where the needs and assumptions were entirely different from our own.

An oral poet had as his stock-in-trade a store of this formal language, suited to every emergency, and he never combined them twice in the same way. His recitals were as freely improvised as Hindu music, within the limits of a given mode. With our books we have the power to look before and after; his audience did not pine for what was not. Nor did these poets learn whole poems by heart. Why should they? They had access to the formal language; and the stories existed as a sort of Platonic idea from which each man made the copy he thought best.

It seems likely, then, that the poems were taken down from Homer's own lips—a piece of prehistoric and most fortunate fieldwork. What we have amounts to recordings of two separate series of Homeric recitals. His version of the stories must have been like stormwaves—endlessly varied and endlessly the same. Surely we can see, then, that a third hero of the epics is the epic language itself. Destroy the formality of that, and while you may have a good story left, what you have is not Homer. The identical phrases must be turned into identical words whether they seem naive or not. This is where the translator must rely on the intelligence and good will of his reader.

The dull truth is that the only way to get alongside Homer is to learn Homeric Greek. It is a short task for the adult, an exhilarating and absorbing one. For by an odd coincidence, those concessions which the oral poet must make to his audience—use of stock phrases, repeated lines for repeated actions, direct and simple thought—are precisely those which help the learner. He soon learns to rejoice in the return of rosy-fingered Dawn; rests like a listener rather than a reader, when Zeus the cloud-gatherer, answering, addresses grey-eyed (or possibly owl-eyed) Athene. Occasionally, with his daily portion of the text stretching before him, he may falter, only to come on a number of familiar lines strung together which help him to make out the distance. I seem to remember that the last ten lines of book nine—condensed by Mr Fitzgerald to seven—came to me in this manner as a sheer gift. There were grains of sand on the page, I remember, and by my ear, the bristles of marron grass shuddered and stirred their small funnels in the dry, white sand. With that sea beating on that beach, it was not difficult to lie back, repeat the ancient words and hear the familiar surge and thunder.

We have lost the art of the oral and kept only the colloquial. How different they are I can illustrate from my solitary contact with something like the epic world. In 1940, owing to circumstances over which I had little or no control, I spent some time in the company of a three-badge AB of His Majesty's Navy. On one glum occasion he confided his intentions to me. *O moi ego* him, he said, as he poured the water out of his seaboots, when he got out of this *O moi ego*ing ship he would take an *O moi ego*ing anchor over his *O moi ego*ing shoulder and *O moi ego*ing-well walk inland until he met some *O moi ego*er who asked him what he was doing with an *O moi ego*ing pick-axe. There he would build an *O moi ego*ing pub and *O moi ego*ing-well live there for the rest of his *O moi ego*ing life. Those who know their Homer will be familiar with some of the thought. I remember reflecting, as I wrung out my vest, that to this level our oral resources had come. The concept, as Matthew Arnold would have agreed, was simple and direct, but neither rapid nor noble in expression. We have nothing to match a diction which is at once oral and formal.

No. No translation. Or if you must, something as dull and dutiful as Bohn. It will bring you nearer the original.

Custodians of the Real

from the *Listener*, 14 November 1974

For this, their most enjoyable book to date (*The Classic Fairy Tales* by Iona and Peter Opie), the Opies have found us convenient limits in a limitless subject. Out of the infinite world of the popular story, they have chosen the twenty-four most widely known in England, and given each in the words and print of the first text to be found in our language. The book is a compendium of any well-cared-for child's background. The material of that background proves to be most varied, both in source and kind. The texts gathered here range back—the direction seems appropriate—from the nineteenth to the sixteenth century.

The phrase 'fairy tale' means nothing and everything. It is here employed to cover the full scope of stories that have been thought suitable for English-speaking children. Some of the tales are so mysterious and dreamlike that, surely, they must rise from the depths of an unconscious clear of craft. Others are sophisticated short stories from named geniuses like Andersen, Madame d'Aulnoy or Perrault. They may be cheerful tales of adventure, like 'Jack and the Beanstalk', or 'Tom Thumb'—a tale in which the hack author recognized when he and the tale had taken all they could bear and simply came to a stop. They may be thrillers void of magic, but packed with terror and suspense, like 'Blue Beard'. Sometimes they are allegories, like 'Beauty and the Beast', with all the facile grace of that genre. Sometimes they are stories to prickle the hair and chill the blood, like the first version of 'Little Red Ridinghood', where, after the famous dialogue, the child is eaten, and that is that.

The authors have prefixed a learned essay to each item, but the essay ends on a separate page, so the tale itself is unencumbered by their scholarship. The essays tell us enough about each story to give us some bearings in a wide and abstruse subject. We have the source where it is single, and some idea of the spread and variability when it is not. Thus we find that, in 'Goldilocks and the Three Bears', the heroine changed during the nineteenth century 'from an ill-tempered crone to a radiant maiden'. We are told how widespread the Cinderella theme is in space and time, until the genius of Perrault gave us the version we have come to accept as the proper one. We note the occasional toning down of violence, here and there. In the English version, Rumpelstiltskin 'made the best of his way off while everybody laughed at him for having all his trouble for nothing'. The Opies tell us that in the 'original' German, he stamps his whole leg into the floor, then in his rage pulls at it so fiercely he tears himself in two.

The Opies invite us to consider how an earlier, poorer, wilder society is mirrored in certain recurrent themes. Babies are not exposed, but older children are abandoned deliberately. The parents hide from them and thus avoid the guilt of their death. Since so many women die in childbirth or are exhausted by childbearing, there is a steady supply of stepmothers. I think that sometimes their suggestions are a bit on the reductionist side. They say that wells figure so frequently in the tales because the well is the village meeting-place—but surely wells have always been magical and sacred? The best wells were holy wells, and were quickly christened when the White Christ came in. Again, though they say that ' "Jack the Giant Killer" appears to consist of a number of classic anecdotes strung together in the not-so-very-long-ago', it seems to me that they have not considered deeply enough that Jack was a Cornishman. It is wholly appropriate to Celtic mythology that he should kill a giant who is armed with an iron club. It is even more appropriate that he should cut off his head—the head of

Galigantus—and present it to the king. The archaeology of the twentieth century has taught us that the Celts were ardent head-hunters. Jack will have expected the king to expose the head on the wooden posts of his stockade or gatehouse. Inside a fairy tale or out of it, a severed head is a powerful affair; and Jack will not have grasped that King Arthur, though born only a little way up the coast, was a Christian, and not a wild man like himself from the wild country at the Land's End.

Long before you have re-read the stories and looked at the commentaries, you will have been seized on by the pictures. They are so numerous they give the book a deceptively 'coffee-table' appearance. There must be more than a hundred of them, and forty of them are in colour. Unlike the texts, the illustrations are not necessarily the earliest published, but those the editors thought the quaintest or most beautiful or informative. They range right up to our own day. In the earliest times, they were sometimes casual and crude. Sometimes a picture was from a block that happened to be lying about; and the story was adjusted to the picture. The nearer we come to our own time, the brighter shines the devotion, or, at least the relief, with which the artists turned to illustrate the stories which must have been familiar to them from childhood. (On the other hand, I believe that, as the tellers of the tales become more sophisticated, so a certain malaise appears, almost a corruption. Why, Hans Andersen ends the short tale of the 'The Swineherd' with a moral, right out there, spelled out, for everybody to see!)

It is the later illustrations that are so skilled, uncorrupted, and fascinating. Here, from the pen of Doré, is a study of Little Red Ridinghood and wolf that is a masterpiece of potential violence on the brink of eruption. Surely this child, so delicately beautiful and——be it said where no shrink may hear——so *edible*, is the one with whom little Charles Dickens fell so hopelessly in love? The hysteria of 'Blue Beard' is pointed up by John Austen's elegantly mannered illustration to it. The Twelve Dancing Princesses who descend the turret stair confirm what any reasonable child knows: princesses are different. Each princess, I think, is a portrait of the young Princess Alexandra, Tennyson's 'Sea King's daughter from over the sea'. Du Maurier could do no better. Heath Robinson's Beast is as horrifying as a Ghoul Mask from Japan. Of course Arthur Rackham's Jack would exchange a cow for a handful of beans! You can see it in his profile. H. J. Ford's picture of the three heads in the well puts the authenticity of the event beyond question, because no one could invent the look on those faces. Two pictures in the book are a pretentious failure. One is an illustration to 'The Princess and the Pea', which looks like an advertisement for a department store. The other is Walt Disney's sketch for a Snow White who looks like a plastic kind of pre-prep Lolita.

So for your money you get three books in one, the stories, the essays and the ample illustrations, I doubt there will be better value to be found this side of Christmas.

The stories begin in paradox. What has a beast to do with a rose? Why should a young lady, and a wife at that, be forbidden to enter a particular room in her own house? How does it happen that a king, in full possession of his senses, does not notice that the Marquis of Carabas's servant is a talking cat? A beanstalk that goes straight up until it vanishes in the clouds? A glass slipper? *Krapp's Last Tape*, and indeed, Krapp's first tape were never like this! Can it be that the episode with the girl in the punt was *not* the only gleam of happiness in a miserable life? Did Krapp's parent never read him anything, tell him anything? Was he so unnatural a child as to be unable to make a positively eager suspension of disbelief? For the result of having your mind stocked with fairy tales as a child——I say 'result', intending to duck the question of 'purpose'——is to have a mind in some way liberated from obsession with the commonplace. Fairy tales are liberating. They pose us a paradox, a puzzle, a contradiction, and in the end they do not explain it so much as resolve it like discord.

They are liberating; but on the other hand they are not liberal. You are not going to get the point of view of the poor, starving wolf, or the mentally defective giant. The stories are as one-pointed as those psalms in which the singer has no doubt he is surrounded by enemies, who——if he has his rights——are going to get their come-uppance. For though fairy tales resolve, they do not forgive. And the point is, surely, that the stepmother or the ogre has gone beyond humanity or never attained it. They are the principle of evil.

They are not to be forgiven, any more than a disease is to be forgiven. They are to be destroyed.

Fairy tales are concerned with right conduct and its difficulties. They are about courage and cowardice, truth and lies, hatred and compassion. They are about morals; and yet moralizing to a fairy tale is as frost to a flower. At the least breath of that frost, they wither into dull, exemplary lessons as boring as impertinent. What work they perform in the spirit is, so to speak, without benefit of clergy, felt rather than understood. For though the scholar may read and re-read a text, today most people are without that adult experience. It is in childhood that they hear or read the same words over and over again, until whatever it is, this unsubstance we call an individual, has been imprinted and in some way formed by these extraordinary tales. They engage the whole awareness. Our reason, even in childhood, tells us the event is impossible at the very moment we feel its rightness, and we move with our will to accept a cosmos in which these things can have their own validity. This, then, is not just an enjoyable book but a necessary one. It is not a present to give to children but to give to grandparents; who, if they wish to attain or retain any status as ancestors, will make themselves custodians of the real world which, in our more perceptive moments, we know to be the magic one. They may read the stories to themselves and their grandchildren, and the commentaries to themselves; for anything said about the stories must be inferior to reading or hearing them.

Crabbed Youth and Age

The Great War and Modern Memory by Paul Fussell

from *Guardian*, November 1975

Year after year the British Legion gathers at the Albert Hall. The Queen and the leading politicians lay wreaths at the cenotaph. The veterans of Dunkirk return to their place of skulls. There is much solemn carrying of banners and flags.

Yet you might cry, 'England awake!' without evoking any response but laughter. Such an exclamation would seem silly if not downright wicked. It is no longer our style. We contort round the simplest questions—round all questions as I shall hope to show, but one. Really, it seems as though both World Wars have fused and become a foundation on which all our assumptions are based. Life goes on at the conscious level, frivolous, worried, cynical, anxious, amused. But beneath, in some deep cavern of the soul, we are stunned.

Professor Fussell would agree with that diagnosis. Anyone who is curious about the American view of the British when they have one, but does not want to be shocked by too much honesty could do no better than read his book. He sees us brooding not so much on the Second World War as the First. He finds our vocabulary war-ridden. Our conceptual life is dominated by ideas of strategy and tactics, of advance and retreat. Our laws are in some way a hangover from years of civilian deprivation. Our leery and cynical suspicions that the system will do you down if you don't watch it all the time derive from the attitude of frontline troops, who having been conned into the mincing machine and astonishingly escaped with their lives and at least part of their bodies and wits are too fly to let themselves ever be deceived again.

This not very flattering view of us he deduces from a consideration of the change in English sensibility between August 4th, 1914 and the present day. There is some validity in his view but the subject is at once so vast and so delicate in texture that the enquiry seems superficial. For example, his chapter Arcadian Recourses deals with the English preoccupation with flowers and all the gentler aspects of nature, while the next one on Soldier Boys deals with what he considers to be our inveterate homoeroticism. Entertaining as they are, both these chapters have no very close connection with his conclusions. In other respects he makes some astonishing statements of the simplistic sort that will not do in a book with these pretensions. For example, he declares 'In the Great War, eight million people were destroyed because two persons, the Archduke Francis Ferdinand and his consort, had been shot.' That is a bit of nonsense. It is a raucous shout, fitter for the hustings. He prises the Great War loose from the historical chain of circumstances and gives it a look over in isolation as though political and social history were no more than a framework which can be ignored unless useful as a support for a literary discussion. In fact the book, though for all I know it was planned carefully in advance, gives the impression of originating in a set of essays or lectures loosely linked for which some common theme and eventual generalization was later devised.

Since his sources are literary for the most part, Northrop Frye's division of literary succession into myth, romance, high mimetic, low mimetic and ironic makes a useful diagnostic instrument. With the Great War he claims that Myth reappears thus indicating a circular progression, and I shall agree. But I must say that what he labels myth seems to me no more than a melange of rumour, superstition and satire. You would think, to read him, that the Mons Angels were now a settled part of the European Unconscious, rather than of European cynicism. It would be as reasonable to include in a mythopoea the rumours of Russian reinforcements marching through Scotland with snow on their boots.

The Great War was wholly unlike the expectations their upbringing had wished on the eager combatants. It proved to have areas of sheer indescribability. It produced from its poets—since the net was so wide as to include every kind of fish—an unmatched sense of articulate outrage. It reduced them to a statistic and they screamed. It is a good point, but relative. All wars have been felt to be indescribable. As far back as the Odyssey, Nestor, wise and boring old man says to Telemachus, 'Who could tell all our woes? If you stayed here for five or six years and asked all the woes the tough Achaeans put up with you'd grow weary before I finished, and go back home.' C. E. Montague's 'eye under the duckboard' does not even match the awful Homeric picture of the spear standing in the heart and shuddering because the heart was still beating. But the Great War did not have or produce a Homer. Professor Fussell gives us a digest of the careers and an analysis of the work of the three most memorable poets who fought in it—Sassoon, Owen, and Graves. It is far and away the best part of his book, and we could still do with a full-length study from him on this more limited subject. His appreciation is profound and full of insight. On the Western Front, these by no means major poets experienced so violent, indeed, so literally explosive a dissociation of all the elements of normal living that they passed their time, emotionally speaking, in a kind of white-hot plasma. There the satiny irrelevance of the Georgian poetasters was burned away and the forked creatures screamed, if not the indescribable, the unspeakable. Frye's age of Irony had begun.

For the Great War was different from others in its combination of duration and extent. Putting aside the superstitions and rumours and cynicism, indeed, the white-hot plasma, burning as it does in our immediate past, has acquired something of the force and dignity and unconscious influence of myth. At the back of our thinking there *does* lie as an unconsciously accepted absolute, the barrage of the Western Front and the thought that hundreds of thousands of young men went through it to their deaths or came back changed for ever. It is the touchstone of all.

Yet surely the profoundest effect of the unparalleled casualty lists was not as Professor Fussell claims a change in vocabulary, a sense of cynicism and division, but rather the turning of the generations upside down. Before the war, old men were thought on the whole to know best. After it and ever since, young men are thought to have a prescriptive hold on wisdom and decision by virtue of their youth. 'They shall not grow old'. They have not. It is as if they have become part of the young in each generation. It is as if they, the pure and blameless, the eternally sacrificed, now come charging *this* way out of the barrage to bayonet any old man in sight and kick in the crutch anyone with a belief dating from more than five minutes back. Since the very old men of today are the very young men of 1918 that is perhaps the greatest irony of all.

Professor Fussell and I went into the Second World War having read much the same books—*Death of a Hero*, *Goodbye to all That*, and most menacing and admonitory of the lot, *All Quiet on the Western Front*—and with a consequent pack of expectations drawn from what we had found out about the First. Our disappointment at finding it so different was tinged in my case at least with relief. That war had a special and unexpected idiocy in that the Home Front, what with the air raids, was often more dangerous than the Front Front. To come home on leave from a peaceful crossing of the Atlantic and hear your wife describe how she had been chased down the High Street of a provincial town by a flying bomb was to have the whole concept of the heroic fighting man stood on its head.

The Second World War came near to demolishing all the assumptions of the first one and uncovered entirely different areas of indescribability. The horror of the brewed up tank, the burning plane, the crushed and sinking submarine—all that is difficult to describe but the job can be done. The experience of Hamburg, Belsen, Hiroshima and Dachau cannot be imagined. We have gone to war and beggered description all over again. Those experiences are like black holes in space. Nothing can get out to let us know what it was like inside. It was like what it was like and on the other hand it was like nothing whatsoever. We stand before a gap in history. We have invented a limit to literature.

Perhaps, then, those black holes will be part of the future's mythology, like the barrage and the mud of Flanders. Did we discover black holes out there in space because we had already invented them in here? Do we create not only our history but our universe? That way teases us too easily out of thought. At least Professor Fussell has tried to make—if not sense—at least some kind of *process* of it all. He has amassed a store of anecdotes and illustrations and his book is wholly readable; yet somehow for all his apparent amiability a note that can only be called patronizing creeps in. Though the perceptions are acute and subtle the style seems wrong. There is a wide divergence between the awful subject and the insouciant cheerfulness of the manner.

Intimate Relations

There is a cave in the Auvergne where if you peer into a pool you can see a single footprint and by it the mark of a stick in what was once soft mud. That capacity we all have called kinaesthesia, a sympathetic identification with someone else's body movement, interprets the signs instantly. We feel how the person lurched, saved him or herself from falling deeper into the pool by stabbing down and leaning on the stick. It was a woman, perhaps, for, it is thought from some other marks, she had a child with her. Other marks! There are many in the caves, the simplest being the hand impressions, hunter's hands, some with a finger missing. There are obscurities surrounding sympathetic kinaesthesia but it is possible to develop that sense until we have at least a guess at what they did and why they did it. They were leaving a sign; and the obscurity lies in this, that such a sign has latent in it some of what we have called sign, symbol, emblem, metaphor, simile. Some of that same obscurity surrounds the question of why we modern people of every age, rank, calling, sex, belief have left records of one sort or another. We have kept journals.

Why? What does it matter? Is not our limited time more precious than that we should spend it making these spidery marks on paper? What is the impulse to describe and record? Are we trying instinctively to stop time or outwit it? Are we building ourselves a monument? Like the most primitive sign, even the most primitive journal becomes more and more obscure in origin the more you look at it. There was the journal kept for some time by Jimmy Mason. He was about as simple a character as you could get. Mr Raleigh Trevelyan resurrected him, so to speak, from an Essex attic. Jimmy states his reason for writing in the first sentence. He thought someone was going to murder him.

> If I should be poisoned at last, and this book is found, it will explain everything. What bad fellows Tommy took up with and encouraged him to poison his father and now trying to poison me.

Was he suffering from persecution mania then? So it might seem. Certainly he withdrew more and more from even the spare life of an Essex village. Father had been a martinet, a soldier of the queen, a sadist. His mother was almost as vague as her son. The causes of his possible madness are evident or as evident as the causes of madness sometimes are. But *was* someone trying to poison him? He was convinced he only escaped death by detecting the taste of poison in a pie his mother gave him. When he gave the rest of the pie to his spaniel it lay down and died. So where are we? Land was a key to a whole volume of interlocking greeds, fears and hates, for the Mason family had four acres. When Mr Trevelyan went into the matter he found himself stared into *Cold Comfort Farm* at ground or muck-level.

> ——the postman had said that Bacon killed himself by drink. Young Bacon was as bad. The parson had been obliged to turn him away from the Sacrament. They had to lock all the drink up at the Griffin, else if young Bacon got at it he would kill himself in a few days.
> *May 31st Friday*
> This morning T. said J. Sweeting had been found with his throat cut. Burial Monday.

These comments do seem to give a fair picture of village life. Allow me to quote once more from Mr Trevelyan's fascinating book on the subject. Hear what he discovered when he climbed one or two family trees where the Sukebind was a-blowing.

With other witnesses I found myself in the quicksands when I tried to probe the secrets of their own parentage. 'You see, my father and she had the same mother' someone said to me about a native of Puttock's End whom I had always supposed to be his mother. 'Then she was your aunt?' I asked. 'A suppose she was in a way, but my father's name being Y-, I've always called myself Y-; ain't I right? Someone lived with her; you see, he was her father and my father like.'

So whether the diary records the delusions of madness or the criminality of village life is wide open to question. There is another strand in all this. Though Jimmy withdrew so that no one could see him, he had a timid passion for little girls and spied on them through the hedge. Sometimes, if it was darkling, he would carry on a whispered conversation with this one or that and leave country presents for them at the gate—eggs or apples. He suffered from passionate jealousies enough to rock the reason of Othello.

A little past 2 o'clock Ednere gone by up hill with can as for milk. Was coming back in less than an hour. But she was riding in a fishmonger's cart with a young fellow, laughing and going on with him just the same as [she] did with the boy that came to Meril's 2 years ago the end of last July. She was packed in the cart so close to [the] man among fish hampers, laughing and talking and holding her hat to keep wind from blowing [it] off. The name of the cart was Woodley of Dunmow,
    A fish cart never seen this way before—

The diary has now got away from Tommy and the poisoned spaniel. It is a record of what hurts. It is also a record of his rare and tenuous pleasures.

Fanny came [a]cross grass. Looked [a]cross pond and said
goodbye several times. So good did seem.

   She wispered goodbye 3 or 4 times.

   & stop a little.

But like Fanny we must get on. Jimmy lost interest in poison and
little girls and ended as what a great many of the diarists of the world
would like to be—according to the Rector at any rate—'He was a
gentle, lovable, old man, so shy he could hardly bear to look at other
people. He kept bees, grew his few plants and read his Bible. That
was his whole life.' When he was in his eighties and defenceless an
elderly and one suspects insalubrious lady did a few odd household
jobs for him. 'He was very religious,' she said, 'and could pray
lovely.' Someone claimed to have climbed a tree and seen Jimmy
praying among the beehives with the bees climbing over his coat and
face.

   Observe then that the journal occupied only a few fearful and
passionate years of Jimmy's life. He recorded what songs the Sirens
sang to him but not what song he sang unto the Lord. Indeed, to find
a journal that records more than a few years is exceptional. There is a
passion somewhere which dies or fades, changes. Boredom sets in.
Indeed, the diary of a whole life could not but be monotonous and
repetitive. Ripeness is not all. It leads to a disinclination to keep on
treating a personal life as worth recording. For we can see by Jimmy
Mason's journal some of the elements that compel the pen. There is
the awareness of important events—someone is trying to poison
me! There is also the pleasure principal. Psychologists tell us that
many people and it may be all, to some degree or other, increase the
original pleasure by repeating it in their minds or even better,
writing it down. That was why Jimmy makes so much of
those timidly tender whisperings in the Essex dusk. They were all
he had.

   Certainly the pleasure principal will lead us on to the next and
greater example. A particularly choice specimen started in the river
Thames quite a time ago—though Time is almost circumvented in
this case—aboard a large ship. There was a fleet which needed an
admiral and got one. The admiral needed a secretary and engaged a

young, distant kinsman of his who has left us a list of some of his baggage—a list in which we can see foreshadowed several, though not all, of the main interests of his life. He took two violins, a chest containing a quantity of money, warm clothing, blank commissions, pens, ink, sealing wax, his seal ring and the machinery which went with it and much writing paper. He also seems to have taken, though he does not say so, what his editors, Messrs Latham and Matthews, describe as 'an ordinary stationer's notebook which was blotted at the edges—but that of course was later—seven and a half inches tall, with five, raised bands.' The young secretary was Sam Pepys, Mr S. Pepys, Samuel Pepys esquire, who was to achieve fame in his own time as the principal secretary to the Navy but is known to us as the greatest diarist in the English language and possibly the world.

There was not much doubt about Pepys' sanity. He was, of all things, sane and sometimes like his contemporary, Evelyn, almost objectionably so. His editors in the latest and surely definitive edition of the diary attempt to solve the prime mystery of why he did it. He was mountainously ambitious. But he had a past that in those days might get him into trouble. He had been a catholic convert and his wife still was one. Now the extraordinary thing about Pepys is that for all his specific genius he was *not* a literary man. He tells us that he turned up the manuscript of a romance he wrote when young and how he admired his young self, feeling he could no longer write such a thing. Then he burnt the manuscript. I swear no literary man could have done that; or if a literary man had burnt the romance it would be in the expectation of writing another. Indeed, Pepys was unique. He *is* unique. You may dip into him at a free moment but only the deepening knowledge of a desultory acquaintance kept with him over a lifetime can bring you to the feeling of having met the man face to face. That stationer's notebook was to be joined by five others and bound sumptuously, after they had been filled by one and a quarter million words.

The suggestion that Pepys kept his diary because he wanted evidence of what an honest, hardworking member of the church of England he was does not bear close examination. He may have started with that intention but the diary soon became a record which he could never have dared to make public in its entirety.

Authority might have winked at the astonishing record of how quickly his private fortune increased. But—and here one of his life's preoccupations appeared—persons of a lower station in the navy, if I read his diary aright, could get a favour done them if they made a pretty wife available. It seems to me the only interpretation to be placed on some passages. His own wife was understandably watchful and fiercely jealous. No. The record was always intended to be private.

Yet once begun, the record continues for nine years until eye-strain forced him to keep a less compromising journal. The compulsion was surely the word itself in the pursuit of the remembering pleasure—pleasure in gold coins heaped up, pleasure in women, clothes, books, music, scandal, personal achievement. Pepys was by nature not merely a talented and devoted civil servant. He was what the seventeenth and eighteenth century called a 'Virtuoso' or 'Vertuoso', meaning thereby something at once specific and general. A virtuoso was—and I quote—'One who has a special interest in or taste for the fine arts; a student or collector of antiquities, natural curiosities or rarities, etc; a connoisseur; frequently, one who carries on such pursuits in a dilettante or trifling manner.' Musical instruments, jewels, curios, splendid books, he collected them all. He was a natural recorder, too, feeling surely that the word is a thing to be treasured like an elegant coin. He heaped up facts like a jackdaw with glittering things, in petty cash books, letter books, memorandum books. Yet the six volumes of the diary we can see were not meant to be published or examined or even sighted. They were to become what has always been an aim of *virtuosi*, they were to become *objets*, objects of *vertu*. They were not written as was once thought in code but in a seventeenth-century form of shorthand. They were written as neatly as possible. Bound sumptuously with the Pepys' arms embossed they were a collector's treasure. They were intensely private. According to the privacy of a statement he would hide it to one degree or another. The books were locked in a glass-fronted bookcase—one of the earliest bookcases of that sort on record. The words in shorthand were much less understandable than a foreign language. Where the record touched on his frequent sexual adventures they were not only hidden in this way but concealed in a jargon of Latin, French, Spanish and Italian. There is no question but that here is an honest record of dishonesty, a self-revelation of what must be concealed. Here he could unlock, take down and repeat securely all the pleasure of nine busy years. He had, we must suppose, that 'Caucasian loop' in the brain which enables the possessor to think twice before acting, to look twice before leaping. Having leapt he is able to turn round and by remembering enjoy it all over again. Any teacher knows the assiduity with which children will at least *begin* the business of making their own version of a book. They will bring pictures and other addenda from wherever they can find them, turning an ordinary school exercise book into a childish and complicated mass which on that level has everything in common not merely with Pepys' diary but with his whole incunabula, his *objets*, even his library with its collection of broadsheets that no one else bothered to collect. His case of curios was not enough. He wanted everything he could lay his hands on; and words, words, words, beautiful words, page after page, book after book. His whole collection is an historical treasure; and since for all his lack of literary ambition he was brilliantly descriptive his diary lies like a jewel in the middle of it. It is a mirror not just for the seventeenth century but for all time, a mirror in which any man can see at least a little of himself and sometimes a lot and sometimes a whole rueful figure. His lesser contemporary, John Evelyn, produced a journal of great merit but it was buttoned up where Pepys' is unbuttoned and it was intended for publication. So really it could have been reconstructed by an historian of the century.

We come to a prime point of intimacy—a relation indeed so intimate that it has sometimes been defined as a man talking to himself. I mean the sense that men have of God. Pepys had been a convert. He must have had some kind of religious experience. Indeed, he knew shame but it was hardly the shame of a fallen man before his Maker. His drunkenness and whoring, his adultery and corruption troubled him indeed, but mostly, it appears, in the degree to which they stood over against the respectable, organized life of the good civil servant who knows where he will be at a quarter to ten next Thursday. He was worried by his attendance at the theatre—which indeed was sufficiently blue and had just adopted the French fashion of allowing real women to appear on the stage. He kept trying to stay away. He had some success in this, certainly more than he had in stopping his compulsion to follow any pretty face he caught sight of through the streets of London. But the intimate relation is a puzzle. A man trying to convince the world that he was a sincere member of the established church might go to church on Sunday. But Pepys was a sermon fancier. He collected them, you might say, the way he collected broadsheets. He often heard two and sometimes three in a day. How did he square one half of his life with the other? Come to that, how do any of us? What kind of private accommodation did he come to? Did he have a feeling that God was as Thomas Huxley said 'a gaseous invertebrate', a tenuity so indistinct as to be harmless and easily avoidable? Or did he think in a society of such personalized devotion from man to man—*my* servant, *my* master—that as one gentleman to another, God would not look? However it was and with whatever unease, he continued to enjoy sermons and any pretty woman who fell in his way. It must be a matter of temperament, for a somewhat later diarist, journalist, was not so lucky. Samuel Johnson's personal jottings ring with the anguish of a man who *would* be good, *would* be consistent, regular, moral in every conceivable way; but who by temperament could never possibly be so. Unless the wolf was right inside the door he was too indolent, too slothful to work. A lady once saw him pour himself a full tumbler of wine and gulp it down in a second or two. As Boswell says, Johnson could be abstinent but not temperate. Johnson recorded his struggles as if indulging the pleasure principal in reverse—what one might call the pain principal. He says of his sloth, for example, 'I propose to rise at eight, because though I shall yet not rise early it will be much earlier than I now rise, for I often lie till two; and will gain me much time, and tend to a conquest over idleness, and give time for other duties.' It was no good. He still stayed in bed. Where Pepys, that fairly well organized individual, was a churchgoer Johnson, who sometimes scribbled sermons for other people, had the greatest difficulty in getting himself there. He says, 'I have this year omitted church on most Sundays, intending to supply the deficiency in the week. So that I owe twelve attendances on worship.' We are familiar with the looming Johnson, that wise Johnson, the superb and complete Latinist, conversational Johnson, dictionary Johnson, Boswell's Johnson, Johnson of the *Hebrides*, *Rasselas*, *The Lives of the Poets*, of the *Rambler*. Most of all we know Johnson since we are in the business of intimate relations where virtue counts above everything as a man of real personal charity who kept others alive when he himself was near starvation. Yet listen to this.

> When I look back upon resolutions of improvement and amendment which have, year after year, been made and broken either by negligence, forgetfulness, vicious idleness, casual interruption or morbid infirmity; when I find that so much of my life has stolen unprofitably away, and that I can descry, by retrospection, scarcely a few single days properly and vigorously employed, why do I yet try to resolve again? I try, because reformation is necessary and despair criminal; I try in humble hope of the help of God.

Here, surely, we find intimacy with Johnson if not with his Maker. You would think the heavy grief of his self-diagnosis would disarm criticism. Not a bit of it. The diary when it was published reached the poet, William Cowper, at Olney. Cowper was to die of religious depression and despair and the signs of it were already on him. He showed little understanding, however. He has this to say on the matter in a letter to a clergyman friend.

> [Johnson's] prayers for the dead, and his minute account of the rigours with which he observed church fasts, whether he drank tea or coffee, whether with sugar or without, and whether one or two dishes of either, are the most important items to be found in this childish register of the great Johnson, supreme dictator in the chair of literature, and almost a driveller in his closet; a melancholy witness to testify how much of the wisdom of this world may consist with almost infantine ignorance of the affairs of a better.

> I remember a good man at Huntingdon who, I doubt not, is

now with God and he also kept a diary. After his death, through the neglect or foolish wantonness of his executors, it came abroad for the amusement of his neighbours. All the town saw it and all the town found it highly diverting. It contained much more valuable matter than [Dr Johnson's] journal seems to do; but it contained also a faithful record of all his deliverances from wind (for he was much troubled with flatulence) together with pious acknowledgements of the mercy. There is certainly a call for gratitude, whatsoever benefit we receive——but it would have been as well if neither my old friend had recorded his eructations, nor the doctor his dishes of sugarless tea, or the dinner at which he ate too much. I wonder indeed, that any man of such learned eminence as Johnson who knew that every word he uttered was deemed oracular, and that every scratch of his pen was accounted a treasure, should leave behind him what he would have blushed to exhibit while he lived.

The truth is that Johnson had a soul, in the greatness of which Cowper's own would have rolled around like a pea in a drum. I believe he would have replied to Cowper, 'Such a man I was and may God forgive me.'

The honesty in Johnson, in so far as it led him to an indifference to what other people might think of him, was part of his complex character and simple goodness. The indifference was the prerogative of a whole class of persons who were Johnson's contemporaries. I mean the aristocrats of the eighteenth century. God does not come into their relations at all though they were often enough intimate in another sense. It is worth while looking at the journal of a sea-faring aristocrat who, without knowing it, was a rationalist before his time. He was Admiral Hervey. The Herveys were an outstanding and outrageous example of social privilege——enjoyable in retrospect, perhaps, because they are so far away from us. The first one was a favourite of Sarah, Duchess of Marlborough, and the title Earl of Bristol was revived for the family. The first Earl's children included the hermaphrodite or perhaps merely homosexual transvestite rather unfairly satirized by Alexander Pope as *Sporus*. He was John Hervey, whose goings-on contributed to the contemporary saying that there were three sorts of creature, men, women and Herveys. He left memoirs ticking like a time bomb since they were full of scandal. Another son is thought to have been the cuckolding father of Horace Walpole. Admiral Hervey's journal does not concern itself with the inner life at all. He was a successful politician, an extraordinarily brave seaman and a Casanova whose exploits make the furtive adventures of Pepys seem like Postman's Knock. He was an aristocrat in the best and worst sense of the word as it applied to the eighteenth century. At the age of twenty he was married off to a lady of his own class, a maid of honour, a woman of great beauty and easy virtue. The reason for the marriage was that Augustus's family thought the lady's financial prospects were good. She was Miss Elizabeth Chudleigh, as typical of her time and class as her young husband. As David Erskine, the editor of Augustus's journal, says of the marriage, 'It was the work of a third party who had procured the union of a bride of promiscuous habits with an impecunious youth about to spend the next two years abroad.'

During the next two years, they graced separate scenes and both had some adventures, Miss Chudleigh's being perhaps the more exciting and certainly the more profitable. We have a splendid account of her appearing at a fancy-dress ball as Iphigenia. Miss Elizabeth Montague wrote, 'Miss Chudleigh's dress or rather undress was remarkable; she was Iphigenia for the sacrifice but so naked the high priest might easily inspect the entrails of the victim.'

Indeed, there was a kind of cheerful insouciance, a zest and indifference to criticism about the whole class of people, principally because it never occurred to them that they need fear criticism either from below or above. They were costly, destructive and creative. This might well have been illustrated in some eighteenth-century garden by a bust of Janus, the two-faced god looking in both directions at once and what we could now call the acceptable and unacceptable faces of privilege. Coming from this class when he joined the Navy Augustus Hervey did not have to bother about promotion or, as he would have called it, preferment. Unlike Pepys, who rose through merit, Augustus floated upward effortlessly. The Royal Navy was his oyster and he made a brilliant job of it as, it will annoy some of my listeners to hear, did many of the officers appointed through sheer influence. There is something ineffably boyish in his glee when it came to manoeuvring at sea and in his gusto with which he grabbed any prize, a female, a ship or prize money. His diary is less well known than Pepys's so it is perhaps worth quoting a bit here and there.

> Being young and much about, it was not surprising I got hold of some things; the Galli and Camioni, both famous in their way on the stage, admitted my attentions. The latter was beautiful, and as she would accept nothing from me, being kept by the Count Hass Lang, I found it most suitable as well as most agreeable to stick to her, and only when I went away, gave her a diamond ring.

After all, noblesse obliges. However, Augustus treated the allegedly serious business of his profession in just such a cheerful fashion. We are all familiar—perhaps too familiar—with the solemn yo-hoing stuff of false colours, lights in tubs, hair-breadth escapes, boarding parties and the rest from Smollett to Hornblower and beyond. But in Hervey's journal, and it seems likely in fact, the war at sea becomes a huge rag.

> The next morning I was off Peverel Point and saw a sail that I perceived was chasing me. I concluded him a French privateer, and therefore judged it best to decoy him. I therefore made from him and towed many things alongside to stop my sloop's way which succeeded; I hoisted a Dutch flag and he answered me with a Danish, I then spread a French ensign and pennant and fired a gun to leeward; then hoisted a jack at my gaffend and threw out a French signal of distress; he then bore right down to me, and as soon as ever I had him under my guns I spread my English colours; he then fired at me his broadside, but soon after mine he struck his colours and surrendered.

Now you would think, would you not, that he would go on from there to commend the crew for bravery, describe any damage or

casualties, hint, in a manly and understated fashion, at his own
coolness under fire et cetera. Not a bit of it. His very next sentence
describes what happened to his prize.

> She was sold the next day at Plymouth and Mr Morsehead came
> off and paid the people; my share £149 for her, each man has just
> one guinea.

It is true, as well, that he could show cool, personal bravery, not to
say heroism, and not mind describing it himself. A ship caught fire in
Leghorn harbour. She was crammed with gun powder and no one
would go near her. Hervey went aboard, cut her cables, towed her
out with his own clothes on fire. She was just clear when she blew
up. Miraculously Hervey was unhurt, though scorched; and through
his action no one else was hurt either. His brother, *Sporus*, when he
heard of it asked his father to send Augustus a letter of
commendation. The letter was sent; but the covering letter to
Sporus was typical Hervey family.

> I have sent you since you desire it of me, a letter to your brother
> Augustus though I found it a little against the grain as a parent to
> be paying where I owed nothing, having never heard from him
> but when he wanted money—

Augustus Hervey fought much for his country, spent much of his
own and other people's money, enjoyed life with an expensive
honesty that would have astonished Pepys. His battles, his politics,
his debts and his *amours* can only be called blatant. As with Pepys, his
journal occupies only a short period of his life and his time at the top
of his profession was all to come. Meanwhile his no more than
nominal marriage had come notoriously unstuck. Elizabeth had gone
the rounds from one noble lover to another. Augustus's comment
seems to me to be amusing and, for once, unconsciously. In
December 1747 he returned to England and has this to say about her.

> [I was] very much displeased with many things I heard of Miss
> Chudleigh's conduct, especially from her own relations, too,

which put me out of humour, and made me mind several little circumstances that perhaps would otherwise have passed me as nothing.

They parted. Bribed, it is said, with sixteen thousand pounds Augustus deposed before an ecclesiastical court that Miss Chudleigh had never been his wife. She thought this made her free and immediately married the Duke of Kingston. It is alleged that Augustus himself was present, remarking that he had come to take a last look at his widow. However, an ecclesiastical court is not the same as a law court and Elizabeth was indicted for bigamy. She fled abroad and after an eccentric existence at various courts died, it is said, 'demented'.

It was a strange affair and worthy of the family. I cannot resist recounting one more story of them. Tom Hervey, Augustus's uncle, eloped with the young wife of his godfather. Then, from a safe distance, he carried on a debate in pamphlet form with the injured husband in the course of which he referred to the lady as 'our wife—for in heaven, whose wife shall she be?' Yet there was the acceptable Hervey face, notably a streak of generosity and a power to recognize merit which made them help the young, unknown and struggling Samuel Johnson who said afterwards in later life, 'If you call a dog "Hervey" I shall love him.'

The Herveys must have been impossible companions for most of the time though at this distance they have acquired the posthumous merit of providing a source of constant entertainment. Since, I have heard it whispered, the common requirement for a thesis is the detailed study of some eighteenth century character, it seems to me that a young person could do no better than to examine an aspect of one of the Hervey family. For impossible as they may have been to live with, they can nevertheless keep their staider posterity in a state of shock and, be it said, hilarity.

Pepys was solidly middle-class. Augustus Hervey belonged to the aristocracy. If the relationship of Pepys in the privacy of his journal with God seems less than intimate, at least the observances of religion bulk large. Hervey seems never to have heard of them. The name of God may have occurred here and there in his journal and letters but only as an expletive, sedulously expurgated by a later and one guesses lesser Hervey. Augustus Hervey was a rationalist born before his time—a rationalist so rational that he did not bother even to formulate his rationalism, at least not to his written-down self. He was like Pepys an indefatigable pursuer of women and art objects. His was a material world in which one could be sure of some *funning* here and there. Not for him those gloomy excursions that sometimes set Pepys walking away from his misdeeds rather than sins when his Puritan ancestry tapped him on the shoulder. He would have agreed, had he read it, with an unforgettable sentence of Pepys, 'I am in a strange slavery to the beauty of women and music.' Yet Pepys's intimacy was, in the end, with himself. Augustus was sunnily at one and intimate with the whole of life, the whole of the world. There seems just as little reason for his journal as for Pepys's and we are reduced to the simplistic explanation that as a naval officer he was so habituated to the keeping of a *log* it had become natural.

All this has really revealed little about the act of recording when the soul faces the white paper. It seems to have little to do with the impulse to create, something with the impulse to collect, perhaps a little with the desire to be remembered, perhaps a little with them all; and yet that list is not inclusive.

We started, as far as the written word is concerned, at the bottom of the social scale with naive Jimmy Mason. We have ascended gradually both in the complexity of mind and in the social scale. We may now go to the top socially and take some of Jimmy Mason's naivety with us though certainly not his other qualities. Another diarist, who like Augustus was much concerned with the Royal Navy, has left us accounts of voyages and journeys. This diarist did not build ships like Pepys nor sail them like Hervey. She owned them. She owned them all, for it was the 'Queen's Nav*ee*' and when Victoria took her diary off in the Royal Yacht she was accompanied by the ship *Pique* 36 guns, the sloop *Daphne* 18 guns, the steam vessel *Salamander* with the carriages on board, the steam vessels *Monkey*, *Shearwater*, *Black Eagle*, *Lightning* and *Fearless*. If this seems a large escort for one young woman, her husband and children, it must be pointed out that times have changed. The young woman's eldest son, King Edward VII, once turned up *incognito* at Naples with an escort of twelve battleships.

The remarkable thing about Victoria's journal is that it is so colourless as to be almost invisible on the page. This is not entirely her fault as it was heavily edited, leaving in only what was proper for a young lady and queen. When extracts were published, concerned mostly with her family and their holidays in Scotland, the public were disappointed. It contained little but a series of royal bromides with everywhere the implied notice to the public of KEEP OUT. I believe we need not be quite so disappointed. We can get a glimpse here and there of Victoria's intimate relation with God and Prince Albert, the two later to be so deeply and inextricably mingled. In addition, we can gather a series of little pictures by the way that provide interest, not perhaps on the Hervey or Pepys scale but nevertheless sufficiently entertaining. Prince Albert figures prominently as indeed he ought. Albert, highly intelligent, humourless and if anything over-educated had recognized with resignation his fate come upon him. He was not popular. Highly educated people seldom are with the great mass of the British people. Albert saw that he would never be British however much the queen had him legally naturalized unless he conformed to the national custom and went out, every day, rain or fine, and shot something. I find Victoria's adoring accounts of his exploits delightfully and, I think, quite unconsciously funny. Albert was dutiful but not an enthusiastic hunter.

Albert set off immediately after luncheon deer stalking and I was to follow and wait below. We sat down on the ground, Lady Canning and I sketching and Sandy and Mr Oswald in Highland Costume. After waiting some time we were told in a mysterious whisper that 'they were coming' and indeed a great herd *did* appear on the brow of the hill when most provokingly two men who were walking on the road—which they had no business to have done—suddenly came in sight and then the herd ran back again and the sport was spoilt. My poor Albert had not even fired one shot for fear of spoiling the whole thing but had been running about a great deal.

Two days later Albert is out again all day with Victoria waiting for him, on a country road.

Meanwhile (she writes) I saw the sun sink, gradually, and I got quite alarmed lest we should be benighted and we called anxiously for Sandy, who had gone away for a moment, to give a signal to come back. As the sun went down the scenery became more and more beautiful, the sky crimson, golden-red and blue, and the hills looking purple and lilac, most exquisite, till at length it set and the hues grew softer in the sky and the outlines of the hills sharper. I never saw anything so fine. At length Albert met us and he told us he had waited all the time for us, as he knew how anxious I should be. He had been very unlucky and lost his sport for just when he could have shot some fine harts the rifle would not go off.

Perhaps the experience soured Albert somewhat for now we hear him hunting close to Balmoral.

When I came in at half-past six, Albert went out to try his luck with some stags which lay quite close in the woods but he was unsuccessful.

Albert was determined, indefatigable. Perhaps salmon were easier to come at? Victoria says, 'Though Albert stood in the water for some time he caught nothing; but the scene at this beautiful spot was exciting and picturesque in the extreme. I wished for Landseer's pencil.'

However, persistence must have its reward. There came the day when Albert justified his naturalized status and became a true Briton. Victoria was delighted.

We turned to the right when out on the moors where I got off and walked; and we seated ourselves behind a large stone, no one but Macdonald with us, who loaded the guns and gave notice when anything was to be seen as he lay upon the ground. The gentlemen were below in the road; the wood was beat, but nothing came, so we walked on and came down a beautiful thickly-wooded glen; and after a good deal of scrambling to get there and to get up the other side of the glen, we sat down again.

We then scrambled over to the opposite side where we again concealed ourselves; in this beat Albert shot a *roe*, and I think would have shot more had they not been turned back by the sudden appearance of an old woman who looked like a witch and came through the wood with two immense crutches and disturbed the whole thing. Albert killed the roe just as she was coming along and the shot startled her very much; she was told to come down which she did, and sat below in the glen having covered her head with her handkerchief. When two of the beaters were told to take up the roe, they first saw the old woman and started and stared with horror—which was very amusing to see.

Let us leave the scene with Albert triumphant. Victoria saw it.

Albert fired—the animal fell but rose again and went on and Albert followed. Very shortly after, however, we heard a cry and ran down and found Grant and Donald Stewart pulling up a stag with a very pretty head. Albert had gone on, Grant went after him, and I and Vicky remained with Donald Stewart, the stag, and the dogs. I sat down to sketch and poor Vicky unfortunately seated herself on a wasp's nest and was much stung. Donald Stewart rescued her for I could not, being myself too much alarmed. Albert joined us in twenty minutes, unaware of having killed the stag. What a delightful day!

But I have been led astray by my personal delight in this account and have lingered too long by a Scottish burn; only pausing to remark that neither Pepys nor Hervey nor Johnson nor any of our cast and comedy would have described a sunset as Victoria did. Dutifully—for had she not said at her accession that she would be good?—she sees the scene as contemporary artists were seeing it, with all its mountains, mists, heather and monarchs of the glen. Yet the diary, if it were possible, might have been written by one of those pretty little figures you see in antique shops, a figure surely of hard, white porcelain.

Nevertheless, the remarkable thing is that when we look for the particular intimate relation in the diary—one the editor and censor would pass—and view Victoria before her Maker, an extraordinary thing emerges. Not for her the indifference of a Hervey nor the accommodation whatever it was of a Pepys. We can find places where Victoria records her relationship with God and there is no deference. She expects God, like the rest of her retainers, to deliver a service. He is not gaseous or personal. He is a servant.

> At the service the second prayer was very touching; his allusions to us were so simple, saying after his mention of us, 'Bless their children'. It gave me a lump in my throat as when he prayed for the dying, the wounded, the widows and orphans. Everyone came back delighted; and how satisfactory it is to come back from church with such feelings!

The Royal party's optimism and cheerfulness was vindicated only a few days later with splendid news from the battlefield in that most futile of all wars, the Crimean campaign. Victoria received a telegraphic despatch saying, 'Sevastopol is in the hands of the allies.' She describes what followed.

> Immediately Albert and all the gentlemen in every species of attire sallied forth, followed by all the servants, and gradually by all the population of the village—keepers, ghillies, workmen—up to the top of the cairn. Ross playing his pipes and Grant and Macdonald firing off guns continually; while poor old François lighted a number of squibs below, the greater part of which would not go off. About three-quarters of an hour later, Albert came down and said the scene had been wild and exciting beyond anything. The people had been drinking healths in whisky and were in great extasy.

There we must leave the pretty little figure. It is a good place; for that figure was not to change. Only when Albert died the white porcelain cracked and fell apart.

It seems clear enough why Victoria kept a diary. She had been directed to do so when a girl and her sense of duty did the rest. But she has little to tell us, little to contribute to the quest for deep reasons for recording daily life. A more faithful portrait of any person emerges from their diary, if it is kept for long enough, than they are aware. What will stand out above all is a ruling passion. In Pepys, if that passion is really discernible, it must be the instinct to collect. In Victoria it was the instinct to possess—to possess people, then things, then in a way the whole world. The more we look, the more collecting and possession seem deeply rooted in a journal. Cobbett, that John Bull-like figure, rides about the countryside and in his journal seems to embrace and possess the very soil, not in a sentimental way but with a hard and passionate grasp. Had he any intimate relationship with anything but with the new, green blades showing their tips through the fertile earth?

The original question of why a diary, why a journal becomes more obscure the more of them we read. Journals of Wesley, Fox and Elizabeth Fry, of Evelyn Waugh, Thomas Merton, and a dozen others try to lay the same kind of hard and passionate grasp on God. Novels and plays may be shaped into consistency. But the diary reveals not that to err is human but that to be mixed and mixed-up, to be inconsistent, irrational, clever and sensible is in general what we are. Fox, mad and hugely merciful and sane, Johnson, with his tics and jerks, his desperate war on his own nature, Pepys, in his own unforgettable sentence, 'in a strange slavery to the beauty of women and music'—they wear our own face, their heartbeat is ours. Once, at Plymouth I seem to remember, Elizabeth Fry saw Great Britain's huge concourse of warships, the old wooden walls lying at anchor. She was a Quaker and dedicated pacifist. Yet she burst into tears. They were hot and unwanted tears for part of them sprang from pride in her own country's power and the majesty of its fleet and she knew that pride was a sin but could not control it; and there was also compassion in those tears for she saw these ships, patched up and contradicting the elements, as a metaphor of the human condition, of the voyage we are all bound on whether we like it or not.

History, where trends and groups and parties are named, is like a landscape with figures that have the assiduity and anonymity of ants. Biography moves in closer and shows us a single human face, and one man's opinion of it. But in diaries people paint a careful, injudicious and often unconscious portrait of themselves. Year by year, date by date, the picture, the portrait builds up. It is not merely the closeness of the pen to the subject, it is the minuteness of the strokes. From Jimmy Mason up to Queen Victoria, and from Elizabeth Fry across to Augustus Hervey.they cannot but, if I may be colloquial, 'give away their game.'

We have come a long way from the footprint in the pool and the hand prints on the cave wall. I have conducted a search through what material occurred to me to find a motive and believe I have failed; or if not failed, come up with a mixture of motives so wide as to be no motive at all. A journey without an end, then—but at least it has been fun.

Rough Magic

University of Kent at Canterbury, 16 February 1977

These are some elementary and mostly technical remarks about the novel and the writing of one. They are elementary remarks because I cannot think of any advanced ones. There is no inbuilt reason why it should be possible to talk about an art because you can practise it. If I were to ask a ballerina how she managed some particular virtuosity of movement and grace I should be wholly sympathetic if she replied in some such words as, 'Well, I get up on my points and keep time to the music.' Elementary remarks then, but at least they are from a practising novelist; they are from the horse's mouth. Unfortunately the older I grow the less I seem to know, the more blurred and trammelled with qualifications the slick or downright injunctions appear. The older I grow in the practice of an art the less I can find to say and the more often I am asked to speak about it. However, novelists do not write as birds sing, by the push of nature. It is part of the job that there should be much routine and some dull daily stuff on the level of carpentry.

On that level, I suppose everyone here would agree that all arts have necessary conventions, unrealities to which the audience assent in advance so that they may be ushered into the presence of more vivid reality. This has been defined as the willing suspension of disbelief, though it might be more accurate to call it the substitution of one level of belief for another. Lovers of the ballerina's virtuosity, or opera-goers, to take outstanding examples, know well enough how perilously suspended in a gossamer web of conventions are the things they attend to for their enjoyment. Even the spoken drama, though it has fewer conventions still has enough to make it astonishing to a rational but unimaginative mind how our attention can be held by such a two hours traffic; but held it is, and always has been. Let me throw in some fighting talk straight away and declare that far from liberating art from its conventions we ought to guard them as precious things and even add to them where we can. Let us claim that the more restrictions a man finds on his art—other things such as talent being equal—and the more he has to fight these conventions, use them, outwit them, defeat them as in Judo by allowing them to defeat themselves, the better his art is likely to be. The finest Egyptian statue was carved from basalt, the hardest stone available to them and one they must have found almost impossible to work.

Now if we look round the circle of writers, the word-smiths, we find their conventions unlike those to which the sculptor must conform in nature but the same in result. The conventions have, like basalt, the virtues of their defects and *vice-versa*. The simplest way to get alongside the conventions in which the novelist works is to compare them with the conventions which apply in an art to which the novelist might find his work akin. Let us first set up the conventions in which the dramatist works. I do not mean the fourth wall, the speeded-up time, the unnatural positioning of characters so that people who supposedly are not even present can both hear and see. I mean the convention so vast we seldom think of it at all. Here we have human beings, physical beings, pretending to be someone else. Obvious, is it not? Yet it is not simple. This is the profoundest limitation and advantage of the dramatist's approach. The advantage is an immediate appeal to our eye and ear. Half the job of persuading us into an absorbed interest is done by our first view of these people, who are so solidly and demonstrably there. At ground level, so to speak, they do not have to do much or say much to convince us, because real people sometimes behave like that. Any acuter movement or more entertaining dialogue is sheer gain. Well then, if the advantage is so great why do some writers bother to write a novel when they could write a play and get most of the job done for them by the loan of half-a-dozen talented people? But conventions have the virtues of their defects. Remember the over-hard Egyptian basalt. The playwright with his talented actors is facing a next-to-impossible task. If you should be so anti-social as to enter a theatre during a performance and find a person lying prone in that perambulatory area at the back of the auditorium——and not only lying there but gnawing the nylon carpet——you may be sure it is the unfortunate author of the piece who has just heard one of his talented actors reverse the meaning of a speech by the use of an inflection he has thought up himself. The playwright who has tried to control his work and tried to keep his own hand on it, who has tried to preserve the original force and intention of the thing he once saw so vividly in his own mind, finds instead that he is wrestling with Proteus, the Old Man of the Sea, who changes shape and nature constantly. I have been through this experience myself and I know what I am talking about. In a sentence, the playwright has solid people there but cannot control them.

This is our direct way into a consideration of the novelist's contrasting job. It is the true opposite of the playwright's. The novelist has no servant to carry a character about with him. We, readers now rather than spectators, each of us a separate awareness in the circle of a skull, each willing to have what the author offers inside the circle, but needing thereafter to be wooed and tickled constantly by something or other as a reminder that the book is there in front of us——we allow him one bite like a dog. After that he is on his own. He must, like a sorcerer, raise up appearances, simulacra in our circle of skull, which will take on the likeness of individual men and women in whom we may become deeply interested and whose strictly unreal, paper fate may inundate us with amusement, curiosity, joy, grief. As Samuel Richardson's *Clarissa* came out volume by volume, the whole of London seemed to hang on what would happen next. In the novel, poor Clarissa suffers a fate worse than death and the London public seemed as outraged as she. When it became evident that Clarissa would die, strong men did not weep, merely, they threatened Richardson with physical violence. Even his first novel, *Pamela*, evidently hit on an archetypal situation, for Mistress Pamela's adventures were followed throughout the country as if every girl's personal fate depended on them. In a Yorkshire village, a lady asked her maid why the church bells were ringing so joyfully and got the reply, 'Oh madam! Mistress Pamela is married at last!' Could any author ask for profounder attention or more generous recognition? Evidently the absence of some more or less reliable body to carry your character about for you is not too much of a handicap. Yet this kind of sorcery, this raising up of spirits in the mind of another is so common we tend to forget how mysterious a thing it is. Did we not see how dogs dream of rabbits I should be tempted to define man as the image-making animal; but at the least I believe homo-sapiens is in part distinguished from the rest of the world by his ample supply of the invisible material necessary for this strange traffic between us.

Now since the novelist has invented his characters they cannot provoke him with a wrong inflection. He can put his intention beyond doubt by creating inside our skulls—once, that is, he has effected an entry—the very tones and actions of the speaker. He is what the playwright would often like to be, that is, actor- and director-proof. I offer a few of these aids to precision, taken at random from a handful of paperbacks.

'Yes, you may well look sheepy,' Ortheris squeaked to the boys.

'I thought Caroline had aborted you,' he said baldly. 'Mother said the child had been got rid of.'

Here is one I owe to *You're a Brick, Angela!*

'Did you hear?' she remarked. 'They actually want to join the Dramatic!'

'Cheek,' murmured Consie, and the others giggled.

'And why shouldn't we join?' flamed Gladys Wilkes.

'Why? Because you're day-girls and the Dramatic's only for boarders. That's why.'

If you belong to a dramatic society or drama workshop, it might be illuminating to take these descriptions literally, perform them and see how much it can teach you about the difference between theatrical action—theatrical in its root sense—and verbal narration. How about this?

'Will you tell me your name?' Sir Anthony said gently.

'It is Prudence, sir. In truth, I know no more. I have had many surnames.' There was no hint of bitterness in her voice, nor any shame. It was best the large gentleman should know her for the adventuress she was.

'Prudence?' Sir Anthony was frowning now. 'So that is it,' he said softly. She looked up, searching his face.

'You are not very like your father,' said Sir Anthony. She gave nothing away in her expression, but she knew that he had very nearly the full sum of it.

There fell a silence. 'Prudence——' Sir Anthony repeated and smiled. 'I don't think you were very well named, child.' He looked down at her and there was a light in his eyes she had never seen there before. 'Will you marry me?' he said simply.

Now at last there came surprise into her face, on a wave of colour. She rose swiftly to her feet and stood staring. 'Sir, I have to suppose you jest!'

Or if there is a member of your company you think would be better employed in some less demanding occupation, you might try him with this.

'Oh God it is unutterable! I *cannot* live without my life! I *cannot* live without my soul!' He dashed his head against the knotted trunk; and lifting up his eyes, howled, not like a man, but like a savage beast getting goaded to death with knives and spears. There were several splashes of blood about the bark of the tree and his hand and forehead were both stained; probably the scene was a repetition of others acted during the night.

Those of you whose acquaintance with the English novel is as yet, so to speak, in the egg, may be interested to hear that the extract, badly written, implausible, ridiculous, is from one of the most famous of our novels, I mean *Wuthering Heights*.

But I am doing novelists a disservice. Let us leave these amusing trifles and see how a really experienced novelist can keep the precise action and tone of the narrated drama going on inside us.

'I'd better knock,' thought Tom, 'sooner or later; and I had better get it over.'

Rat tat.

'I'm afraid that's not a London knock,' thought Tom. 'It didn't sound bold. Perhaps that's the reason why nobody answers the door.'

It is quite certain that nobody came, and that Tom stood looking at the knocker; wondering whereabouts in the neighbourhood a certain gentleman resided, who was roaring out to somebody, 'Come in!' with all his might.

'Bless my soul!' thought Tom at last. 'Perhaps he lives here and is calling me. I never thought of that. Can I open the door from the outside, I wonder? Yes, to be sure I can.'

To be sure he could, by turning the handle: and to be sure when he did turn it, the same voice came rushing out, crying 'Why don't you come in? Come in do you hear? What are you standing there for?' quite violently. Tom stepped from the little passage into the room from which these sounds proceeded, and had barely caught a glimpse of a gentleman in a dressing-gown and slippers (with his boots beside him ready to put on) sitting at his breakfast with a newspaper in his hand, when the said gentleman at the imminent hazard of oversetting his tea-table, made a plunge at Tom, and hugged him.

'Why Tom, my boy!' cried the gentleman. 'Tom!'

'How glad I am to see you, Mr Westlock!' said Tom Pinch, shaking both his hands and trembling more than ever. 'How kind you are!'

And so on. In dramatic terms that is a little dialogue with a mass of stage-directions. Observe however with what docility we obey the directions. We would no more dream of substituting some other actions, some other mood for the one the author has designed for us than we would dream of reading the book backwards. Indeed we *could* not read and substitute at the same time. At least, I could not. But take that small dialogue, throw away the prose surrounding it. Reinflect the speeches and you could produce a version for instance in which Pinch and Westlock detested each other because of a covert homosexual feeling against which each was unaware he was fighting, or some such; strip them naked and get your dramatic version of the book declared to be a fresh and uninhibited examination of the text. Pity the poor playwright! He is the last person to be considered, unless he is dead, when the whole thing may undergo a further convolution. But within the covers of his novel the novelist is king and we his obedient subjects. He can bring on an earthquake with as little trouble as make a cup of tea. If a character gives him trouble he can have him shot. He is lord of birth, of love, of death, those three dimensions in which all story, all succession operates.

It would seem at first sight would it not, then, that the author of a novel has everything his own way. We invite him in and let him do what he likes. But observe. It is easier to put down a book than it is to leave the seat of a theatre. The novelist can doodle as much as he likes, but may come to with an awful start to find nobody is listening. The playwright can see his audience if he cares to look, count them and calculate, can assess their every response. But to the novelist the people who read his books are as remote as creatures of the deep sea. So there is a behest to be engraved over the novelist's door. Have one hand holding your pen and the other firmly on the nape of the reader's neck. That is rule one, to which everything else must be sacrificed. Once you have got him, never let him go. How this is achieved differs from writer to writer—the stunning opening sentence, the witty preamble or the plunge into the middle of things—it is all a matter of judgement and there are no rules other than the one I have enunciated. It is all story, that is, succession of events. Yet story is not enough. Now of course story is natural to man. It is a distinguishing mark of his mind—but the natural story, unadorned, has little to do with what I am saying. Natural story is a generalized concept which might contain, say, ballad, epic, even saga, fairy tale. We are concerned with the type of story *we* call a novel in the Western world and the twentieth century. An epic hero is no more than a changeless state of mind and usually rather hysterical, as witness his mixture of brutality and tearfulness. A creature in a fairy tale is one aspect of things, as it were, crystallized out from the rich solution of human character and existing in a state of chemical purity. But the novel, a form evolved for the peculiar circumstances of our literate Western civilization, though it may have something in common with all these forms and indeed with myth and fable and allegory too, has some particular requirements which are not found spread out through all narration. The main one, to my mind, is not found anywhere else except perhaps in classical drama with its catastrophe: the novelist's characters must be seen to undergo a change. He or she must change in a way that is credible and before the very eyes of our spirit. The novelist may, if he dares, spend a little time with his character as a static phenomenon but not much. Remember how easily that book can be put down! The novelist shudders—a goose has walked over his grave—he remembers how often he has heard the casual remark 'No, I couldn't seem to get on with it.' All that effort, devotion, to hang on such a whim! So that the great and necessary ingenuity of the novelist's craft, his journeyman's craft I would say, since this is no more than how to keep the edge of the wood straight or make a chair stand on four legs without rocking, is how to raise up the character as the Witch of Endor raised up Samuel, raise him, describe him and set him moving and changing all at once. There's judgement for you! That calls for a good eye and a steady hand. For the character must be introduced somehow, there's no help for it or you will hear the ghostly whisper of voices, 'No, somehow I couldn't seem to get *into* it.' How much description can we afford? If your story-teller has pleased you before with some other performance so that you have some faith in him, he may risk a little static description. You allow him his first bite, like a dog. If the first sentence is witty or the description acute or both our audience will hold our book just that much longer, may be beguiled—but not very long, these days, with all the competition from the aerial on the novelist's roof, which is driven into the brick or thatch, a self-inflicted wound.

It is a truth universally acknowledged that a single man in possession of a good fortune must be in want of a wife.

Come now, we may stay with this; and so we should. Let us look at some others.

In the days of high-waisted and muslin-gowned women, when the vast amount of soldiering going on in the country was a cause of much trembling to the sex, there lived in a village near the Wessex coast two ladies of good report, though unfortunately of limited means.

Interesting, we think, the immediate evocation of a fashion; but doubtful, that consciously substituted word 'sex' for 'women' or 'ladies' or 'female sex'. But Mr Hardy's *Under the Greenwood Tree* entertained us just sufficiently—Yes. We will allow this book its first bite. Or if the word 'Wessex' has already aroused in us the faint feeling of weariness that a later generation may feel to surround such a name as 'Bloomsbury', down goes the book and we pick up another. What's this?

To the red country and part of the grey country of Oklahoma the last rains came gently, and they did not cut the scarred earth. The ploughs crossed and recrossed the rivulet marks.

So it goes on, a description of nature that is professional, seductive. It does not let go. It moves from a generality to a specific. It is *not* static. On the first page it takes us through nature's normal rhythm suffering an interruption, the coming of a drought, though significantly everything is active not passive—the rains actively did *not* come.

Then it was June and the sun shone more fiercely. The brown lines on the corn leaves widened and moved in on the central ribs. The weeds frayed and edged back towards their roots.

Now we move up from the botanical to the animal.

> In the roads where the teams moved, where the wheels
> milled the ground and the hoofs of the horses beat the ground,
> the dirt crust broke and the dust formed.

Only then do we see our first human being, and they are legendary as
it may be Cain and Abel, they are like some painting by Blake. They
are 'the people'. In particular if we were American we might pick up
on that first page some resonance from the wheels milling the
ground. The hoofs beating it and the dust forming, not only because
of the 'dust bowl' with which we are all too familiar but because we
understand that this ground is being trodden as *The Grapes of Wrath*.

> Every moving thing lifted the dust into the air; a walking man
> lifted a thin layer as high as his waist, and a wagon lifted the dust
> as high as the fence tops, and an automobile boiled a cloud
> behind it.

The great theme of the book has been laid before us, a sun caught in
rising clouds of copper and grey and bronze, men like trees walking.
Successive pictures will bring us nearer and nearer to the people and
then to individuals. It is a magnificent illustration of sheer daring,
insolence almost, in the management of story-telling and qualifies
Steinbeck for the 'I could not put this book down' prize.

  Yet most authors I believe would avoid this approach which
might be described as Miltonic. They get to their characters as
individuals as quickly as they may. Encouraged by Steinbeck we
might look a bit further back in American writing to see what it has
for us.

> Strether's first question when he reached the hotel, was
> about his friend; yet on his learning that Waymarsh was
> apparently not to arrive till evening he was not wholly
> disconcerted. A telegram from him bespeaking a room 'only if
> not noisy', reply paid, was produced for the enquirer at the
> office, so that the understanding they should meet at Chester
> rather than Liverpool remained to that extent sound.

What's all this? We grasp a rather limp hand when we embark on reading *The Ambassadors* by Henry James though that hand can exert extraordinary strength if we accommodate ourselves to it. But if this is the first of his books to come our way we shall be uncertain whether the elaborately negative language makes the invitation worth the journey. The journey *is* worthwhile but you cannot say that the author made it an easy one to begin with and here and there further on, the hedges of elaborate prose seem to meet impenetrably across the pathway of narration. It is the verbal opposite to the characterless bloods, the sex and violence brigade, published shall we say by Messrs Bang and Bang and designed for a short railway journey. James does really expect too much from the average reader. Like James Joyce he might say, 'All I ask from my readers is a life time's devotion.' Unlike James Joyce, at least as far as *The Ambassadors* is concerned, he seldom gets it and that is a pity.

In general what grabs the reader is a character who is doing something; or if not doing something at least being something. It is all very well for Steinbeck to delay with dust as Dickens in the same emblematic way delays *Bleak House* with fog but these are inspirations rather than professional and necessary carpentry.

But I am no further on than the first page of a book. We must get on. I said that a character when the person appears must move and act because he must change and develop later on. He must be living. Forgive me if I turn to Jane Austen again; but she is the novelist's novelist. Hear what she does for us in the first sentence of *Persuasion*.

> Sir Walter Elliot, of Kellynch-Hall, in Somersetshire, was a man, who, for his own amusement, never took up any book but the Baronetage; there he found occupation for an idle hour, and consolation in a distressed one; there his faculties were aroused into admiration and respect, by contemplating the limited remnant of the earliest patents; there any unwelcome sensations, arising from domestic affairs, changed naturally into pity and contempt, as he turned over the almost endless creations of the last century—and there he could, if every other leaf were powerless, read his own history with an interest which

never failed—this was the page at which the favourite volume
always opened: 'Elliot of Kellynch-Hall.'

And so on. Miss Austen dares not only to give his entry in the book
but she amplifies it with his whole pedigree—because his pedigree is
most of the man and on the first satiric page she gets him for ever and
the reader with him. I say satiric; but where a satirist like Pope
destroys his victims with flashes of lightning, Miss Austen often
roasted her victims over a fire so slow and nicely judged that the
thickskinned feel no discomfort on their behalf at all but only a
gentle tickling; which is why Jane Austen's epitaph in Winchester
Cathedral is the *possibly* satiric sentence, 'Her tongue speaks wisdom
and in her heart is the law of kindness.' Indeed, she roasts her
readers in the Regency sense. Some have argued that these stories
are simple romances with no hurt in them so that we see her as the
ultimate enchantress and her spell a kind of continual and delicate
ambiguity. We might murmur to ourselves what Falstaff said to
Mistress Quickly—we should never dare to *say* it to Miss
Austen—'A man knows not where to have you.' Yet somehow for
all her ambiguity, objectivity, inscrutability, she brings us little by
little to a great friendship for them and a need to know what will
happen to them. Does not our dear Emma—a cousin, one feels, to
everyman—change all the way in a process which is life itself,
discovery, rebuke, self-examination, contrition? Have we not come
to so close a knowledge of her that part of our affection for her is
rooted in exasperation, amusement, and the wry knowledge that in
some unwritten volume she will come to do it all over again? In such
a book and with an author of such genius, event and character are
nicely balanced. They produce each other but the emphasis is on
character. The changes in character are the very substance of the
book. That is why the stories of the *One Thousand and One Arabian
Nights* in four thick volumes, where character is sacrificed to event as
it must be in an oral tradition, seem to sink away into the sand after
we have read them, leaving nothing behind but a kind of magical
iridescence, while the year or so of Emma seems like a
well-remembered period of our own lives. Change of character is
essential. The point need not be laboured since the examination of

any respectable work, from Dorothea in *Middlemarch* to Fagin in *Oliver Twist*, will demonstrate it.

Still, change must be carried. Change is event, and in a novel time must never have a stop. If we were to look through the novelist's window and catch him at his work we should see that he had a clock and operates in a constant awareness of it. I do not mean datelines, or so many words a day, though they will be a preoccupation. I mean he knows that he must operate in an awareness of movement, of succession. How fast or slow is up to him, his individual and let us hope informed opinion. One novelist of my acquaintance thinks always of this movement in the deliberately down-to-earth terms of 'what the traffic will bear' or 'will they wear it', 'they' in this case being the mass of his readers. But the movement can be fast or slow so long as it is continual. It can be of awful, cataclysmic precipitance or minimal, the one movement following the other as in a set of musical variations. You may have your earthquake or your battle; and the louder and swifter it all is, the gentler the movement that may follow. That is obvious. Can we not imagine a chapter about a man seated at a table? If he thinks, merely, unless he does so with sparkling wit, we notice things are not happening, and what is all this? How should we fill this chapter? He must decide something, an interior movement if nothing else. Must we have a minute and physiological description of the processes involved? I do not discount the idea but do not feel myself drawn to it. Let us seat him at the table, then. He is deciding to write a letter. He picks up his spectacles to do so. Finally he decides not to write the letter and puts them down again. Between the picking up and the putting down, there is the long *active* holding of the spectacles and the long interior debate as to yes or no. There were hesitation, half-decisions, an attempt at balancing arguments for and against, reconsiderations until at last, with a perhaps defeated gesture he puts down the spectacles, end of chapter seventeen. The letter may have been crucial in the development of story and character, the movement forward apparently minimal, yet the whole weight of the story may have lain on it. Without the spectacles the story would have stood still and the reported interior monologue become an essay. Our author who has raised up the spirit of the man with the spectacles in our skulls could get away with it once, perhaps, but not more. If we set aside such one-off examples of virtuosity as *Tristram Shandy* in which the chapter on noses is an essay and practically thumbed in the face of the reader, there are not many stories as such in which the author makes a habit of delay and survives through it. You will remember I hope that the last chapter of *Ulysses* is sixty-five pages long. For a great deal of the chapter, Molly Bloom's soliloquy, nothing happens at all. The key to this literary outrage lies not in the printed words but in the full stop at the end. The author was very particular as to the exact size of the full stop. In my copy, alas, it is full stop and no more. James Joyce, however, wanted it to be, if I remember correctly, three-sixteenths of an inch in diameter. It was to represent the final nothingness, unconsciousness, for what happens to Molly Bloom is that she falls asleep; and it is sometimes a close run thing between Molly Bloom and the reader.

I have laid it down as a necessary convention of the novel that action must advance at one pace or another but that the advance must be continual. Of course, even if we do not commit a Shandian outrage and write a novel with a preface, a wandering middle and no end we can still cheat the reader for his own good. As Haydn said, 'Gentlemen, rules are my very obedient, humble servants.' Halfway to a flouting of the rule of continual advance is an apparent indifference to it, a delay that lulls the reader who does not know that we propose to clout him good and hard. If a great event is toward, then at the very moment of crisis the author can delay, can indulge himself in some, what shall I say, some rhetoric if you like, some eloquence, some diversion or divergence; and he can do it for precisely as long as his reader's excited interest and suspense will last. That is a very pretty calculation and can go disastrously wrong, particularly nowadays when novels are not read first of all as serials but come in one thick volume. If the writer has overestimated his own cleverness the reader may simply skip the writer's most cherished pages just to get on to see, for example, whether they did or didn't. The most successful example of the delaying tactic I can recollect offhand is in *Vanity Fair*. For the author knows what we do not; which is that something has indeed happened and that it will strike us all of a heap. Only after Thackeray has described the whole course of the Battle of Waterloo does he reveal to us that Amelia's husband is lying dead, with a bullet through his heart. That is technique. Thackeray keeps us in suspense and ignorance for our own good, so that when the revelation comes the story shrinks terribly from a wide panorama of history to the fate of a single man. Inasmuch as we have been caught up in the play of characters, his death is as terrible to us as our involvement has been deep. The spirits Thackeray raised up have become so real that we truly grieve with them.

But in the language of chess, we have got, without quite knowing how, from the opening into the middle game. We are in the richness of the novel. I spoke of rhetoric just now, then substituted the word eloquence; but in truth, both words have been unjustly blown on. Rhetoric, the art of persuading by means of words and the acceptance of that means of persuasion, is part of the contract we entered into when we invited the writer to invade the circle of our skulls and raise up his appearances there. Of course rhetoric in this sense is the fabric of the novelist's craft as wood is of the carpenter's. We forget it most of the time and should be made to forget it. The deliberate cunning of the novelist as a rhetorician exercised as it is on our behalf must stand with change of character and movement and those 'stage directions' as a component. Indeed, it is often most markedly present when it seems most absent. Theodore Dreiser's deliberate clumsiness and Hemingway's monosyllabic and threadbare vocabulary are in fact examples of rhetorical artfulness. The man sounds so dense, we feel, he *must* be feeling deeply! He *must* be sincere! No one with as much poster art as that can possibly be phoney! As far as I am concerned the question remains open. But whatever may be the true stature of the novelist in question, the artlessness is an attempt at least at the art that conceals art. It is the novelist's equivalent of the playwright's ingenuity when he made Cordelia say—

> unhappy I
> who cannot heave my heart into my mouth.

—saying more thereby than Regan and Goneril get out in a whole page of blank verse.

A character dressed in the plain or ornate fabric of eloquence, subject to the swift or slow, the racing, jolting or loitering hands of the novelist's private clock, and changing as he moves forward through a succession of events either does or does not impinge upon our consciousness as real; and if real, the real in one of a whole set of degrees of reality. The trappings, the uniform may be real enough, the exterior appearance convincing. Yet in a curious way that I find difficult to describe, these trappings when we have found them in the author's prose tend to fade away into unimportance. Is not our memory of Mr Pickwick's appearance based more on the original illustrations than on the description of him in the text? Yet whatever reality Pickwick has as a character arises from his movement through the book's rhetoric in a series of actions of monumental stupidity. The true reality of Pickwick that stays with us is Dickens's own discovery that inside the drawing of a pathologically fat and complacent fool there is a core of steel. Mr Pickwick goes to jail rather than comply with an unjust demand for damages. In those days of serial publication the change was not foreseen by Dickens but it turns Pickwick from an impossibly farcical figure into a man. That was not done by engravings but by rhetoric deployed *in extenso*. True, in our present world unjust imprisonments do not always end as happily as Mr Pickwick's but Dickens wrote for a wide popular audience. T. S. Eliot, never one, I always felt, for giving undue admiration to the common man, declared that we cannot stand much reality. In a novel, provided the clock does not stop and the character cease to change we can stand as much reality as talent or genius can give us.

There have been recipes for achieving that reality. Did not Conrad lay it down as a prime aid that the writer must know something about each character that he will not put in the book and will not reveal to any reader or critic? It is as if Conrad felt he could play the God and that this secret knowledge was akin to breathing some kind of life into clay. A rational explanation would be that this awareness gives the character depth; and the writer, feeling that depth will allow himself his own mystification and deal with the inscrutability of the character as if he were writing of a quote real unquote person. But then, in the mess and confusion of a novel's begetting and bringing to birth there are few things less satisfactory than a rational explanation. Ernest Hemingway, early in his writing life—he does not seem to have continued or improved the claim for method that he made to, I think, Fitzgerald—Ernest Hemingway, excessive in everything but vocabulary, said you should have a complete unwritten story running along under the written one. I can only remember one story in which he did try the method—I believe it is in the collection *Men without Women*, and the method, far from being hidden sticks out like a sore thumb—a singularly appropriate simile, if you read the story. Another aid to the raising of fictional spirits in the charmed circle is for the writer to be aware of some touch in his story, some thing however slight it be, that actually happened out there in the real world. The event may be disguised, may become an enigmatic sentence that puzzles the critic, but it will lie in the bed of the river of words like a stone, itself invisible but making a swirl on the surface. It can be a remark, perhaps; and in the inevitable hours when the writer suffers the anguish of doubting the plausibility of his own inventions it can be a sheet anchor—that last anchor kept for the ultimate emergency when the ship is driving towards the rocks. On the other hand, no less a writer than Henry James, that man of infinite talent, ingenuity, sensibility without genius, talks of 'the fatal fatuity of the fact'. Clearly these hot, practical tips, hints, recipes for concocting an acceptable fiction, contradict each other. Like tribal laws—which in some way they resemble—there are many ways of writing novels. There is no help for it. If you want to write you must choose among the tips or invent your own.

Then is that appearance no more than an appearance, a juggling trick, the sleight of hand which is quicker than the eye? The question is worth asking since novelists among the innocent—I mean those who have not written a novel if there are any left—novelists have a reputation for seeing further through a brick wall than most. Some people believe, or at least in my own experience pretend to believe, that a novelist does, as it were *see* people for what they are. A member of the presumed non-writing public will even approach such a man with a degree of trepidation. He wishes to discover if there is any mark of Cain, any visible connection between the fleshly creature and the printed page. Those eyes—do they in fact see? Behind those pebble glasses do other mortals pass as before a seat of judgement?

The question is not as preposterous as it looks. You could argue that the novelist, preoccupied with his inventions, has really dissolved people into a sort of mush out of which he fishes his characters like unlicked cubs. Among writers there is fair agreement that most real characters are useless for the purposes of fiction. No one would possibly believe in them. They must be toned down. The question is as wide and impossible to answer as some such fundamental enquiry as 'what is man that thou has made him?' We can see how the trappings of character could be come by. The author does notice, he does take notes if only mental ones. The man has a red nose, is balding, and plainly believes that the world of horse racing is the only one of any importance. Into the book he goes, fawn waistcoat, binoculars, check trousers and all. The details are heaped up until we can visualize the character from the elastic sides of his pull-on boots to the ginger hairs that project on either side of his head. But is not the author now in the helpless position of Michelangelo before the completed figure of Moses? Should he not cry 'Speak!' and hurl his hammer or his pen at it? What would happen? A chip flies off the statue and there is a blot on the page, no more. The statue must move as we mention it. It must pull on those boots, the ginger hairs must rise again as his hand passes over them. Is this what the occasional common man or woman means when he credits the novelist with a special and specific kind of perception? Certainly the trick—for it is no more—can be very convincing. Kipling was particularly good at it. He was a noticing man. He was better, though, at observing than at perceiving. Perhaps he did not dissolve the whole human race into the necessary soupy mush; but if he did not take physical notes about people he certainly had something like a total recall of them. Though his people move stiffly sometimes they move by very refined clockwork. Why should not clockwork entertain us, you may ask, as much as the genuine live thing? Nor—since we are not dealing with the mathematically demonstrable—is the clockwork movement always to be distinguished from raw life. I have enjoyed Kipling too much to denigrate him. Let us remember Private Ortheris cuddled down by a rock, muttering of fifteen hundred yards and a dropping shot, as he takes his expert aim at the lover climbing the side of the opposite mountain! Then, after the marvellous craftsman's shot and the crumpling of the distant body, his silent, satisfied stare—an artist contemplating his finished handiwork. Trappings? Clockwork? Do I really know what I am talking about? It is a question to which you might give a dusty, a short answer.

And yet, and yet, there is a better thing. It is what the innocent enquirer had at the back of his mind, with his trepidation before the novelist though he will not find that better thing in more than one novelist in a thousand—what am I saying? One case in ten thousand! The thing without which the run-of-the-mill novelist with a whole international reputation can pass his life amid respect and admiration—that better thing is a passionate insight. Like all phenomena on the very edge of awareness and differentiation it defies analysis, though not perhaps exemplary description.

I am about to do a dangerous thing. I am going to talk about saints or some of them—one of them. My own personal qualifications for talking about them are non-existent except in so far as saints do sometimes exhibit a quality which today would ensure them a wide reading public, continued and respectful academic analysis and a whole series of invitations to be writer in residence at this establishment or that. What would not a university department give for a series of lectures on the perception of character, if they were given by the Curé of Ars, Jean Vianney? Admittedly, he was near enough a half-wit but that drawback could be accommodated. He was quite unable, for example, to learn Latin. The inferences to be drawn from that today are less evident than they were in the last century. Let us come to what was most important in our context about him. He knew about people, not in the way of the trappings and exterior appearances—even the exterior actions—but in the nature of their very vital processes and movements, the beating of their spiritual hearts. As a confessor he was able to see clean through his penitent in a way you may call miraculous or inexplicable according to your individual taste. There is no arguing the fact. If it is not true, then no fact of his century is true. Or put in another way, the facts of Vianney's inexplicable power are as well recorded, documented and undeniable as any other fact of the nineteenth century. Step delicately as you may through the history of that time, take any system of belief or disbelief along with you and you will still break your shins over the fact of Vianney's extraordinary intuitions. Now I must perform a trick never done before, I think, on any stage and get novelists and saints into the ring together. For below what we are told is the purer vision, perception, of the saint there lies that curious region of the occult, of psychokinesis, extrasensory perception, second-sight; a region endlessly debated, fruitlessly investigated, and coming down at the end it seems, to a matter of individual opinion. Below that area again are there not in us all, hints and—not flashes—but sometimes sparks of the inexplicable, fleeting suggestions that of all things the human mind, its whole volume of mentation still remains the mystery of mysteries? May it not be, then, that the greatest of our novelists, the Flauberts, the Stendhals, the Dickenses, the Eliots, the Austens and Dostoevskis may find in themselves a tincture of that quality which exists in full power among the saints? I do not know, but think it possible. Remembering *Madame Bovary*, *Middlemarch*, *Crime and Punishment*, I have at least to constate some power that the average writer can admire but not comprehend. I surmise that those greater writers did not understand it either but were happy with the gifts the gods gave.

I have suggested places where that power of intuition may exist among the literature I am acquainted with. But the questions that follow the suggestion, the distinctions to be made, are oversubtle. Let the thought lie there to be developed or forgotten as you please. For the average writer as for the reader there is a lifeline that will take him along through most novels without the handicap of a too exquisite sensibility. The comfort is that as human beings I believe we are far more like each other than we are different. It is for that reason that the action of a novel may be hurried forward since necessary speeches can be put in the mouth of anyone. In an ideal world and perhaps in an ideal novel, any word, be it yes or no, or what or why would be said in a way peculiar to one person and to him alone. In the workaday novel common speeches and common action can be performed by any character because I dare guess that the pressure of awareness, the raw act of conscious living is ninety per cent the same for everybody. We insist on the ten per cent difference and call it character. But once introduced, Raskolnikov, Emma Bovary or Fabrice will carry *our* ninety per cent of common humanity along with them. This is the true aid to sympathetic identification. When we come on the flash of insight, the true genius, we have helped the author thereby to his triumph. The author who has attempted to dive down through the complexities of living to find a curious creature not usually found on the surface—that is, the creature half-emerged from its shell and so, vulnerable to investigation, I mean the human being going defencelessly about his business, must either bring back a photograph or a living memory of it to the surface again. He must keep it alive in the aquarium; or more mysteriously and dangerously he must allow the strange creature to live and develop in his heart and head. I find I have entered an area to which my powers of description are inadequate. The metaphors if they are to convey anything at all must be so mixed that our daylight awareness is under a strong compulsion to dismiss them as merely silly. I will add only one consideration and that in a kind of despair at my inability to treat of more than elementary and technical considerations in my own craft, or, if I essay something subtler and of more value, my inability to say what I mean. Perhaps these subtler things are not to be said. I have treated the craft of writing a novel as if it consisted of parts that are divisible. Indeed that is so. The parts are divisible or what are the technical terms for? There is character, movement, plot, method, development, intention and discovery. There is irony, peripeteia, catastrophe. Of *course* a writer can plan the map of what lies before him, having already in his mind some idea of the characters who will traverse it. He will indeed sometimes write a synopsis of what is supposed to happen in the next chapter; and if the unexpected event *does* break in will either accept it with gratitude or frugally put it away in a bottom drawer for a rainier day. But if we are to judge from the ample but strangely uninformative explanations of their methods that have been left us by the novelists who stand out from the rest, then it would seem that the act of creation is as strange to the writer as to his reader. Faced by the white blank page, isolated, separated in thought, feeling, even sensation, from the phenomenal world about him he creates not by a judicious arrangement, a calculation and balance, an engineering job of girders and interlocking forces. The act of creation is a fierce, concentrated light that plays on a small area. It is, though not to be set above the other capacities of the human spirit, nevertheless different from them. It is a single, lambent thing; and those with most experience in that area have been the ones who said least about it since they had better things to offer than lame explanations of how they worked.

In philosophy, and more precisely in the study of logic, I believe there is what might be called an ordering of languages, meta-language after meta-language. If I, who am no philosopher, have got this right, the situation may be stated as follows. Beyond each logical language in which a statement may be made there must be a further or higher language in which we may assent to or dissent from a statement made in the lower one. I am in a mess. This knowledge is too high for me. But there may be some analogy here in the world of the arts. They are orders of language, of communication in which statements of varying value—I will not be deterred from using the word value—statements of varying value may be made to the human intellect, or coming more nearly to home, to the human heart. For all the complexity of literature there is a single focus in literature, a point of the blazing human will. This is where definition and explanation break down. We must call on a higher language. The strength, profundity, truth of a novel lies not in a plausible likeness and rearrangement of the phenomenal world but in a fitness with itself like the dissonances and consonances of harmony. Insight, intuition. We are at a height—or a depth—where the questions are not to be answered in words. The greatest of all writers who between the green sea and the azured vault had set roaring war—for whom graves had opened and let forth their sleepers, did at last come to abandon the rough magic of his own creativity; and required after that, music, a solemn air, nothing but music; which remembering some high moments, you may now supply in your own hearts, leaving to the speaker the easier task of providing the necessary silence.

My First Book

from *The Author*, July 1981

In 1934 Messrs Macmillan published among their shilling series of 'Contemporary poets' *Poems*, by W. G. Golding. It ran to thirty-four pages and the verses ranged from four lines to twenty-eight. Today, in 1981, the book has been on offer in the United States at 4,000 dollars. This is nothing but value by association.

I have had a lifelong love of rhythm, sound, and in particular, rhyme. At my dame school there was a thing called 'recitation' where each age, from six to ten years old, stood up in turn and said the piece they had learnt by rote. I learnt everybody else's piece as well as my own, by listening. I had in a developed degree the 'flypaper memory' of childhood and never forgot what I had heard once. I had, too, a direct appreciation that verse was an important deed, though of course I never thought to formulate the feeling and probably could not have done so. Doctor Foster went to Gloucester and it was deliriously funny that he should take *that* name to *that* place, and quite appropriate that he should step into a puddle deeper than puddle ever was in a world gone clownish. And then—*Boot, saddle, to horse and away* was more of a rush than Brooklands, or fighter planes flying at more than a hundred miles an hour. Then, *Who will stand on either hand and keep the bridge?* I knew that I wouldn't stand on either hand but I could recognize and enjoy someone else's courage.

And so on. Of course the change came with the ugly word, that rearrangement of personality, additions of emotion, perception, joy, pain. Poetry began to speak to the whole man, or boy, rather. My first *adult* appreciation at thirteen or fourteen was of the more accessible sonnets of Shakespeare, *Shall I compare thee* of course and perhaps another half a dozen, together with the songs. I began to scribble after that—scribble at verse, I mean, for I had always been a scribbler of prose.

These verses were bits of lyric. I had a Wordsworthian belief in the primacy of the lyric. The lyric could be short and simple—the simpler the better. It is easier, on the whole, to read the poetry of a European language than its prose. Except in aberrations like metaphysical poetry the ideas, proclamations, celebrations, invocations, are not confused and detained by any close reasoning.

I quite early came to understand that poetry was a matter of what I will call *interior stance*. A man was either swept into that stance or willed himself into it. It might be called, in the case of the adolescent lyricist, the *vocative stance*. In my own case the oh's and ah's were fervent. Nevertheless, though Wordsworth would have condemned my habit of invoking the mighty dead rather than the living, he would have recognized the stance as would most of the romantics. It was to be many years later that I read and at last understood Cleanth Brooks's assessment of the stance where he points out how narrowly it limited the feelings and subjects thought worthy of poetry.

What had I that gave me any genuine relationship to the job? It was a small thing, I believe and not altogether helpful. I passionately enjoyed, lengthily savoured the *phrase*. It might not be *a jewel five words long* and was more likely to be two words only, a noun with attendant adjective. It would be a phrase that recreated by some magic the phenomenon that lay under its hand. This kind of phrase was the opposite of the Homeric epithet, which having done its first work of evocation was thereafter repeated as a moment of rest for the listener and was finally assimilated to the noun and became an accepted part of it. My phrases were not repeated—*multitudinous sea*, ανήριθμον γέλασμα, *sable muet, dew-dabbled poppies!* These were (and are) more precious than stamps or birds' eggs or crystals or jewels.

Out of *Thyrsis whose sweet art hath oft delayed the huddling brook to hear his madrigale*, my ear and eye and imagination took 'huddling brook' and saw (as it still sees) the very thing conjured by the words.

Let me call such a phrase a 'unit'. The capacity to invent a unit which was at first sight an advantage was in fact a hindrance when I came to essay extended verses. The verses tended to huddle like the brook rather than flow. They became so dense as to be opaque. They clotted rather than formed round the unit. Combined with the *vocative stance* they permitted no more than a brief comment on some idea so approachable, so universal as to be commonplace. Spring is coming or here or over, winter is about somewhere, how sweetly sad autumn is, how heavy summer by comparison. I was conscious that I said nothing but was uneasily preoccupied with how I said it.

Now this was particularly difficult at a time when——whether the word was current or not——a poet was supposed to be closely 'engaged' to social questions. I was quite disengaged, bar a very mild feeling which I got from my parents that the Labour Party was Our Side. I lacked the generosity of spirit that would give all——not merely life but writing too!——for the betterment of mankind. I was stuck with the unit. Even to think of getting the two words apart for alternative use in the same poem created in me a sympathetic muscular tension as if I were using chest developers. Indeed, to tear them apart would have violated the only thing I had. What was lacking in me——though I may have developed it later——was a certain mobility of outlook, the power to walk round the back and see the thing from the other side, to walk away from and see it in relation to what was all around. I could see what short verses were but not what by alteration and perhaps extension they might become. I lacked the attitude of the chess master, who, finding a good move, is not content, but looks for a better one. I have always been a curious mixture of conservative and anarchist. Translated into an attitude towards verse-making, this means either being content with a minimal result or destroying the thing petulantly.

Today, some of my units seem less jewels than pebbles; but after all, a pebble is a jewel of a sort. To take an example, the phrase 'twisted violets' seemed to me to have the proper magical immediacy of evocation though it has not much power over my mind now. If there is a concordance to the sort of poetry which contents adolescents I might well find that the phrase was not my own for such associations of adjective and noun stick subliminally like advertisements. I search my mind for a few moments and come up with violet-embroidered dale, *sweet as Cytherea's eyelids*, and *the year's first violet white and lonely* though there must be hundreds more. Perhaps I *was* the first who ever put *twisted* and *violet* together!

This preoccupation with the minutiae of the craft was interrupted and now and then subsumed in another experience more like true eloquence—not I mean in value but in method. There were moments when a positive and coherent thought rose up with emotion and brought both rhyme and metre—it seemed in that order—to the surface of my mind. It was my first meeting with the mystery of the mind as not so much giving *to* airy nothing a local habitation as creating *out* of airy nothing. It was the unconscious (of which I had not heard) triggered by emotion—hardly to be distinguished from the involuntary phrases, ejaculations, admonishments, prayers, runes and spells that can be heard from the lips of a man talking, as we say, to himself. I will make a watery comparison and liken myself to a pipe furred with phrases that occasionally allowed squirts of liquid past to demonstrate that the tube was almost wholly blocked.

Clearly, if the cork could be taken out or the fur removed there would be some flow. I experienced it once, a remarkable example of how pure the flow could be—pure, as it were, in terms of hydrodynamics rather than in the intrinsic value of the resultant fluid. I wanted to go back to Cornwall and the sea but was in Wiltshire. While walking on the Marlborough Downs where now there is a memorial stone to Edward Thomas, Alfred Williams, the 'railway poet', and Charles Hamilton Sorley, I saw what was rare in those days, a seagull come swooping down along the wind. I was fourteen or thereabouts. With the sight there rose in my mind as an automatic expression of what I felt, the following rhymes. They have their absurdities of course but they show that the flow was there.

Across the sunlit downs the west wind sings
    Its ocean melodies. I stand and see
You wheel the white flash of your long, swift wings
    And for this moment being I am free:
As one who holds a shell against his ear
    And listens rapt until the sullen roar
Seems in his soul to echo faint and clear
    The slow surf-murmur of a distant shore.

Memory, of course, was working overtime. I have heard somewhere else of a man who held a shell to his ear and 'for this moment being' is no more than a filler, like 'as of this moment in time'. Yet the flow was there.

I knew even then, how strong in me would be the impulse to rewrite in an inferior manner the more accessible romantics. Uneasily I wrote my seagull lines down, not daring to alter a word—I have not done so now—although I understood their imperfection. Uneasily as time passed and I fiddled with my two word phrases—my units—I saw the engagement of my contemporaries move farther and farther away from what was important to me. I had no interest in politics, none in the USSR, none whatever in tractors. I felt the whole generous movement was wrong but knew that I could not be right. One solitary adolescent! And yet—

The trouble of course was Tennyson. I devoured him and had done so right back to the time when as a seven year old I had taken home 'hafaleeg hafaleeg hafaleegonward' as some wonderful stuff the seniors had learnt. As an adolescent I fell for *splendour falls* and *willows whiten* and *now sleeps the crimson petal*. Only *Come down O maid from yonder mountain height* troubled me. I knew the poem faced the wrong way for all its verbal magnificence—I knew that even if someone could not *glide a meteor by the blasted pine* he should not persuade someone else from that height or let on he could not reach it himself. Besides, Tennyson, I knew, was *out*. As a child, boy, adolescent, young man, I still loved him in the face of all criticism. I knew his deficiencies. It will be a bleak world when we love nothing but perfection. I could understand Tennyson, readily enough, since after a brilliant boyhood he never again got his intellectual feet wet. He was wholly accessible. He was a master of the phrase but spread his thought nearly as thin as Swinburne did. His *stance* was more rigid even than mine. His instinct was to keep things as they were. In a word, he was *bourgeois*, which as much as anything else was why he was *out*. I was not to know how often he would be in and out during my lifetime.

Like Tennyson I lacked intellectual mobility or if I had any intellect and mobility I was too lazy to use it. I went on writing my sub-Thomas, sub-Keats verses. I fashioned them as if from precious metal. The eloquence of immediacy appeared less and less often. It came sometimes in moments of savage contempt, as when I heard people lusting after murder cases and executions. I acquired a mass of odds and ends in the way of verse. I moved from school to university, still young for my age and ineffably naive. The flow seemed heavily blocked.

Yet there was a pressure somewhere. I can be sure of that because of an experience analogous to the one with the seagull which I only now recall to mind after a lapse of exactly fifty years. In my first year at Oxford I met a man who dabbled in hypnotism. I was eager for any experience that would release me from an increasingly grey daylight and from the labs where the frogs twitched and the rabbits' guts swelled in the hot summer humidity. I embraced his proposal that he should hypnotise me and he made his passes. I knew it was no good but pretended in a curious way which I think must apply to all subjects under hypnotism—a cooperation and a pretence that was only half a pretence. When the light of the room became normal again I saw that my acquaintance was looking pale. I raised my eyebrows at him. He wiped his forehead with a handkerchief which I remember was rather dirty.

'It was like a chapter of the old testament.'

I never saw him again.

A friend lent me a typewriter. Another sent a sheaf of my verses to the publisher. They were not the ones I would have chosen, merely those to hand which I had already typed. I received a letter from a Captain Macmillan offering me five pounds and a place among my contemporaries, Yvonne ffrench, Hugh Macdiarmid, T. W. Ramsey, R. C. Trevelyan, Norman C. Yendell. I kept the secret and waited for the day of publication, like Peacock's Mr Skythrop and like Skythrop was disappointed, for of course nothing happened. My experience was that of tens of thousands of other would-be poets. I sent off a second collection of verses written since the others and also including many that had missed the first volume but Captain Macmillan was no longer interested. He may well have been right.

A Moving Target

Address to *Les Anglicistes*, Rouen, 16 May 1976

I am very conscious of the honour done me by your invitation and a little intimidated by it. In the first place, since I was forced to send you a Title before I had thought of anything to say we may be a long time in getting anywhere near the advertised one. More than that, what, you might ask, has a story-teller to tell but a story? Even more to the point, what has he to say to a gathering whose daily business it is to dissect, illustrate, appreciate, explain and vivify the best that has been written in the English language? I remember the mountains of critical work that fills our libraries—a mountain with which I suppose you to be far more familiar than I am, and my heart goes near to failing me. I contrast your, shall I say, *deliberate* learning with my own meagre equipment in that field, with my own knowledge which is so very uncritical, so wide and so shallow. If I have any insights to offer they may well be those a teacher, a critic, an academic would think too obvious to need stressing.

Yet by this time I ought to know something about the journeyman's job of keeping the covers of a book apart by sticking a story between them. Then again, no novelist in the second half of the twentieth century can be anything but part of a wide literary world that stretches from journalism into academia. Some elements in this world cancel each other out but some result in cross-fertilization. There is nothing in that world existing wholly to itself, nothing of crystal simplicity. There is no one who is creative without being just a little dissective, no one who is a mythologer of the unconscious without also being to some extent an analyst of the process by which he gets his daily bread. Indeed, I doubt that there ever has been a maker, a wordsmith in the wider sense, who has sung as the bird sings, warbling his native wood notes. Homer, most unliterary of story-tellers, though he did not have the benefit of the critical and explanatory library that has grown up round his work, must have known well enough what would draw old men from the chimney corner, what would keep an audience silent in hall and what ensured that he would be asked again. The story-teller must have this Homeric third ear, this equipment. To be without it would be unprofessional. I should have no excuse for having nothing to say, then. Nor—and here we touch on a situation with which Homer might be unfamiliar—nor can there be any rigid distinction drawn between the speaker and his audience, between me and ye. The academic world, the literary world, the world of journalism and that Bohemian world once called Grub Street, are now inextricably mixed, not just in the same country or city but, more often than not, in the same person. There must be the occasional sport, *ludus naturae*, but casting about in my mind for an example I could only think of Guiseppe di Lampedusa to test my rule. It is an impossible discovery, a writer who does nothing but exist in a state of passionate creativity. Of course all of us, writers, teachers, critics, though I cannot discover why, have a feeling that the wordsmiths ought to exist and we have, do we not, a desire, half romantic, half reluctant, to find them. Do we not feel that somehow we ought to be able to produce one, a test-tube example for our readers and pupils? I remember how, a good many years ago, I took a lecture of mine round the deeply trodden path of the American academic scene. This was at a time when those same campuses were still reverberating like a struck gong from the passage of the late Dylan Thomas. What stories we heard! What Bohemianism! What a picture of the wild man, the artist, destroyed as a kind of human sacrifice, almost a kind of Christ-substitute hung on the cross of his own art. It was Villonesque, that picture of a man who died in the poetic sense that we might have and respect poetry!

But if one enquired further, insisted a bit, the picture was not so clear. It was always a story from up the road, from somewhere else. At the next campus they say he did such and such—and look! Here is the very hole his cigarette burnt in our counterpane! But here, here where we were? Oh no! Curiously enough, here he had behaved well, had asked to be allowed to sleep, yes, all things considered, he behaved very well, rather dully in fact, like a man who has a schedule to keep. I began to understand then the deep need we feel for the sacrifice, for the creator rather than the critic. I came to the conclusion that this deep need accounts for the new trade of Writer in Residence—a trade in which a degree of eccentricity is accepted and even expected and in which some moral confusion is tolerated if not condoned. The truth is that in the West we fear the wells of creativity are running dry and we may be right. We are prepared to pay a good price for the creator and exhibit the creature in our universities, on a leash indeed, but a fairly long one. But money cannot buy the writer who produces his work—as John Keats said—as easily as the leaf comes to the tree. We must put up with what we can get—the man who is like an oak which puts out one green leaf now and then and apparently with much labour. In a large view one might even suggest that civilizations die and their literature with them. Man must not be stifled under paper. Perhaps the various burnings of the Alexandrian Library were necessary, like those Australian Forest Fires without which the new seeds cannot burst their shells and make a young, healthy forest.

You have told me, through the medium of the British Council, what you expect of me. First, you wish to know—and I quote from a voluminous correspondence—'What I think of the novel'. I interpret this to mean not that you want to know what I think of the history of the novel because you are more familiar with that than I am. Nor, I hope, do you expect me to talk about my contemporaries. Dog does not eat dog. No. I believe you to mean what do I think of the future of the novel—in fact, do I think it has any?

I am by nature a pragmatist with a touch of empiricism. First, then, I will avoid all theory and give a down-to-earth definition of what I include in the word 'novel'. I mean a story which is at least in part a fiction and which is not seen on a screen or heard through a loudspeaker but written down in a physical book. Down-to-earth as we are, let us first consider a book. I mean not a *teuchos* or *volumen* but a *codex*, the thing we have in our mind's eye when we use the word 'book'. Once, when I asked a friend of mine what he thought to be the greatest human invention, he immediately replied, 'The symphony orchestra'. I had not expected that answer; but I think it shows an innocence of vision which I hope we can all exercise on the present occasion. What a piece of work is a book! I am not talking about writing or printing. I am talking about the *codex* we may leaf through, that may be put away on a shelf for whole centuries and will remain there, unchanged and handy. We are so accustomed to crediting books with personality you will forgive my excursion into the pathetic fallacy when I speak of books as lying to hand with the obedience and humility of all harmless and useful beings. Of course, in a large library or bookshop we may see hundreds of yards of books and mutter, 'Good God—who would want ever to add to that lot?' But this is the reaction of surfeit. The book, the stack of conveniently arranged pages, is an invention, in its physical nature as near as anything can be to remaining beyond criticism. We have them so often before our eyes that we tend to forget the ingenuity concealed in their apparent simplicity. Our world is voracious and still becoming more so. Sooner or later, unless we exercise a care and forethought which is seldom evident in the mass of human beings, we shall be left with little more than village or small town economy. It is worth noting, therefore, that the making of books can be a cottage industry. If the need is there, anyone could learn that careful swirl of the tray and flick of the wrist that distributes the pulp evenly over the mesh and gives us handmade paper. Flax, leather, cotton, silk—the heart warms at the thought of them in our era of alloys and plastic. I say all this because I sometimes hear people say that the age of the book is past; and I suppose these statements to come from people who have a couple of thousand television sets on their shelves. But it will be a very advanced village industry that can manufacture a television set. Tapes, cassettes, records, radios, television sets are with us, certainly; but he would be a wise man who could predict how long we shall be able to afford them. Nor have these objects beauty in themselves. I think of a book that I bought for a few pence, second-hand. It is the *Odyssey*, published in 1800. It is printed on handmade paper and in the most exquisite Greek fount of the early eighteenth century. I do not collect books for their rarity or beauty but I come across such books sometimes. That one is a delight not just to the eye and the intellect but to the hands, with its leather binding, still supple after more than a hundred and seventy years. A luckier friend bought for only a few pounds a book within a few years of being five hundred years old. I held it in my hands, opened it, and the immense words were there, still clearly to be read on the near-white page.

Would that the ship Argo had never sailed—

As long as we value the simple and durable, the unobtrusively convenient, we shall make books available to us. For they will hold in perpetuity something as dull as a date or as proud as a poem. There lies, perhaps, some tedious record; or there will blaze out at us some passionate expression of the human spirit, not dulled or obscured by time, but clear as ever it was. As long as we are physical human beings with an inclination towards the acceptance of physical convenience and with a pleasure in touch and sight, there will be physical books.

If you remember, the first part of my working definition of a novel was a story which is in part a fiction. Here I go on strike, I withdraw my labour, I take industrial inaction. It is one thing to ask you to look again at the physical nature of a book, for by your work in libraries and classrooms you are the very people for whom the satiety stemming from too huge a heap of books is an occupational hazard. But I refuse to dig deep into what is meant by a story or fiction. We all know what we mean by the words—or if we don't what are we doing here? It would be better to go home.

Well. Are people going to go on constructing stories that are in part fiction to fill these paginated servants we shall always have with us? I believe we shall, and the reason is simple. It depends on direct observation of the human creature. We like to hear of succession of events; and, as an inspection of the press will demonstrate, have only a marginal interest in whether the succession is minutely true or not.

Like Mr Goldwyn, who wanted a story that began with an earthquake and worked up to a climax, we like a good lead in but have most pleasure in a succession of events with a satisfactory end point. More simply and directly still in the examination of our nature; when children holler and yell because of some infant tragedy or tedium, at once, when we take them on our knee and begin—shouting if necessary—'Once upon a time', they fall silent and attentive. Standing as we do in some way tiptoe at the apex of the animal kingdom, story is in our nature. There will always be stories written and published.

So much for the first part of my brief. My answer has been pedestrian perhaps but you *did* ask. The second part comes nearer home and is not so simply answered. How do I as a writer find my themes and how do I go on from there? I have given much bumbling thought to the question, for the relationship between theme and story is vague indeed. I consulted various dictionaries in your language and mine without much profit, for the small French dictionary, which was all I had by me, gave six definitions of theme. When I turned to that inestimable quarry, the Oxford English Dictionary, I soon gave up. I do not seem to mean by theme anything in the dictionary. I think of a theme as that which exists as a first movement, a seed, as it were, the first tiny indication that somewhere, some time, provided you hold your breath and do nothing unpropitious, there floats in the air the spiritual, or should I say the ideal image, the imagination of a possible book. If indifference or sheer laziness does not intervene, this can become a point of entry.

I can look back over many years and remember these occasions of prospective authorship though the great majority have been abortive. I experienced the state first at the age of seven. I wished to write a play about Ancient Egypt but was struck at once by the thought that my characters would have to speak Ancient Egyptian, a language I was unacquainted with at the time. I started to learn the language, therefore; and somewhere in Wallis Budge's ill-constructed book *The Egyptian Language* my play vanished without trace. I see now, with a certain rueful amusement, that I could have claimed that the theme of my unwritten play was language itself and that I was about half a century ahead of the field both in critical evaluation and in the direction of my creative work. I was a structuralist at the age of seven, which is about the right age for it. However, I ended with no play and only a minimal acquaintance with the *Book Of The Dead*. I do not remember the details of my literary career for a few years after that, except for the usual small boy's interest in *paronomasia* but I do remember the prospect of my first novel when I was thirteen. This work was to be in twelve volumes; and owing to the political preoccupations of my parents was to incorporate a history of the Trades Union Movement. I can, as it happens, recall the first sentence of volume one.

I was born in the Parish of St Mawes, in the Duchy of Cornwall, in the year 1792, of rich but honest parents.

I read that on the page, was overcome by its wit and saw it was a standard I could not possibly maintain. I decided, therefore, to start with volume two. What should slide off the nib of my pen but the apothegm 'Proverbs are the refuge of the inarticulate.' I was defeated by my own brilliance. All twelve volumes joined the long, long shelf of the works I might have written had I been someone else.

Someone else. There's the rub. It *is* possible to be someone else. When you are young, in the literary sense it is all you *can* be. Was it not Robert Louis Stevenson—I think it was he—who called the process, 'Playing the sedulous ape'? These are the involuntary parodies to which the young writer is so subject. One of the trials of the academic life in my experience of it is the obligation to read these student works; works which however valuable they may be to an individual in helping him to appreciate the difficulty of the job—and, if he will be a writer, are a necessary preliminary to his own mature work—are nevertheless embarrassing and dreadful to evaluate. English, or at least English-speaking universities are full of promising students who will never write an original word in their lives but are nevertheless capable of writing perfect T. S. Eliot. However, T. S. Eliot has already written T. S. Eliot. Of course, absolute originality is impossible. I remember writing some years ago what I thought to be perceptive review of someone else's book and thinking that one of my sentences was particularly good. Only after the review was published did I discover that George Bernard Shaw had liked the sentence too. My unconscious memory had lifted the sentence straight out of one of his prefaces. I was very worried about this until one day I was reading Jonathan Swift's *A Modest Proposal* and discovered where Shaw had found the sentence. But the student's true struggle through his parodies is towards that thing a writer must have more than a room of his own—though Jane Austen never had one—which is a voice of his own. Yet the student who is parodying other writers is likely to be your best student. He or she has fallen in love with a writer. His or her parody is passionate. He will think nothing as important as to have had a book printed and so he will look always for a theme where other people have found it. I have to own to being one of those students and to have committed these necessary follies so often as to make me a prize example of the process. The sedulous ape wrote whole novels. Like inferior paintings they might be called 'School of —'. In the only book of mine which achieved publication before I was forty—a book of verse—I could now pick many pages and name for you the great originals. Perhaps I was stubborn. But I should prefer to think that I loved poetry too well, if not wisely. But it was in a state of some despair that I wrote the following paragraph—the despair of a man who has found no voice of his own and no clear view of the sort of theme nearest to him.

When I have tried all ways and found them shut, I can think of one last thing to do. I shall take my manuscripts aboard a ship and go to Egypt. I shall carry them up the Nile, walk into the hot, dumb desert to Oxyrhynchus and bury the lot in the town rubbish heaps. In the year two thousand five hundred and fifty they will be excavated by a team of archaeologists from the University of Pekin and published among the five hundred volumes of *Vestiges of Western Literature*. No one will read them of course, any more than they read Erinna or Baccylides. This preoccupation with writing is pointless as alcoholism and there's no Authors Anonymous to wean you from the typewriter.

Nevertheless, during this period I did move towards my own area and began to develop my own voice, guess at my own themes. Turning over old papers, I find odd sentences and suggestions for possible books that came to nothing—words which when I read them, conjure up the place and time, the bright, the over-bright vision, the *Fata Morgana*, the glimpsed *Will o' the Wisp*. Sometimes these jottings are the length of a paragraph; and I think how good the idea might have been for someone else; for I know now you see it was never for me, not my *metier*, I couldn't do it. On three occasions the jotting went further and became whole novels, each of which had already been written by someone else; and it was only then that I perceived, in my slow wits, the folly of writing other people's books for them. I was tired also of the recurrent thud as returned manuscripts fell on the mat in the morning. It was always a depressing start to the day. I felt there was no point in going on, yet knew I couldn't stop writing. I determined to write, but for myself, since no one else seemed interested.

Since Eliot, books do not merely furnish a room, they are a mental furnishing that has spilled over into his poetry.

> 'This music crept by me upon the waters'
> And along the Strand, Up Queen Victoria Street.

It was not surprising therefore that a novel written to please myself should not so much imitate someone else's book but, so to speak, 'kick off' from it. I moved at last into my own area and found my own voice thereby. The book is one with which you are all familiar, *Lord of the Flies*.

And now you will feel, I suppose, that at last this lecture is about to get somewhere, may even come up with a pearl worth passing on to students. You are waiting for me to explain the theme of the book. It was at this point in composing this lecture that I swung round in my Fischer-Spassky chair and looked at the row of books written about the books I have written and already more numerous than them. I was, as always, a little flattered by the sight, a little awed, and still astonished; and at that point also a little apprehensive. For the truth is *Lord of the Flies* has either no theme or all theme. In terms of external happenings the following is a summation. More than a quarter of a century ago I sat on one side of the fireplace and my wife on the other. We had just put the children to bed after reading to the elder some adventure story or other—Coral Island, Treasure Island, Coconut Island, Pirate Island, Magic Island, God knows what island. Islands have always and for a good reason bulked large in the British consciousness. But I was tired of these islands with their paper-cutout goodies and baddies and everything for the best in the best of all possible worlds. I said to my wife, 'Wouldn't it be a good idea if I wrote a story about boys on an island and let them behave the way they really would?' She replied at once, 'That's a first class idea. You write it.' So I sat down and wrote it.

A story about boys, about people who behave as they really would! What sheer *hubris!* What an assumption of the divine right of authors! How people really behave—whole chapters in that row of books behind my chair do little in the last analysis but agree to or dissent from that first casual remark. How then do I choose a theme? Even then, did I know what I was about? It had taken me more than half a lifetime, two world wars and many years among children before I could make that casual remark because to me the job was so plainly possible.

Yet there is something more. In a way the book was to be and did become a distillation from that life. Before the Second World War my generation did on the whole have a liberal and naive belief in the perfectability of man. In the war we became if not physically hardened at least morally and inevitably coarsened. After it we saw, little by little, what man could do to man, what the Animal could do to his own species. The years of my life that went into the book were not years of thinking but of feeling, years of wordless brooding that brought me not so much to an opinion as a stance. It was like lamenting the lost childhood of the world. The theme defeats structuralism for it is an emotion. The theme of *Lord of the Flies* is grief, sheer grief, grief, grief, grief.

There are of course other routes to a theme and themes different wholly in quality—intellectual themes, one might call them. So I cannot generalize even among my own books. For my second book was written to a proposition, while my third one, *Pincher Martin*, was written and rewritten before I knew what it was about at all. Indeed, if I am asked about that book I have to embark on a theological exposition that bores me as much as my questioner.

You might think that another of my books, *The Spire*, was an easier case. Indeed, before I began it I thought so too. In a kind of prelude I did once declare what I was setting out to do, though when the book was finished I abandoned it. If you wish to measure the intention against the achievement you might read this prelude which has never been published before and compare it with the book—always providing you have read the book. Here, then, is my intention.

I have often wondered how it was that Anthony Trollope should write so much about our city, or Barchester as he called it, without even considering that object for which the city is celebrated beyond all its other things. Trollope, of course, was interested in how things are. He could pass a very pleasant life without worrying how things were, what they had been and what they would become. He was not much interested in *meaning*, or so it seems to me. It was not so long ago that I stopped on his bridge, the grey stone bridge, Harnham Old Bridge, where he recounts how he once paused, with the Cathedral Close near him and allowed to bud in his mind and then to flower, the concept of the Barchester Novels. Below me the river performed its endless necessities of overfall and adjustment, bore the customary lilies and stemming trout. The sun looped and shattered and swam in it. We could say, in a way, we leaned over the bridge together—for what after all is a hundred years in Barchester—and I saw that he had left me a corner of his job to fill in. For no one can live in Barchester without one eye cocked upward. It is a sort of spiritual squint. You may fall into a habit which consciously ignores our astonishing symbol but the unconscious which carries you about knows better. You are like a Swiss who is so used to the Jungfrau that he no longer looks at her. But she conditions him all the same. Her angle is built in. So in Barchester, we look to the spire sometimes, for the weather. Humidity greens the moss and algae and strengthens the moulding like eye-shadow. Low cloud, mist, fog, inflate the spire so that it loses definition and looms like the promise of mountain country. Dry heat and light bleach the stones to a bone white against blue sky, the immensity of which brings out the delicacy and fragility of the structure. Odd combinations of lighting produce effects that can stop you in your tracks. Not a Barchester man or woman but has half a dozen of them tucked away in his memory like an album of private snapshots: the lightning conductors, glittering like a chain of emeralds against the brown smoke that had drifted in the weather of that fantastic summer all the way from burning Dunkirk; the midsummer madness of a shivering spire fevered by mirage; the floating spire when mist has severed it from the earth; the drab, factual spire of rain and cold and wind; the enchanted spire that was lit at sunset or near it by the reflection from twenty acres of open daisies. It is natural as you go about your business to glance up to accept like the recognition of a friend that glimpse beyond the gables. Coming into Barchester by train it is natural to search the southern sky for a glimpse of the red aircraft warning light that tells you you are home. Walkers on the downs sweep the appropriate quarter with their binoculars to see if even here—seventeen miles from the city—the tip of the 'finger pointing to heaven' is still visible.

For the spire has no natural advantage in position. The city lies in a meeting of valleys and a web of rivers and in every direction there are hills. The spire must fight its way up to a level where it may compete with the hills for attention, perhaps by a virtuosity of architecture, perhaps by some other method; perhaps by some combination of methods which defies analysis but appeals more directly to the imagination. Yet whatever its history, man-made and man-maker, it is there.

I say, 'Is there'. But I write these words at a hot point of the Cold War when nothing is even as certain as usual. These words, then, may never be printed; or if printed, never read. Certainly the spire *was* there; and certainly there must come or has come a time when the spire passes away. But it was built; and in the building made or broke the men who built it. It stood, changing men and being changed by them. It was part of us and we were part of it, experimenter and the experiment, the observer and the object. No one who lived in Barchester with that juggling act of stone thrown up to poise and peer over his shoulder was ever quite the same as he would have been without it. Whether he was dean of Barchester with the spire as his pride and headache; whether he was a surveyor, confounded by the fluidity of the circumstances that made his measurements always a little less than exact; whether he was a schoolmaster with the spire outside the classroom window; whether he was a poor painter who lived by selling accurate paintings of it or a housewife who found it blanketed her television reception; whether he was a garage hand who had it nagging at him through a grimy skylight; whether he was a consulting engineer called in to inspect it and stunned by the mystery that kept it up——*whoever* we were in the radius of that influence, we had the heart of some huge question at our shoulder. It was familiar as a wife, loved, ignored, essential. It was a date which was there to be kept.

Now I am far enough away from this prelude which has become a postlude to find it agreeable enough in an essayish sort of way. Yet I cannot say after all that it conveys more than the information that I and the spire spend a long time in each other's vicinity. Why write about it? After all, there used to be a gasworks in the same area with a chimney that looked nearly as high as the spire. Why did I not choose the gasworks? Indeed, I can think of a number of contemporaries who *would* have chosen the gasworks. More than that, is the novel that eventuated about the spire at all? The quality I was concerned with was how a mystery presented itself to me and raised the question of how far a novelist knows what he is writing, a question to which the right answer seems to be, 'Some more, some less.' In the extract which I have just read to you there is one word missing, deliberately missing. I believe you would not find the word in the book, either. The book is about the human cost of building the spire. Is the theme of the book something that is missing from it? In the book the protagonist forces through the building of the spire against all odds, not counting the cost to himself or anyone else because he thinks he does God's will. He does not think of beauty——might never have heard of it. He only sees it part by part and when it is finished cannot bear to look at it because of the folly and wickedness the job forced on him. Only when he is dying does he see the spire in all its glory; and the sight reduces him to understanding that he had no understanding. Theme! What is a theme? Where was that one? Yet the book is simple as a book could well be. If the reader, the critic does not understand that after all the theology, the ingenuities of craft, the failures and the sacrifices, a man is overthrown by the descent into his world of beauty's mystery and irradiation, flame, explosion, then the book has failed. The theme is not there.

I am uneasily aware that you may be wondering what all this has to do with the title of my lecture, 'A Moving Target'. The fact is, I wrote the title, owing to your urgency, before I had considered whether I had anything to say about it! Yet the title has been there floating about somewhere; and now it occurs to me I might attach it to the last few paragraphs. But that would be lame. I must do better. Certainly one switches one's aim from target to target, but that is the rifle not the target that is moving. Now I remember where I heard the phrase and a possible application of it. Let me keep it for the end.

To start with a theme and then write a book; or to write a book, find a theme afterwards so that the book has to be rewritten if not reorganized in the light of it—I have tried both and they both work. Empiricist and pragmatist, you will observe. My approach to a novel, then, is a confusion in itself, a hand-to-mouth thing. Men do not write the books they should, they write the books they can. These approaches to writing in my experience, are wasteful of time and energy and for all I know there may be a better way, an easier way. If there is I would be happy to adopt it. But my confused methods have been applied to novels during a generation in which the unreasonable, the confused and haphazard are loose in the world and raging there. It seems to me no wonder that even in my fumbling, mess and hesitation I should mirror the world round me.

What then of the future? I have said that I believe the novel will survive as long as man does; but the question I am considering now is a more limited one. What of my own future? Is there a novel about anywhere that I can lay my pen to? Well, there is something in my experience I would write of if I could—shall write of if I can. Only recently, travelling through Egypt, I grew first weary, then irritated then angry at the colossal statues of Rameses II who was so outrageously unaware of his own brutality and egotism. At Abu Simbel he fronts the rising sun, all four of him preserved at vast expense. He stares across the Nile, or rather across what is now Lake Nasser, as calm and as smugly imperceptive as a Second World War general sitting down to write his memoirs. But there were also, lower down the Nile among the green fields the stones that sang immemorially until the Roman Empire washed over them and ebbed away, the singing stones of Memnon. They sit hugely in a field. They have suffered all time's indignities except absolute destruction. Their faces have been struck away. They are like some modern paintings, some modern sculpture in which the distortions tell a truth that an exact reproduction would miss. For we are in the age of the fragment and wreckage, those timbers, it may be, washed up on some wild seashore. Not for us the well-clad gentleman with his bronze walking-stick and bronze top hat, doffed for the occasion, but held by his side, crown up so that the pigeons cannot nest in it. Not for us the studio portrait and the social grin. These huge stones that once sang are seated kings. Ruins as they are they may yet convey by a metal-language what we have left for a future and what we may build on. I say their faces have been struck away as if blasted by some fierce heat and explosion. All that is visible there is shadow. Their heads preserve nothing but a sense of gaze, their bodies nothing but the rubble of posture on a royal throne. Here might be an image of a humanity indomitable but contrite because history has broken its heart. It may be that in a reading of these broken stones lies an image of a creature maimed yet engaged to time and our world and enduring it with a purpose no man knows and an effect that no man can guess.

What can I say then about my choice of theme? Ideas come easily enough. I scuff with my foot and turn up themes like a pig rooting for truffles. Why are some truffles and some useless bits of stone? At the last I am driven to a wry conclusion. The writer does not choose his themes at all. The themes choose the writer.

A moving target. A year ago my wife, as happens to the wives of writers, found herself sitting next to the vice-chancellor of a university. He told her a story about the very new university at Port Moresby in New Guinea. This university is organized along tribal lines. Each tribe has its chief in the university who is responsible for his people's behaviour. Now it happened that a man from—let us say—the Mountains, insulted a man from—let us say—the Shore people and the insult was of such a nature that it could only be wiped out by a ritual murder. The vice-chancellor felt this was going too far, but the whole university was soon in an uproar. He decided therefore to call the chiefs together and see if over a little food and drink the insult could be atoned for in some less spectacular way. Finally the chiefs agreed that a sufficiently lavish feast provided by the insulting tribe for the insulted one would see the matter at an end. The tribes sat, therefore, in war paint, before the verandah of the vice-chancellor's house. He and the chiefs sat on the verandah facing them. The open space was piled high with fruit, sucking pigs, fish, coconuts, fruits of all kinds. Everyone sat in solemn silence waiting for the feast to begin. At that critical moment and for some unknown reason, a roast sucking pig slipped down from the top of a pile and lay at the vice-chancellor's feet; whereupon the chief of the Mountain people turned to the chief of the Shore people and said, 'Doesn't all this rather remind you of *Lord of the Flies*?' I tell this story with reprehensible complacency. It makes me feel successful and global. But it also enables me to point out to you that for better or worse my work is now indissolubly wedded to the educational world. I am the raw material of an academic light industry. I should be disingenuous if I pretended not to be flattered and to discount the financial benefits which accrue. Nevertheless the situation is not without its drawbacks. The books that have been written about my books have made a statue of me, fixed in one not very decorative gesticulation, a po-faced image too earnest to live with. Nor is this all. A fall-out from my use as educational material means that I get a supply of letters not just from the wider public or from university students but from children as well. For twenty years I have had letters from boys and girls all asking the same questions. Sometimes I think they must still be the same children. Even more dangerous are the post-graduate students in search of a thesis. We are close now to the title of this lecture. Now I think it is time we drew right up and so to a conclusion. It was not long ago that I received a letter from a young lady at a famous English university. She had, as far as I could make out, just straightened out her professor. She was, you see, looking for a subject for her thesis. The poor professor had not succumbed without a struggle but he had lost in the end. He had recommended her to do a thesis on someone who had known Dr Johnson—in fact, on *anyone* who had known Dr Johnson. However, she was an advanced student and knew that everyone who had known Dr Johnson was now dead. You can, I suppose, guess what she was after. She was not going to write a thesis on anything as dull as a dead man. She wanted fresh blood. She was going out with her critical shotgun to bring home the living. She proposed I should bare my soul, answer all her questions, do all the work, and she would write the thesis on me. But years first of reading theses on me and then more years of not reading theses on me have made me more elusive than a professor. I wrote back at once, saying that I agreed whole-heartedly with her professor. I was alive and changing as live things do. She would find someone who had known Dr Johnson a most agreeable companion who would not answer back and would always stay where he was until wanted. She could guarantee filling him with a shower of critical small-shot at any time *she* wanted. But as for me, I am a moving target.

Utopias and Antiutopias

Address to *Les Anglicistes*, Lille, 13 February 1977

Ladies and gentlemen, you see before you a man, I will not say more sinned against than sinning; but a man more analysed than analysing. One book of mine has been subjected to Freudian analysis, neo-Freudian analysis, Jungian analysis, Roman Catholic approval, a kind of implicit *imprimatur*—protestant apprisal, nonconformist surmise, Scientific Humanist misinterpretation, to say nothing of the dialectic, both Marxist and Hegelian. An anonymous gentleman from the state of Texas accused me of being un-American, an accusation I must bear with what fortitude I may. I thought, after that, that the list was complete. But one dark night, after a lecture in Brisbane, Queensland, Australia, a curious figure loomed up—I never saw his face—and told me I wrote Science Fiction. Clearly there was life in the list yet. Then, a few days ago, I received your invitation to this meeting. I welcomed it, as my wife and I welcome any excuse to visit your country whether it be agricultural France, or industrial or academic or all three at once. But before I had read very far in the literature that accompanied the invitation two new feelings came over me. In the first place, I saw that the addresses to be given by the other speakers were of awesome, if a little narrow, profundity. Truth lives at the bottom of a well, but these were oil wells, miles deep and only a foot across. What was there about me that would be a qualification for speaking in such company?

However, a partial answer to that question emerged late in the literature. I felt like the gentleman who discovered he had been speaking prose all his life. I was, I discovered, an 'antiutopian'. Indeed, as I read on, for an awful moment or two, I even thought myself to be diagnosed as a 'dystopist', and setting aside the questionable etymology of the word, it seemed to describe some terrible disease or perhaps a vice so disgusting its name was not to be found in the dictionary.

Antiutopian seemed clear enough. But what was I to say about it among scholars boring so deep for some oil or other? Clearly it was useless for me to try to as we say 'get the subject up'. You have got it up, all of you. All I could do, then, was to glance back over a lifetime of desultory reading, of casual enjoyment rather than dedicated effort and see what antiutopian and utopian might mean to me. That backward landscape was blank first. You have limited yourself to the last hundred years but I freed myself with a bound and looked wherever I chose. Still, the backward landscape of the mind was blank and dark; but then, of course, Plato began to glimmer. Thomas More came into view. As my eyes accepted this new constraint of choice the whole landscape came into a kind of halflight. Suddenly there were names in neon lighting—Butler, Swift, Voltaire, Defoe, Shaw, Wells, Huxley, Orwell. The field was absurdly wide. The only way in which I could enter it was to take with me the reason why you must have asked me, that book, *Lord of the Flies*, which by now I have gone near to surrounding with commentary the way Dante surrounded the *Vita Nuova*.

When I realized that I felt mutinous and much inclined to talk about something else even at the risk of boring you and behaving like a man who is invited to dinner because his wife is so beautiful but who insists on telling his funny stories whether anyone wants to hear them or not. So I abandoned immediate consideration of my own books—I have written more than one, after all—and looked at utopias not as they are explained and ticked off in some literary continuum but as human aspiration to be set in and with what Wordsworth called the still, sad music of humanity. We must remember first of all that when a utopia glitters all gold in the memory it does so against a background of social darkness, of

misery, want, deprivation at every level. Yet there is a universal seed
or root natural to the soil of the human mind from which all
endeavour, all working towards a happier order of things rises and
sometimes flowers. So when I gave that first glance back at my own
memory it was poetry, not prose that seemed to lie behind the works
we have named and others we shall name later. It was Pindar's
Hesperides where, to use Tennyson's superb translation,

> Where falls not hail, or rain, or any snow,
> Nor ever wind blows loudly; but it lies
> Deep-meadowed, happy, fair with orchard-lawns
> And bowery hollows crowned with summer sea—

It was Alcman. Two hundred years before Plato abandoned poetry
and talked philosophically of the perfected society, Alcman gave the
longing for human happiness a lyrical expression. You will find the
lines somewhere in the anthology; and true to my determination not
to read anything, study anything, look up anything specially for this
lecture, I can only give you a paraphrase of them. He, you will
remember, would like to be transformed into the *haliporphuros ornis*,
the sea-blue bird of the spring. But he was old, was he not, like our
civilization, and crying out that his limbs, like our institutions, were
weak and no longer able to support him.

But this look far back brings up too much. We might stay with
Hesiod and a golden age or even with Ovid. I broke away, flipped
three thousand years, near enough to *The First American Gentleman*.
There, the father when asked by his child what happened to people
after they died, replied that they became brightly plumaged birds,
flitting and singing and feeding and making love for ever among the
branches of endless flowering trees. From that, I myself flitted to
Swift's *Laputa* and Defoe's *Libertalia*, then by way of Voltaire's
Eldorado to Shelley. I was behaving like a ball on a pin table, bouncing
from one contact to another and, to tell the truth, not scoring very
much. I began to appreciate the common sense of restricting us to
the last hundred years and determined to return myself to it.

Might we agree that both utopias and antiutopias must form
under the pressure of ruling ideas? Those ideas enforce a simplicity
of outlook so that in utopias at least, character gives place to the idea

of humanity. We have castes, or classes rather than people. This enforces a simplicity of outlook that might be called simplistic. The anonymous and faceless gentleman who approached me in the darkness of a Brisbane Street with his talk of Science Fiction may or may not have been aware of the utopian element in that genre. Science Fiction, SF, is related to the mainstream of writing much as ghost stories were related to it in the past. Possibly tales of the supernatural were a by-product of a waning religious faith and possibly SF is a by-product of our increasing loss of faith in science. The writer's view of character in SF is as two-dimensional as in a utopia. Though SF generally has a utopian element in it because it tends to deal with the human future, the machinery of life, of the hypostatized world is the important thing. At the lowest level SF is about as utopian as a glossy magazine. The hero and heroine ride off into the sunset of a perfected society in an old familiar fashion not much altered by the fact that the noble steed is an anti-gravity machine and the sun a green one. The trouble with the writing of SF is its complete freedom of manoeuvre. Once you accept the premise of knowledge and power increasing world without end you are carving in butter rather than stone. There are hundreds of dully competent SF writers who can just keep your attention as cards just keep it when you are playing patience. It does not matter much whether you say a city is on the moon or Alpha Centauri when the inhabitants are paper cutouts and the story recognizably one of cops and robbers. Perhaps SF is also running out of steam, the way ghost stories seem to have done. It is notable that empires are back in. Read Gibbon's *Decline and Fall* and you can find the history of all the galactic empires right there in every detail. I strongly suspect one or two hack writers, to say nothing of script writers, of being secret addicts of Gibbon. If not, I offer them the idea for free.

There are, of course, many better things than that in SF. Ray Bradbury's story the *Fire Balloons* is utopian in its way. Mars is a sort of Hesperides where you could say the ethereal inhabitants toil not neither do they spin. But—and here we come to a point I wish to elaborate later—in most science fiction the idea of evolution is deeply embedded because SF is post-Darwinian. Writers, after all, are children of their age. Arthur C. Clark illustrates this very well. In an early book of his, *Childhood's End*, he makes us all evolve into a higher form of life. The whole of the human race coalesces as amoebas do. The super-creature strips the world of life, leaving it dead as the moon and takes off to do whatever it may do in the pastures of deep space. Indeed, SF may have taken over a bit of the religion that tales of the supernatural left lying about, for in the book *2001* Clark shows us a man moving towards a higher state and becoming something very like an archangel. If you find that hard to believe of something that falls so demonstrably in the realm of SF please note that Clark himself says the work is theological. In fact, when discussing the film of his book he has a quiet snigger at what the producers would have thought if they had known they were investing tens of millions of dollars in a theological subject. But it is worth noting that this child of his century has succeeded in writing about God and man without any discussion at all of good and evil. After all, two-dimensional people would find it difficult to engage in more than two-dimensional sin.

My complementary and contrasting example is C. S. Lewis, a fully-fledged apologist for and advocate of the Church of England. He was a man of vast erudition, both literary and theological. His utopia is peopled with God's unfallen creatures. They are not prelapsarian but unfallen and we are to witness in one book their rescue from the fall. Where Clark's book tells us nothing of how his evolved creatures are to disport themselves in the future, Lewis's creatures have been disporting themselves ever since they were created and we see them in their paradise. It is Mars and Venus—both now, owing to space probes and photography, useless as possible paradises, like those lost civilizations in Africa. The picture Lewis paints has much appeal. God has created on Mars three classes, benign intellectuals, jolly hunters and energetic artisans. No class is top class. They do not interbreed, but find much enjoyment in each other's company and difference. Co-operation is complete. They do not study theology for that, after all, is a postlapsarian requirement. On Mars, God Himself is present and meets his people in a holy place, while His angels hover as it were always on the fringe of visibility. Lewis himself had a deep, and one might think morbid, fear of dead bodies; and certainly there are few people unless they are doctors and trained to it who can claim complete indifference to those sad and sometimes repulsive relics. It was Charles Lamb, I believe, who lamented that our bodies cannot disappear like the Cock Lane Ghost 'with a sweet smell and melodious twanging'. On Lewis's Mars the dead are made to disappear in just such a seemly fashion. Throughout Lewis's fantasies we may detect not so much his opinions but his very nature, his moral anguish and private disgusts. One cannot ask too much of a book which does not claim to be more than a popular romance. But his utopian bent is undeniable however; and he does seem to me to invite our questioning by the pervasive devotion and moralizing of his books. Unlike Clark's books, Lewis's are always set against a background of good and evil as warring principals. For all his vast learning, his faith, his polemical theology, I believe the impulse behind his writing takes us back not to More or Plato, not even to the New Testament, but further back, where we began with Pindar and even more, with Alcman. Alcman was growing old, his limbs were no longer able to sustain him—would I were a halcyon flying over the flowers of foam, a sea-blue bird of the spring! Lewis was growing old too. The world had a narrower and narrower place left for his orthodoxy and dark war was looming. He might well feel—would I were an unfallen Sorn or Hrossa or Fiffltriggi and not this poor man whose end is so disgusting and so dark! Yet observe how Lewis is also a child of his post-Darwinian century. In *Perelandra*, the book renamed for the popular market *Voyage to Venus*, the whole thing ends with a paean, a vast hymn which sketches out the future evolution of the species saved from sin, even though the evolution will take place in a Christian heaven or seventh heaven. The ruling idea of the century, simplistic as it may be, seems here to stay.

Now you may wonder how all this links up with the idea of utopias in the last hundred years. The answer is that utopias do not have any evolution, merely an endless, changeless future. They do not have any past, either. They were always there it seems. They did not evolve except in one or two rare examples. They were come across. Thomas More simply came across his Utopia as Candide came across his Eldorado. Plato's Atlantis is hearsay. In general when a writer says how it all came about he is not writing about Utopia, but somewhere else. I can only think of one—let us call it Utopia—which has a past. Shaw in his huge trilogy *Back to Methuselah* gets a Bergsonian life-force combined with Lamarckian evolution to mould men until by action and interaction they can mould themselves. Shaw's thesis is that we shall only become wise when we have two hundred years or more to learn in. I must say that he lived long enough to cast doubts on his own thesis by the evidence from his own longevity. In his trilogy men, or, one supposes, women have become oviparous, immortal though not indestructible, plastic and mathematical. The final section of the trilogy is called *As Far As Thought Can Reach*; and has left at least one reader thinking that if that is as far as thought can go, the sooner it comes back again the better. The Marxist is quite right to insist on the *how* of Utopia even if he is hazy about the what and when. Utopians, with their pretty pictures, their indifference to the fact of human nature and their assumption that even in a book it is possible to ignore the Heraclitean flux of things, are a feckless if good-humoured lot.

However, utopias are presented for our inspection as a critique of the human state. If they are to be treated as anything but trivial exercises of the imagination I suggest there is a simple test we can apply. Let us set evolution aside for a moment, even ignore Humanity with a capital aitch, abandon all thought of bosses and workers and intellectuals and political parties which are the parody infrastructure of our real lives. We must forget the whole paraphernalia of social description, demonstration, expostulation, approbation, condemnation. We have to say to ourselves, 'How would I myself live in this proposed society? How long would it be before I went stark staring mad?' Unfair as this may seem when the test piece is not more than an unpretentious romance it does, and in a very startling way, reveal the defects in an ideal construction. But as a personal reminiscence I remember reading *Men Like Gods* by H. G. Wells when I was boy and I remember feeling with a positive surge of joy that I myself could walk straight into such a society and live there. I do remember asking myself in my innocence—or ignorance—why the world was not like that and was too young to know the answer. We should be poorer genetic material if our boys and girls did not sometimes feel like that, no matter what happens to them later on. For the cruel fact is that had that boy walked into the perfected society, to him would have come out of his blood the hates and loves—no, on a less epic scale, the antipathies and greeds, the jealousies and ambitions, the misdirected energies and deadening sloths; and not just his but those of other people all working with, through and against each other. This is why your true Utopia is a timeless, changeless thing. Did it move off the printed page into living reality there is one thing certain we can say about it. The instant it moved it would change. I do not say it would evolve, since the implications of that word in its technical sense are too restricting, but it would change, warp, harden, fragment. These things and good things along with them would operate like viruses in the blood.

Here is an extended metaphor for the nature of life as I suppose it to be. If someone else, or many other people, have used it I can only apologize to you for boring you; but at the end of a conference in which the papers, erudite and fascinating as they unquestionably have been to the few people qualified to engage their attention to a particular one, you must nevertheless have had some practice as I have in projecting an image of profound engagement while your thoughts were somewhere else. I offer my extended metaphor, then, as a period of rest to those present who have heard it all before.

Consider a man riding a bicycle. Whoever he is, we can say three things about him. We know he got on the bicycle and started to move. We know that at some point he will stop and get off. Most important of all, we know that if at any point between the beginning and end of his journey he stops moving and does not get off the bicycle he will fall off it. That is a metaphor for the journey through life of any living thing, and I think of any society of living things. To confuse the issue I might add in parenthesis that I believe in another spiritual dimension which crosses that journey at right-angles, so to speak; but it is not relevant here and we must forget it. What a delicate, ineffably complex and intuitive ability this riding of a bike is! Definitions and theories and systems are inadequate to its description. They do nothing but get in the way of the act. Yet a small child can perform this wonder and think little enough of it after his first triumph.

Now how does the utopian fit into the metaphor? He is like a man who takes a snapshot of the action. He will tell us that to ride the bicycle for ever the riders must have the pedals just so, with the machine leaning, perhaps twenty degrees one way or the other. But we know well enough that the bicycle that stops as in the snapshot, and no longer relies on the balance between change and stability, will fall in the road; and a society of the same sort would fall clean off the world and vanish with the dinosaurs. We are not to be taken in by the snapshot, pretty as it may be. We have a movie film of the ride and know that bicycles do not keep themselves up as if frozen.

That we should fall off the utopian bicycle is clear enough. Perhaps the writer himself does not mean to concern himself with reality? Did Voltaire think those elders and their younglings in Eldorado would remain the same if they discovered the power latent in gold and jewels? Or was there a touch, a feather brushing him as he wrote, of the *haliporphuros ornis*? Certainly from the musical made of *Candide* it would be easy enough to suppose so. Sometimes the modern utopians give a sketch of the history that led up to their utopias but it has never seemed convincing to me. Wells gave a sketch in *The Shape of Things to Come* and more romantically in *The Sleeper Awakes*. Indeed, during the last hundred years the utopian has had hanging over him always the brooding question from Marx, 'How are you to bring it about?' That Marx found the wrong answer does not lessen the importance of the question. The question leads us from Utopia, a little further on. It leads us on by way of two works to which time has already brought a vagueness of outline. Are they utopias? Surely not, you will say! What, *Erewhon* and *Brave New World*? Surely they are satires? But I believe we ought to be careful before we put them into that pigeonhole. *Erewhon*, where disease was a crime and crime a disease is not with us in full extent; but it is remarkable how many of the situations and conversations in the book could come nowadays out of a court. After each case and before sentence the social worker stands up and explains that the unfortunate person in the dock is not a criminal; or if he does happen to have criminal tendencies, why, a long history of this and that has proceeded and produced them. I do not mean to deride this practice in any way. I merely point out that if *Erewhon* is a satire civilization has produced a situation somewhat like it; for do not those of maturer years regard our thickened waistline as evidence of crime? Of sin? It is wicked to be unhealthy, wicked to be fat, and if we have a tendency to the rheumatics, why we should have learnt to adopt a correct posture early on. As for the whole question of teeth—but I have said enough, I hope, to let you see what I mean when I say that *Erewhon* today looks less like a satire than a progress report. The case of *Brave New World* is similar. It was, and I suppose still is, taken as a satire on society and the way society was going. It differs from *Erewhon* in that Huxley gives it a bit of a history. There had been a war and it had so sickened the world that it ended up gratefully under the benign eye of Our Ford. That was a pleasant jibe; but having lived through two world wars, after each of which the worldwide cry was 'never again', and in spite of which we still face the ghastly possibility of a third one, I take leave to doubt the validity of the historical assumption Huxley made to get humanity to the brave new world. The third war, unthinkably ghastly, will certainly be followed by a feeble moan of 'never again' from the few unhappy survivors. But as before, in the face of intransigent humanity I doubt that 'never again' will mean more than it did before. Now as far as the satire in the book is concerned, it has suffered something of the same sort of fate as *Erewhon*. Truth has not caught up with it wholly but is on the way. A dullard, living now and enmeshed in the scene of any of our great cities would recognize a great deal that he tacitly approves of. It is a world of consumer goods and television quizzes. *Brave New World*'s combination of games, sex, interminable pop music varied only by orgiastic revivalism prompts the ungenerous thought that Huxley believed most people needs must love the lowest when they see it. *Erewhon*, as I remember, is timeless. But if Huxley's society was not going to last for ever, at least by building on the lowest common denominator of human appetite, it did promise a state that would be able to last longer than most. In the pride of education, intelligence, perceptivity, aesthetic enjoyment, creativity, we ought to be careful that we do not find ourselves like Lewis's Sorns, living in the last tenuities of a planet's atmosphere. Huxley's world, an apparent satire, hideous for the intellectual, for the religious, for the scientist and the artist might claim that it did at least promote the gross contentment of the many; and that is not wholly to be despised. There is, behind the witty surface of the book, what Huxley suffered from as a young man—a contempt for *l'homme moyen sensuel*, for most of us in fact. By the time he wrote *Brave New World*, like Malvolio, he was thinking nobly of the soul. As the clouds of war darkened over Europe he and some of our most notable poets removed themselves to the new world, vanishing, as it were, with a sweet odour and a melodious twanging. There Huxley continued to create what we may call antiutopias and utopias with the same gusto, apparently for both kinds. One antiutopia is certainly a disgusting job and best forgotten. But then, Huxley seems always to have had an equation in his mind between evil and dirt as if morality were at bottom a kind of asepsis. Yet I owe his writings much myself, I've had much enjoyment and some profit from them—in particular, release from a certain starry-eyed optimism which stemmed from the optimistic rationalism of the nineteenth century. The last utopia he attempted which was technically and strictly a utopia and ideal state, called *Island*, is one for which I have considerable liking and respect. He does give his utopia history and a single revolver shot signifies its end. If the drug mescalin has proved more dangerous and less helpful than Huxley thought it would be, the same thing is true of Plato's authoritarianism, More's Christianity, and Wells's scientific rationalism.

What are we to make of it all, then, utopia and satire? It really is difficult to see where one begins and the other ends. We recognize as satire, and savage at that, Huxley's picture of children deliberately bred and trained into being alphas and gammas and the rest. We may see Wells's Selenites in *The First Men In The Moon* as an even savager attack on the industrial deprivations that made men into images of any dirty trade. But Plato's Golden Children are bred and trained into fitness for their task as Philosopher Kings. Is there any difference? Plato drew his image, and a real one it was, from Sparta, Wells from all the mess of the depression and the desperately competitive industry that preceded it. Huxley, I suppose, thought in some scientific terms or other—biological engineering, perhaps. It would seem from the world we have round us that to satirize society by means of a clownish utopia is a dangerous thing to do. Lucian did the same in his journey to the moon. No, you cannot outrun the facts very far. Depict a utopia in which you would not wish to live and you may end like Christopher Wren, whose monument lies all around him.

There is, of course, another thing. Let us accept that Plato's Atlantis, or More's Utopia are what they purport to be—that is paradigms for society. Let us accept that from Lucian to Huxley utopias can be intentional satire however much the event catches up with them. The other thing is the antiutopia. In our generation, or even in our century, the nature of the cosmos, the universal premise is still very much under debate. Perhaps it always will be. It is in the knowledge of that fundamental dubiety rather than single doubt, that infinite regress that surrounds us on every side, that some minds are drawn to work. It is an awareness not exact, but a shared feeling, a *zeitgeist* if you will, as if the proper image of man had its face veiled. It is a sad knowledge that antiutopians share among them. Their hearts are not ebullient as the satirist's, not savage either, but broken. It gave the dying George Orwell no consolation to write *Nineteen Eighty-Four* as an illustration of the monstrous social thing that could happen when political theory and humanity are out of step. He knew it *was* happening, just across the road, so to speak, under Joseph Stalin. H. G. Wells, so sanguine as a historian, or would-be historian, had unfathomable depths of darkness in him when he really let his imagination run loose, as anyone who has studied his scientific fantasies, his SF, must be aware. *The Time Machine* is as terrible, no—a more terrible picture of what man might become even than Orwell's. Wells died among all the horrors of a universe running down in cold indifference to a pointless end. That is how he saw it. For his last book, *Mind at the End of its Tether* is misery and a barely concealed terror. Yet he did not write it with the desire to make other people unhappy by forcing an unhappy truth on them. It is at this point that we come, I believe, to the true reason for the invention of an antiutopia. It is at once a cry for help and a cry of despair. The antiutopian wants to be proved wrong. No antiutopian desires to hurt. But he has looked into the face of man rather than statistical humanity. He knows, too, that the clock does not stop.

And now, though I do not like to be posted into a pigeonhole like a letter, I have done it in this essay to so many other writers it is only fair that my own turn should come. I must own that you could argue reasonably enough that one of my books, or the tone of it, is antiutopian. It was a book stemming from what I had found out during and for a few years after the Second World War. You can connect the two easily enough in your own minds so I will not elaborate. It was an experience that fell to the lot of my generation. I used children because I knew about them and they were to hand. I described no particular child, for a novelist does not work that way; and in any case, to do so would have been unfair. But I did conduct an experiment, allowing a class of children as much freedom as possible and only intervened when there seemed to be some possibility of murder being committed. That, and the war and its aftermath were all my research. As for the elaborately described island, it was an escape to a part of the world I had never seen but wanted to, a tropical island. I made myself a *haliporphuros ornis* and flew away from rationed, broken England with all its bomb damage, flew away across the flowers of foam to where the lianas dropped their cables from the strange tropical trees. It has convinced some people because it convinced me. I was there; and sometimes it seemed a pity not to enjoy the place rather than allow the antiutopia to take over. But take over it did.

However, time marches on. I no longer feel so antiutopian. Of course, we shall have to get off our bicycle sooner or later. A precise theology has defined the moment as when the last trump is blown. A less precise political science will define it as when the red button in the presidential holdall gets pushed. A precise science tells us that we shall have to dismount when the sun hots up. Another precise science tells us we shall get off when the sun cools down. In any event as I said before, if we do not dismount with dignity from our circling planet—and I would define that dignity as a calm awareness of the majesty of our consciousness and the sheer drabness of indestructibility—*if*, I say, we do not get off, then either theologically or politically or scientifically we shall be pushed. I do not find the prospect distasteful. It is not just that I shall not be there anyway. It is that all these questions deal with Humanity, whereas what matters is the future of you and me and our children's children. Besides, though Heraclitus declared that *everything flows* and that *you cannot bathe twice in the same river* he also said, anticipating by more than two thousand years a hymn well known in schools, that *the sun is every day new*.

As a diagnosed and perhaps condemned antiutopian I offer you the distilled wisdom of fifty years. It is my only contribution to political thought and it could be inscribed on a large postage stamp. It is simply this. With bad people, hating, unco-operative, selfish people, no social system will work. With good people, loving, co-operative, unselfish people, any social system will work.

It is, then, a moral question. Well, we have had *australopithecus*, *homo habilis*, *homo neanderthalensis*, Mousterian Man, Cromagnon Man, *homo sapiens*—has nature done with us? *Surely* we can search that capacious sleeve and find something a bit better! We had better *decide* we are Lamarckian and make it work. We must produce *homo moralis*, the human being who cannot kill his own kind, nor exploit them nor rob them. Then no one will need to write utopias, satires or antiutopias for we shall be inhabitants of utopia as long as we can stay on the bicycle; and perhaps a little—not much, but a little—dull.

Belief and Creativity

Hamburg, 11 April 1980

Mr Chairman, ladies and gentlemen:

It gives me particular pleasure—I might say peculiar pleasure—to address you today in Germany, home of exact scholarship, because it was a German reference book which announced my death in 1957. The announcement was premature but, of course, no more than that. Mark Twain, on a similar occasion, remarked that the report of his death was exaggerated. I do not know whether I can claim to be as lucky as he was. I do not refer to what has been called the burden of the years but to something more unusual. For a quarter of a century now the person you see before you has undergone a process of literary mummification. He is not entirely a human being; he is a set book. Of course that is a great personal benefit but not without its drawbacks. The creature lives and breathes like some horrible Boris Karloff figure inside his mummy wrappings which year by year are tightened. A statue, an image stands in his place. To some extent we are all victims of a similar fate. The teacher may create his own image for the purposes of discipline and find himself unable to creep out of it. In the end, he may consent and become the image entire, at last the parody of a schoolmaster, don, lecturer. Indeed, people live by their image sometimes and cherish it. The actor, the politician—since our global television suburb is not so much bookish as imagist—must think first of an action, 'How will it affect my image?' Watch the box and you can see it happen. Constrained by the necessities of his trade he will adjust either his action or his image so that another figure of fantasy mops and mows in the social space. That space, our divided but communal awareness, is so full of the image, the real unreality or unreal reality, it is a wonder men can breathe. Perhaps we cannot. Perhaps it is our fate as human beings that none of us knows what it is to draw a lungful of psychically unpolluted air, to look and to examine innocently the crowded impressions on every sense with which our individual selves cope, suffer and enjoy as the essence of being. My image as author of a set book goes near to solidifying my public self into a statue. The other day a little boy wrote to me and said, 'It is a fine thing to be able to write to an author while he is alive. If you are still alive will you answer these questions?'

I am still alive; and today it is my purpose to peer out of my wrappings and speak out of a centre which for all the impediment of bandages has gone on living and changing. It is my hope that some of what I say will be displeasing to some people.

I am subject to rages. They are not always explosive. They are sometimes what in a splendid phrase the Americans call 'a slow burn'. They are rages of a particular quality and set against particular circumstances. From Aristotle onwards—even from Hecataeus and Herodotus—the glum intellect of man has succeeded in constructing bolts and bars, fetters, locks and chains. In a world of enchantment that glum intellect has nothing to say of the fairy prince and the sleeping beauty but much to say of the tower and the dungeon. We have had great benefits from that same intellect but are having to pay for them. I say we have erected cages of iron bars; and ape-like I seize those bars and shake them with a helpless fury.

We have spoken of images. Looking out, I see with continuing astonishment the huge images, the phantasmata that condition our world. Generally these images and phantoms are connected to a single person, our demi-gods and our heroes. It was at a particular moment in the history of my own rages that I saw the Western world conditioned by the images of Marx, Darwin and Freud; and Marx, Darwin and Freud are the three most crashing bores of the

Western world. The simplistic popularization of their ideas has thrust our world into a mental straitjacket from which we can only escape by the most anarchic violence. These men were reductionist, and I believe—peering out from the middle between the bandages, saying not what I *ought* to think but what I find my centre thinking honestly because in spite of itself—I do indeed believe that at bottom the violence of the last thirty years and it may be the hyperviolence of the century has been less a revolt against the exploitation of man by man, less a sexual frustration, or an adventure in the footsteps of Oedipus, certainly less a process of natural selection operating in human society, than a revolt against reductionism, even when the revolutionary, or it may be the terrorist, does not know it.

One of the most bizarre and photogenic, or should I say filmic sights in the West is, or was, *Macey's Parade*. When I think of a procession truly emblematic of the twentieth century my memory turns to that parade but you can, I suppose, substitute some gross example of your own. I do not mean those processions which seek to preserve historical associations and which may retain a degree of dignity, but those shows which are an extended version of an advertisement for the store or company in question. The procession I saw had, towering above it, gas-filled figures of rubber or plastic. They were tethered to people walking in the procession. These gigantic objects came lurching, ducking, swaying down the main street, Mickey Mouse, Uncle Sam, Yogi Bear and a number of other folk heroes though I could not identify them. They were alike only in their grotesquerie, idiocy, their floundering, grinning, bobbing, swaying, reeling dominance of the whole scene so that they turned the scale of the people walking beneath them to that of ants. I remember one figure began to lose gas, its gross rotundity wrinkling. I remember how its attendant ants scurried round in a desperate attempt to rescue it from dissolution, tried to prop it, hold it up as they might have attempted to rescue a fading reputation or a political system in which they had invested such belief as they had, but which plainly would not work. Little by little that procession with its totemistic figures has become my metaphor for the processional life, the hurrah for X the hero, the low common denominator of belief. Down the main street of our communal awareness they come. They dwarf the human beings, dwarf the buildings. Here comes plastic Marx, bearded and bellied with 'workers of the world unite' across his vest. Darwin is inscribed with 'natural selection'. Freud stares with Jahvistic belligerence from behind his own enormous member. Whether we are in the procession and holding one of the ropes that support our idol, whether we are among the crowd on the sidewalk, or whether we work in the offices that line the street we all know to one degree or another—are *forced* to know to one degree or another—that these simplistic representations of real people are what goes on and what counts. They, inept, misleading, farcical, are what condition our communal awareness.

It may seem to you that I am exempting myself from the ant-like creatures that watch or scurry in attendance on the three major figures. Believe me, I am not. At one time or another in my life I have walked in the procession, held a rope and felt the upward tug of the gas-filled balloon. It can be a happy and perhaps rewarding experience. I may be addressing many rope-holders. Let us agree I have been one: and yet at no time could I succeed in convincing myself. For among the many rope-holders attendant on the three major figures I laboured under a singular disadvantage. I had assiduously read some of the writings of all three. It came to this at last, that I left the procession and went looking for my own belief.

Belief and creativity. Creativity and belief.

What *is* a belief? Is the act of believing definable? Certainly we can agree that most people have a simple belief that as they walk on the surface of the earth their successive steps will meet a continuing solidity. Even a molecular chemist—I mean one who is interested in them as well as constructed of them—who would assent to the proposition that the process of walking is one statistical complex meeting another, will not keep it in his awareness as he goes about his private rather than his professional business. It will be in his mind, we might say, but not in his awareness. The belief, then, is occasional, is accepted and put away. What about a political belief? Persons whose daily life is one of comparative privilege—privilege of education, intelligence, position—people whose daily belief, if they may be said to have one, is in their own rarity, their own elevation above the hurly-burly of the street, will nevertheless consider which candidate, which system they should vote for every few years and begin to decide with quite genuine feeling that they, for example, believe in democracy. The belief is taken down from the shelf as it were, dusted, used on the fourth or fifth year, used, then put back again. What about religious belief? It may be that there are still people—I cannot vouch for this but suspect it to be true—who take down a belief every Sunday morning but have it tucked away again comfortably by half-past twelve. Now people will die for democracy and die for their belief in God. But please observe I am not talking about people who have what I would call, for want of a better phrase, a genius for belief. The rare mystic who can succeed in what has been called the practice of the presence of God, regretfully, with him I have nothing to do. Some people can murder for democracy. With them I have nothing to do either. Alas, we do not pass our lives among the geniuses of belief, perhaps we may pass a long life and never meet one. If we were to meet one, it is my guess that his passing would scorch us like a blow-torch. We, the community, pass our lives with whole high-rises, whole congeries of belief inside us, seldom knowing which is going to govern us at a given moment. We do, some of us at least, muddle along through a mixture of probabilities and some plausibilities. We are too easily exhausted for the passion and fury of concentration which appears to be the way of life among the rare, uncomfortably elect. Perhaps the best analogy would be among the racing fraternity. Would I, for example, back the horse called Democracy among the many political runners of today? Well, yes. But I believe I would hedge my bets, I would back democracy for a place, I would back it both ways. I would not, like the geniuses of belief, put my shirt on it. On the other hand if you asked me whether I believe the paper before me will continue to obey the rules of physical existence I would stake any money I have on that, if only because the money would be a part of the same physical existence. But how many beliefs are of that order? The generality of us are not rash enough or brave enough or foolish enough to hurl ourselves through the open mouth of a consuming belief. Life after death? What would you bet? What a pity

pity the result cannot be monitored! We must be content with our muddling and our cloud of ignorance.

And yet, and yet. I have set over against the geniuses, the generality of us more concerned with the daily job, the effort in confusion, than with first and last things. But even that division as you know very well, must be qualified. On any of us the moment may strike, the awareness of something not argued over but directly apprehended, perception that the sun makes music as of old. As we pause, like Leopold Bloom after that long Odyssey of a single day, we may look up and be pierced by the sight of the heaven tree hung with humid night blue fruit. Music may present us with its passing ineffable proposition. We may stare through a rectangle of canvas into a magically perfect world and get a touch of paradise. Yet we must be content with memories of one level of intensity or another, memories of moments of absolute conviction, or prayer, it may be, that seemed to pierce the blank wall. That it may be of the same sort among the rare elect is illustrated in the anecdote told of Pascal. He, you will remember, had a mystical religious experience of such profundity and force, such intensity and height that he was prepared to shape his life from it. Yet he knew he would not always feel so and therefore scrawled the hopelessly inadequate words, *feu*, *joie*, on a piece of paper which he had sewn into the lapel of his coat. Then he knew that at moments when the confused levels of daily life obscured the crowning moment of it he could finger his lapel, feel the crinkle of the paper, and if not recreate the moment, at least remember the words. How can we say, simply, what he believed? How could he dare to say it and define it himself? The act of believing, the ground of believing rather than the structure built on it grows more mysterious it seems to me, the more I examine it. It grows more irrational.

What has all this, you may ask, to do with the talk a novelist might be expected to offer? More particularly, what has it to do with the writer you see before you? You may remember how, in a mutinous state, he abandoned the procession with its carnival figures. Once out of the procession and off the sidewalk a man may find himself lonely, inside if not out. The consolation of that state is a kind of riotous impiety in the face of popular, or perhaps I had better say

accepted, adages, those lighted sky-signs of the main street, its
sacred advertisements and didacticisms. These are and were the
sentences and phrases familiarity with which is sometimes taken as
evidence of a full and educated mind. Treating these catchphrases
simply as they were presented, playing their game in fact, I saw that
if beauty is in the eye of the beholder, why then, so is everything else.
Again; it was a prime tenet of classical psychology at that time that
imagination is the rearrangement of material already present in the
mind. I knew something about imagination. It was one of the few
things I felt I had experienced. Suddenly, one evening I saw that I
simply did *not* believe that tenet; and that my disbelief was as positive
as the experience. My disbelief was a positive negative. It was
passion. Here, then, was freedom! Disbelief could be as irrational as
belief and as passionate. I had left the procession, I had opted out of a
world so sane as to make nothing but nonsense! Seated one day on
the stump of a tree in a beech forest it was borne in on me that the
dialectical materialism before which we had all fallen down had feet
of clay. For though quantity did occasionally change into quality the
process was not universal and invariable. The corollary omitted by
our political simplicists was that the result of the change was
unpredictable. I have no doubt that Marx said this somewhere. He
seems to have said most things according to those who have
examined his work closely; but the crude system extracted from his
corpus of work omitted this unpredictability. I could, by including
it, account for the fact that Marxism always got the future wrong
and excelled in predicting the past. The whole of its illustrations of
human conduct was what our fellow sufferers, the French, have
called *l'esprit de l'escalier*, an expression drawn from a common
experience——the brilliant retort that occurs to us after an argument
when we are going down the stairs. Reason, when it is refined into
logic, has something to offer but only in terms of itself and depends
for its effect and use on the nature of the premise. That useful
argument as to how many angels can stand on the point of a needle
would turn into nothing without the concept of angels. I took a
further step into my new world. I formulated what I had felt against
a mass of reasonable evidence and saw that to explain the near
infinite mysteries of life by scholastic Darwinism, by the doctrine of

natural selection, was like looking at a sunset and saying, 'Someone has struck a match'. As for Freud, the reductionism of his system made me remember the refrain out of *Mariana in the Moated Grange*—'He cometh not, she said, she said I am aweary aweary, O God that I were dead!' This was my mind, not his, and I had a right to it. It was and is, surely, an impossible outcome of philosophy that Occam's razor should always shave so close there should be no reason allowed for phenomena other than the one that happens to be simplest. We question free will, doubt it, dismiss it, experience it. We declare our own triviality on a small speck of dirt circling a small star at the rim of one of countless galaxies and ignore the heroic insolence of the declaration. We have diminished the world of God and man in a universe ablaze with all the glories that contradict that diminution.

Of man and God. We have come to it, have we not? I believe in God; and you may think to yourselves—here is a man who has left a procession and gone off by himself only to end with another gas-filled image he tows round with him at the end of a rope. You would be right of course. I suffer those varying levels or intensities of belief which are, it seems, the human condition. Despite the letters I still get from people who believe me to be still alive and who are deceived by the air of confident authority that seems to stand behind that first book, *Lord of the Flies*, nevertheless like everyone else I have had to rely on memories of moments, bet on what once seemed a certainty but may now be an outsider, remember in faith what I cannot recreate. Here is no sage to bring you a distilled wisdom. Here is an ageing novelist, floundering in all the complexities of twentieth century living, all the muddle of part beliefs.

For I am only a novelist during a fraction of my time. Nor can I illustrate the link between belief and story from the novel, the quotations to be of any use would be too long. I must turn to poetry for that. Poets, I conceive—and, what is more, with a good deal of envy—are different. In the lyric at least they seem to emerge from some depth entire and effortless. We, with our huge pack of words on our backs are pedlars, the poets' poor relations. Yet we have something in common. The heart of our experience is not unlike that of the poet at his height. There is a mystery about both trades—a mystery in every sense of that ancient word. Argument, debate, exposition, can seem to come from the poet or novelist in his proper voice, voice of the householder, lover, begetter of children, traveller, swimmer, swindler, drunkard, libertine—whatever a man or woman may be; and then there will come another voice so that we hardly recognize it as the same or the person who uses it, a voice of authority, power.

We have got round at last by way of belief to creativity. It is that second voice, most succinctly to be heard in the poet.

> Hear the voice of the bard,
>   Who present, past and future sees,
> Whose ears have heard the holy word,
>   Walking among the ancient trees.

I once sat next to an eminent cleric who confided to me that apart from his hope of heaven his ambition was to retire and read the whole works of Walter Scott. I have hardly recovered from the bewilderment left in me by that remark. Indeed, Evelyn Waugh built the end of a novel round something of the same situation, so I could not even use it. But Scott was a poet—and would he had stuck to it! But listen to this which is Scott, of all people, putting the pack of a hundred thousand words into a few lines that say it all.

> Proud Maisie is in the wood,
>   Walking so early;
> Sweet robin sits on the bush
>   Singing so rarely.
> 'Tell me, thou bonny bird,
>   When shall I marry me?'
> 'When six braw gentlemen
>   Kirkward shall carry ye.'
> 'Who makes the bridal bed,
>   birdie say truly?'
> 'The grey-headed sexton
>   That delves the grave duly.
> The glow-worm o'er grave and stone
>   Shall light thee steady:
> The owl from the steeple sing
>   Welcome proud lady!'

It is that voice emerging from the most unlikely creatures that does seem to ignore all those lolling, capering, billowing figures dominating the main street of our communal awareness in the social procession. There is no argument. However brief the time during which the poet or novelist can lay his tongue to it, here is absolute conviction, a declaration to be held in the face of all the world.

What, then, of the novelist and his approach to that moment? For a great deal of his work must by the nature of the end product be workaday and pedestrian. He must labour at the world of successive events, the world of 'and then'. He lives like everyone else in the near infinite multiplicity of phenomena—in what should be and, thank God, often is, an abundance poured out for enjoyment. Yet somehow, in that abundance he must come not to the crystal of a verse but to the extended replica, map, chart, simulacrum of an abundance which is naturally indescribable. Unlike the lyricist he is a kind of diver. He goes down and it is as if he took sufficient oxygen with him for a short stay only. He is looking for a theme. This dive is something I have undertaken myself on a number of occasions but I still do not know how I do it. Nor is that all; for the diver, having mucked and mulled about down there among a host of creatures and circumstances which like real creatures of the real sea seem at a certain depth to have no real names, the diver has then to reverse and come up again, through the abundance of living to the abundance of writing about it. Nor is the ascent a mirror image of the descent. We sometimes forget that the world even the most realistic of novelists then sets about creating is still as different from the real world as difference could be.

But for all the difference the novelist offers his work in the automatic expectation of its being accepted. I do not mean we expect success in the narrow sense but that we rely on the readiness of people to perform an operation every bit as mysterious as the writing. It is our nature to receive writing. This has been called the willing suspension of disbelief, but to my mind that implies a too conscious decision and effort. A child has to make the effort when he learns, but the adult who has learnt has not. I would prefer to use a phrase of my own and hold up my hands in outright astonishment at what I will call the reader's instinctive complicity. It is his, it is our ability unconsciously to accept the scraps, the hastily gathered observations, the leaps and gambols of language and thereby share some level of reality. It is as if we were to take the stutter of the morse code and not merely hear it as a language but turn it, instant by instant into a world. Think of it! Emma Woodhouse, Fabrice, Raskolnikov are not really people. They are paragraphs in books.

I fumble. I practise a craft I do not understand and cannot describe. For if I find what I have called the reader's instinctive complicity—a psychologist would prefer me, I dare say, to make that 'habitual complicity' but who cares?—if I find that astonishing what shall I say of the facility that nature has thrust on us for the exercise of the craft itself? I will try to outwit the apparently commonplace by inviting you to go with me round the back and ambush a simple fact.

The little, lighted awareness that we call a conscious person is indescribable and incommunicable yet needs neither description nor communication since we all know it and how it is. If we cannot agree on that it is impossible to agree on anything. We are it. *It* is our burden and pleasure. The awareness is not a point, a position without magnitude, but an area. Awareness, like belief, is a matter of position in the area. We are aware perhaps of a person in the room and aware too of the wallpaper but that awareness is not in the centre of the area. This must be so. If it were not, how could the glimpsed and half-noticed events and furnishings of our sensory ambience return to us as dreams which in those nightly flights from the too bright light of full consciousness are in themselves as accepted and perhaps as unimportant as the wallpaper? Inevitably we have used a metaphor; but even the metaphor is inadequate and must change. For another dimension must be added to the area and I do not see how I can present you with a three-dimensional surface. Yet the area is moving through the third dimension of time. The playwright can have a crowd on stage, the supporting multiplicity of life may be everywhere visible be it on the stage or the screen. Who has not marvelled at some time or other to see a man or some people at least wander through the background of someone else's story? But *read* the story and the supportive multiplicity has to trail along behind you as a memory. Even if you can take in a whole page of print with a single sweep of the eye from top to bottom, essentially your reading is successive. You read as the novelist must write, one word at a time.

Well. I have tried to ambush a commonplace and do not know whether I have succeeded or not. But we ought to be up to our eyes in mystery and astonishment and we have only just begun.

Imagine him, this writer, this novelist, this story-teller, spinning a longer and longer string of single words! Imagine him at one of those lambent moments that are his equivalent of the poet's lyric impulse! There is exultation but there is also fear, sometimes a kind of terror, since the method of expression is not a few sentences but pages of them, not stanzas but incidents, an incident, a whole happening in the world that has flared up inside him so that he knows this is it, this is what the book is about, this is what he is for, or to be colloquial as the occasion demands, he knows he is on to something good! So there is terror as his pen races to overtake the event before it dims or smashes, before the details blur or vanish or stand there round him to be set down while the man from Porlock hammers on the door!

One word at a time. But consciousness is an area. There is room in the writer's awareness for more than the simulacrum of abundance however that abundance may seem to blaze. Somewhere—shall we say metaphorically?—somewhere in the shadows at the edge of the area stands a creature, an assessor, a judge, a broken-off fragment of the total personality who surveys the interior scene with a desperate calm and is aware how he wishes it to proceed. He is all the time controlling things, admonishing them. He is a divided creature. Then it may be, if he has—what? Luck? Grace? Lightning? the new thing appears from nowhere. We will stick to the spacial metaphor that I have used because here it is at the very centre. The new thing appears from a point in the area of his awareness, from a position without magnitude, which of course is quite impossible. Yet this is the occasional operation of creativity. You will remember that I said earlier how I knew that the psychologist's proposition that imagination is only the rearrangement of material in the mind, was not true. Here I present the denial again and do not argue it. The moments of genuine creativity must argue for me, if not with everybody at least with those who have experienced those moments or appreciated them; but my hope is better. The writer watches the greatest mystery of all. It is the moment of most vital awareness, the moment of most passionate and *unsupported* conviction. It shines or cries. There is the writer, trying to grab it as it passes, as it emerges impossibly and heads to be gone. It is that twist of behaviour, that phrase, sentence, paragraph, that happening on which the writer would bet his whole fortune, stake his whole life as a *true* thing. Like God, he looks on his creation and knows what he has done.

A truth. *An* unsupported conviction. *Like* God. You observe that if I am trying to give the story-teller his due I am also trying to give him no more than that. Poets in the search for that real thing may assert the same knowledge but more proudly and with Bardic aplomb.

> Mock on, mock on, Voltaire, Rousseau,
> Mock on, mock on, 'tis all in vain.
> You throw the dust against the wind
> And the wind blows it back again.

Or perhaps, proudest and most enigmatic of all:

> 'J'ai seul la clef de cette parade sauvage!'

We, the story-tellers, must produce a more bumbling truth and it has to be sought for in that extended co-operation that must go on between the novelist and his reader. Yet our feeling that we have *a* truth, if it does not shake the world is worth having on our pedestrian level. Indeed, coming up from the deep sea or back from one of those rare moments of insight one will see Macey's parade, the human procession and carnival, the 'parade sauvage' that dances down the main street of human awareness if not with a God's-eye view, then with a worm's-eye view. Your emerging literary worms are your true heretics. They have a kind of confusion about them that often cripples them for the integrated and calm traffic of daily life. Yet ironical as it may sound, the emerging worm will feel himself to be the true human being. Those of you who may still remember Peter Brook's production of the *Marat-Sade* may remember how at the end the mad men and women on the stage rushed downstage and applauded us. For we, the audience, were the true actors there where we sat in our respectable rows with all our natural instincts and impulses subdued and civil. A novelist, having gone down from the confusion of daily experience to the supportive multiplicity beneath it and down once again to the magical area of his own intuitions will come up to the scaffolding, the supportive machinery of his story. Then, finding himself faced with those carnival figures wallowing along the street will slash them to bits.

Those of you who are acquainted with anything I have written are likely to have read *Lord of the Flies*. I am not going to explicate the book for you. That has been done so often by others, has been subjected to Marxist, Freudian, neo-Freudian, Jungian, Catholic, Protestant, humanist, non-conformist analysis and opinion, has been buried with its author not just in a German reference book but under a pile of not always sweet-scented international criticism there is nothing left to say. The book yields readily to explication, to instruction, to the trephining of the pupil's skull by the teacher and the insertion into the pupil's brain by the teacher of what the pupil ought to think about it. I would like the pupil or anyone else to enjoy the book if he can. For my own part I have moved on to other books. I have always felt that a writer's books should be as different from each other as possible. Though I envy those writers who can go on writing the same book over and over again it is not something I can do myself. I do not see myself writing a book about a group of girls on an island. Yes, I have moved on. Though in general terms I would still assent to the philosophical or theological implications about the nature of man and his universe presented in the book, today, a generation later, I would qualify them as subtler and less definable than I once thought. God works in a mysterious way, says the hymn; and so, it seems, does the devil—or since that word is unfashionable I had better be democratic and call him the leader of the opposition. Sometimes the two seem to work hand in hand. Sometimes neither is on call even if you call them louder. They are asleep or away hunting perhaps—perhaps hunting each other. Not to refine upon it, my mind is all at sea. At those times I feel myself to have committed acts of fearful asseveration. How did I ever dare? Shall I ever dare again? And then—yes, I shall! The moment must return. The bare act of being is an outrageous improbability. Indeed and indeed I wonder at it. A mental attitude to which both heredity and upbringing have made me prone is a sense of continual astonishment. At times I have felt this to be a matter for congratulation. Confirmation of that can be found in most elementary Greek schoolbooks where you will find the exemplary sentence 'Wonder is the beginning of wisdom.' You cannot get straighter speaking than that, and in Greek too! I lived for years, therefore, in the happy conviction that since I had the wonder in ample supply in time the wisdom would follow. But as the revolving years revolved moments of doubt in my mind have become more numerous. Is it possible? Is nothing secure, nothing sacred, not even Greek? Yet a human life seventy years long deserves some attention. Its experience could be called a lengthy experiment the results of which might be approached with cautious respect. I herewith deliver an interim report and announce that it is possible to live astonished for a long time; and it looks increasingly possible that you can die that way too. My epitaph must be 'He wondered.' Or perhaps it should be in Greek where it would be one word only and thus economical for my heirs and assigns. As for my books—shall I adapt my favourite epitaph—that of a canon of Winchester Cathedral of whom his inscription says only 'In this building his powerful voice was singularly melodious.' No, let it be the one word only.

Let us return. What man *is*, whatever man is under the eye of heaven, that I burn to know and that—I do not say this lightly—I would endure knowing. The themes closest to my purpose, to my imagination have stemmed from that preoccupation, have been of such a sort that they might move me a little nearer that knowledge. They have been themes of man at an extremity, man tested like building material, taken into the laboratory and used to destruction; man isolated, man obsessed, man drowning in a literal sea or in the sea of his own ignorance.

I have tried to say how the process of writing such a book appears to the man who does it. You may say I take him, take myself, too seriously. Yet if there is anything of value in those books their richest moments appear to me in their genesis as mysterious as to anyone else. I will take myself and my craft now with a seriousness that may seem outrageous to you and laughable. In my awareness, in the three-dimensional absurdity of a surface moving through time, discoveries, creations appear impossibly from a point, a position without magnitude. This, then, is the terrifying thought to the frail human creature that all creation may be of the same, or a related nature. The novelist is God of his own interior world. Commonly men make God in their own image—he is a warrior, a lover, a mathematician, a father, son, mother, a remote universal and a small image in the corner of a room. Let us add our quota of inadequate description and say that he is of all things an artist who labours under no compulsion but that of his own infinite creativity. Are we, in some sense, his novels? We are said to be made in his image and if we could but understand our flashes of individual creativity we might glimpse the creativity of the ultimate Creator!

See how prose limps after the blinding fact! Verse does it better as usual.

> Flower in the crannied wall,
>   I pluck you out of the crannies,
> I hold you here, root and all, in my hand,
>   Little flower—but *if* I could understand
> What you are, root and all, and all in all,
>   I should know what God and man is.

He comes back at last not to the complexities of explanation but to the simplicity of his own awareness. If there has been any coherent argument in what I have said, it leads to a proposition that could see the end of all literary criticism and analysis, whatever you may think of that possibility. The proposition is that writing, when you get down to it, like running, like eating, like pursuit, is a simple, direct thing, uncomplicated, natural, like the act of *being*, a wholeness which is in itself a defier of analysis. It must be the muse after all!

> Goodbye Piccadilly, farewell Leicester Square;
> Où sont les neiges d'antan?
> Leavis and Trilling lay thee all adown
> My lady cometh that al this may disteyne
> βάλε δὴ βάλε κηρύλος εἴην,
> Drop it, Towser, drop it I say!

If you are a teacher or critic this may seem to you the ultimate heresy, the ultimate pessimism. Indeed, you might have expected some such conclusion for I have been called a pessimist in my time. So you might call the physician who sets out to diagnose a disease though he cannot cure it a pessimist. I should disagree with you; but after such a long, hard haul you have the right to hear what my sense of wonder has led me—not to know—but to guess about the nature of things. Though universe and cosmos are the same thing in the dictionaries I will distinguish between them, making words, like Humpty-Dumpty, mean what I tell them to. I will use cosmos to mean what Tennyson meant with all in all and all in all—the totality, God and man and everything else that *is* in every state and level of being. Universe I will use for the universe we know through our eyes at the telescope and microscope or open for daily use. Universe I use for what Bridges called 'God's Orrery'. With that distinction in mind I would call myself a universal pessimist but a cosmic optimist. The extent of my guesses is outrageous. In their irradiation I manipulate the arrangement of such lucky flashes of creativity as come my way. I guess we are in hell. We can say if we will with Marlowe's Mephistopheles, 'Why this is hell nor am I out of it.' But suffering as he was, Mephistopheles was still cunning enough not to give away the whole game. It would deny the nature of our own creativity, let alone the infinitude of God's creativity, if there were no more than one universe, one hell. There must be an infinite number of them, parallel, perhaps interpenetrating, some ugly, some beautiful, some sad, joyous—most, surely—though this may be the limitation of my own imagination—somewhat like our own, a mixture of the lot and all restless, all sustained by the creatures that inhabit them.

To be in a world which is a hell, to be *of* that world and neither to believe in nor guess at anything *but* that world is not merely hell but the only possible damnation; the act of a man damning himself. It may be—I hope it is—redemption to guess and perhaps perceive that the universe, the hell which we see for all its beauty, vastness, majesty is only part of a whole which is quite unimaginable. I have said that the act of human creativity, a newness starting into life at the heart of confusion and turmoil seems a simple thing; I guess it is a signature scribbled in the human soul, sign that beyond the transient horrors and beauties of our hell there is a Good which is ultimate and absolute.

Well there it is. Who was it said 'If Mr So-and-so has experienced the indescribable he had better not try to describe it?' An amusing remark but at the same time a pusillanimous one. It is our business to describe the indescribable. I prefer and at the same time fear the saying of St Augustine 'Woe unto me if I speak of the things of God; but woe unto me if I do *not* speak of the things of God.' I have tried and it may be, failed, to bring the disparate into equation. People who talk long enough are bound to contradict themselves at some point or a series of them. If you have detected contradictions and some screaming fallacies in what I have said, I wish you luck. I am unrepentant and about to perform the verbal equivalent of the Indian Rope Trick. You may well think that the novelist like the cobbler should stick to his last. I will claim from you the privilege, not of the psychiatrist, philosopher or theologian. I claim the privilege of the story-teller; which is to be mystifying, inconsistent, impenetrable and anything else he pleases provided he fulfils the prime clause in his unwritten contract and keeps the attention of his audience. This I appear to have done, and it is enough for me.

Nobel Lecture

Stockholm, 7 December 1983

Those of you who have some knowledge of your present speaker as revealed by the loftier-minded section of the British press will be resigning yourselves to a half-hour of unrelieved gloom. Indeed, your first view of me, white-bearded and ancient, may have turned that gloom into profound dark; dark, dark, dark, amid the blaze of noon, irrecoverably dark, total eclipse. But the case is not as hard as that. I am among the older of the Nobel Laureates and therefore might well be excused a touch of—let me whisper the word—frivolity. You see, it is hard enough at any age to address as learned a gathering as this. The very thought induces a certain solemnity. Then again, what about the dignity of age? There is, they say, no fool like an old fool.

Well, there is no fool like a middle-aged fool either. Twenty-five years ago I accepted the label 'pessimist' thoughtlessly, without realizing that it was going to be tied to my tail, as it were, in something the way that, to take an example from another art, Rachmaninov's famous Prelude in C sharp minor was tied to him. No audience would allow him off the concert platform until he played it. Similarly critics have dug into my books until they could come up with something that looked utterly hopeless. I can't think why. I don't feel hopeless myself. Indeed, I tried to reverse the process by explaining myself. Under some critical interrogation I named myself a universal pessimist but a cosmic optimist. I should have thought that anyone with an ear for language would understand that I was allowing more connotation than denotation to the word 'cosmic', though in derivation universal and cosmic mean the same thing. I meant, of course, that when I consider a universe which the scientist constructs by a set of rules which stipulate that his constructs must be repeatable and identical, then I am a pessimist and bow down before the great god Entropy. I am optimistic when I consider the spiritual dimension which the scientist's discipline forces him to ignore. So worldwide is the fame of the Nobel Prize that people have taken to quoting from my works, and I do not see why I should not join in this fashionable pastime. Twenty years ago I tried to put the difference between the two kinds of experience in the mind of one of my characters and made a mess of it. He was in prison.

All day long the trains run on rails. Eclipses are predictable. Penicillin cures pneumonia and the atom splits to order. All day long, year in, year out, the daylight explanation drives back the mystery and reveals a reality usable, understandable and detached. The scalpel and the microscope fail, the oscilloscope moves closer to behaviour.

But then:

All day long action is weighed in the balance and found not opportune nor fortunate nor ill-advised, but good or evil. For this mode which we must call the spirit breathes through the universe and does not touch it; touches only the dark things, held prisoner, incommunicado, touches, judges, sentences and passes on . . . both worlds are real. There is no bridge.

What amuses me is the thought that of course there is a bridge and that, if anything, it has been thrust out from the side that least expected it, and thrust out since those words were written. For we know now that the universe had a beginning. (Indeed, as an aside I might say we always *did* know. I offer you a simple proof and forbid you to examine it. If there was no beginning, then infinite time has already passed and we could never have got to the moment where we are.) We also know, or it is at least scientifically respectable to postulate, that at the centre of a black hole the laws of nature no longer apply. Since most scientists are just a bit religious and most religious are seldom wholly unscientific, we find humanity in a comical position. His scientific intellect believes in the possibility of miracles inside a black hole, while his religious intellect believes in them outside it. Both, you could say not wholly in jest, now believe in miracles: *credimus quia absurdum est*. Glory be to God in the highest. You will get no reductive pessimism from me.

A greater danger facing you is that an ancient schoolmaster may be carried away and forget he is not addressing a class of pupils. A man in his seventies may be tempted to think he has seen it all and knows it all. He may think that mere length of years is a guarantee of wisdom and a permit for the issuing of admonition and advice. Poor young Shakespeare and Beethoven, he thinks, dead in their youth at a mere fifty-two or -three! What could young fellows such as that know about anything? But at midnight perhaps, when the clock strikes and another year has passed, he may occasionally brood on the disadvantages of age rather than the advantages. He may regard more thoughtfully a sentence which has been called the poetry of the fact, a sentence that one of those young fellows stumbled across accidentally, as it were, since he was never old enough to have worked the thing out through living. 'Men,' he wrote, 'must endure their going hence, even as their coming hither.' Such a consideration may modify the essential jollity of an old man's nature. Is the old man right to be happy? Is there not something unbecoming in his cheerful view of his own end? The words of another English poet seem to rebuke him:

> King David and King Solomon
> Led merry, merry lives,
> With many, many lady friends
> And many, many wives;
> But when old age crept over them,

> With many, many qualms,
> King Solomon wrote the Proverbs
> And King David wrote the Psalms.

Powerful stuff that, there's no doubt about it. But there are two views of the matter; and since I have quoted to you some of my prose which is generally regarded as poetic, I will now quote to you some of my Goon or McGonagall poetry which may well be regarded as prosaic.

> Sophocles the eminent Athenian
> Gave as his final opinion
> That death of love in the breast
> Was like escape from a wild beast.
> What better word could you get?
> He was eighty when he said that.
> But Ninon de L'Enclos
> When asked the same question said, no
> She was uncommonly matey
> At eighty.

Now let us be, for a while, not serious but considerate. I myself face another danger. I do not speak in a small tribal language, as it might be one of the six hundred languages of Nigeria. Of course, the value of any language is incalculable. Your Laureate of 1979, the Greek poet Elytis, made quite clear that the relative value of works of literature is not to be decided by counting heads. It is, I think, the greatest tribute one can pay your committees that they have consistently sought for value in a work without heeding how many people can or cannot read it. The young John Keats spoke of Greek poets who 'died content on pleasant sward, leaving great verse unto a little clan'. Indeed and indeed, small can be beautiful. To quote yet another poet, prose writer though I am (you will have begun to realize where my heart is), Ben Jonson said:

> It is not growing like a tree
> In bulk, doth make men better be,
> Or standing long an oak, three hundred year,
> To fall a log at last, dry, bald and sere:

A lily of a day,
  Is fairer far in May,
Although it fall and die that night;
It was the plant and flower of light.
In small proportions we just beauties see,
And in short measures, life may perfect be.

My own language, English, I believe to have a store of poets, of writers that need not fear comparison with those of any other language, ancient or modern. But today that language may suffer from too wide a use rather than too narrow a one—may be an oak rather than a lily. It spreads right round the world as the medium of advertisement, navigation, science, negotiation, conference. A hundred political parties have it daily in their mouths. Perhaps a language subjected to such strains as that may become, here and there, just a little thin. In English too a man may think he is addressing a small, distinguished audience, or his family, or his friends, perhaps; he is brooding aloud, it may be, or talking in his sleep. Later he finds that, without meaning to, he has been addressing a large segment of the world. That is a daunting thought. It is true that this year, surrounded and outnumbered as I am by American laureates, I take a quiet pleasure in the consideration that though variants of my mother tongue may be spoken by a greater number of people than are to be found in an island off the west coast of Europe, nevertheless they are speaking dialects of what is still centrally English. Personally I cannot tell whether those many dialects are being rendered mutually incomprehensible by distance faster than they are being unified by television and satellites; but at the moment the English writer faces immediate comprehension or partial comprehension by a good part of a billion people. His critics are limited in number only by the number of the people who can read his work. Nor can he escape from knowing the worst. No matter how obscure the publication that has disembowelled him, some kind correspondent—let us call him X—will send the article along together with an indignant assurance that he, X, does not agree with a word of it. I think apprehensively of the mark I present, once a moving target but now, surely, a fixed one, before the serried ranks of those who can shoot at me if they choose. Even my most famous and distinguished fellow laureate and fellow countryman, Winston Churchill, did not escape. A critic remarked, with acid wit, of his getting the award: 'Was it for his poetry or his prose?' Indeed, it was considerations such as these which have given me, I suppose, more difficulty in conceiving, let alone writing, this lecture than any piece of comparable length since those distant days when I wrote set essays on set subjects at school. The only difference I can find is that today I write at a larger desk, and the marks I shall get for my performance will be more widely reported.

Now when, you may say, is the man going to say something about the subject which is alleged to be his own? He should be talking about the novel! Well, I will for a while, but only for a while and, as it were, tangentially. The truth is that though each of the subjects for which the prizes are awarded has its own and unique importance, none can exist wholly to itself. Even the novel, if it climbs into an ivory tower, will find no audience except those with ivory towers of their own. I used to think that the outlook for the novel was poor. Let me quote myself again. I speak of boys growing up—not exeptional boys, but average boys.

> Boys do not evaluate a book. They divide books into categories. There are sexy books, war books, westerns, travel books, science fiction. A boy will accept anything from a section he knows rather than risk another sort. He has to have the label on the bottle to know it is the mixture as before. You must put his detective story in a green paperback or he may suffer the hardship of reading a book in which nobody is murdered at all; I am thinking of the plodders, the amiable majority of us, not particularly intelligent or gifted, well-disposed but left high and dry among a mass of undigested facts with their scraps of saleable technology. What chance has literature of competing with the defined categories of entertainment which are laid on for them at every hour of the day? I do not see how literature is to be for them anything but simple, repetitive and a stop-gap for when there are no westerns on the telly. They will have a far less brutish life than their nineteenth-century ancestors, no doubt.

They will believe less and fear less. But just as bad money drives out good, so inferior culture drives out superior. With any capacity to make value judgements vitiated or undeveloped, what mass future is there, then, for poetry, for belles-lettres, for real fearlessness in the theatre, for the novel which tries to look at life anew—in a word, for intransigence?

I wrote that some twenty years ago, I believe, and the process as far as the novel is concerned has developed but not improved. The categories are more and more defined. Competition from other media is fiercer still. Well, after all, the novel has no built-in claims on immortality.

'Story', of course, is a different matter. We like to hear of a succession of events and, as an inspection of our press will demonstrate, have only a marginal interest in whether the succession of events is minutely true or not. Like the late Mr Sam Goldwyn, who wanted a story which began with an earthquake and worked up to a climax, we like a good lead-in but have most pleasure in a succession of events with a satisfactory end-point. Most simply and directly, when children holler and yell because of some infant tragedy or tedium, at once when we take them on our knee and begin shouting, if necessary, 'Once upon a time . . .', they fall silent and attentive. Story will always be with us. But story in a physical book, in a sentence, what the West means by a 'novel'—what of that? Certainly, if the form fails, let it go. We have enough complications in life, in art, in literature without preserving dead forms fossilized, without cluttering ourselves with Byzantine sterilities. Yes, in that case, let the novel go. But what goes with it? Surely something of profound importance to the human spirit! A novel ensures that we can look before and after, take action at whatever pace we choose, read again and again, skip and go back. The story in a book is humble and serviceable, available, friendly, is not switched on and off but taken up and put down, lasts a lifetime.

Put simply, the novel stands between us and the hardening concept of statistical man. There is no other medium in which we can live for so long and so intimately with a character. That is the service a novel renders. It performs no less an act than the rescue and the preservation of the individuality and dignity of the single being, be it man, woman or child. No other art, I claim, can so thread in and out of a single mind and body, so live another life. It does ensure that at the very least a human being shall be seen to be more than just one billionth of one billion.

I spoke of the ivory tower and the unique importance of each of our studies. Now I must add, having said my bit about the novel, that those studies converge, literature with the rest. Bluntly, we face two problems: either we blow ourselves off the face of the earth or we degrade the fertility of the earth, bit by bit, until we have ruined it. Does it take a writer of fiction to bring you the cold comfort of pointing out that the problems are mutually exclusive? The one problem, the instant catastrophe, is not to be dealt with here. It would be irresponsible of me to turn this platform into a stage for acting out some anti-atomic harangue and equally irresponsible at this juncture in history for me to ignore our perils. You know them as well as I do. As so often, when the unspeakable is to be spoken, the unthinkable thought, it is Shakespeare we must turn to, and I can only quote Hamlet with the skull: 'Not one now, to mock your own grinning? Quite chop-fallen? Now get you to my lady's chamber and tell her, let her paint an inch thick, to this favour she must come; make her laugh at that.' I am being rather unfair to the lady perhaps, for there will be skulls of all shapes and sizes and sexes. I speak tangentially. No other quotation gives the dirt of it all, another kind of poetry of the fact. I must say something of this danger, and I have said it, for I could do no less. Now as far as this matter is concerned, I have done.

The other danger is the more difficult to combat. To quote another laureate, our race may end not with a bang but with a whimper. It must be nearer seventy years ago than sixty that I first discovered and engaged myself to a magic place. This was on the west coast of our country. It was on the seashore among rocks. I early became acquainted with the wonderful interplay of earth and moon and sun, enjoying them at the same time as I was assured that scientifically you could not have action influenced at a distance. There was a particular phase of the moon at which the tide sank more than usually far down and revealed to me a small recess which I remember as a cavern. There was plenty of life of one sort or another round all the rocks and in the pools among them. But this pool, farthest down and revealed, it seemed, by an influence from the sky only once or twice during the times when I had the holiday privilege of living near it, this last recess before the even more mysterious deep sea, had strange inhabitants which I had found nowhere else. I can now remember and even feel, but alas not describe, the peculiar engagement, excitement and, no, not sympathy or empathy but passionate recognition of a living thing in all its secrecy and strangeness. It was, or rather they were, real as I was. It was as if the centre of our universe was there for my eyes to reach at like hands, to seize on by sight. Only a hand's breadth away in the last few inches of still water they flowered, grey, green and purple, palpably alive, a discovery, a meeting, more than an interest or pleasure. They were life; we together were delight itself, until the first ripples of returning water blurred and hid them. When the summer holidays were over and I went back again about as far from the sea as you can get in England I carried with me like a private treasure the memory of that cave——no, in some strange way I took the cave with me and its creatures that flowered so strangely. In nights of sleeplessness and fear of the supernatural I would work out the phase of the moon, returning in thought to the slither and clamber among the weeds of the rocks. There were times when, though I was far away, I found myself before the cavern watching the moon-dazzle as the water sank, and was comforted somehow by the magical beauty of common world.

I have been back since. The recess——for now it seems no more than that——is still there, and at low-water springs, if you can bend down far enough, you can still look inside. Nothing lives there any more. It is all very clean now, ironically so——clean sand, clean water, clean rock. Where the living creatures once clung they have worn two holes like the orbits of eyes, so that you might well sentimentalize yourself into the fancy that you are looking at a skull. No life.

Was it a natural process? Was it fuel oil? Was it sewage or chemicals more deadly that killed my childhood's bit of magic and mystery? I cannot tell and it does not matter. What matters is that this is only one tiny example among millions of how we are impoverishing the only planet we have to live on.

Well, now, what has literature to say to that? We have computers and satellites, we have ingenuities of craft that can land a complex machine on a distant planet and get reports back. And so on. You know it all as well as and better than I. Literature has words only, a tool as primitive as the flint axe or even the soft copper chisel with which man first carved his own likeness in stone. That tool makes a poor showing, one would think, among the products of the silicon chip. But remember Churchill. For despite the cynical critic, he got the Nobel Prize neither for poetry nor for prose. He got it for about a single page of simple sentences which are neither poetry nor prose but are what, I repeat, has been called, finely, the poetry of the fact. He got it for those passionate utterances which were the very stuff of human courage and defiance. Those of us who lived through those times know that Churchill's poetry of the fact changed history.

Perhaps, then, the soft copper chisel is not so poor a tool after all. Words may, through the devotion, the skill, the passion and the luck of writers, prove to be the most powerful thing in the world. They may move men to speak to each other because some of those words somewhere express not just what the writer is thinking but what a huge segment of the world is thinking. They may allow man to speak to man, the man in the street to speak to his fellow until a ripple becomes a tide, running through every nation, of common sense, of simple healthy caution, a tide that rulers and negotiators cannot ignore, so that nation does truly speak unto nation. Then there is hope that we may learn to be temperate, provident, taking no more from nature's treasury than is our due. It may be by books, stories, poetry, lectures that we who have the ear of mankind can move man a little nearer the perilous safety of a warless and provident world. It cannot be done by the mechanical constructs of overt propaganda. I cannot do it myself, cannot now create stories which would help to make man aware of what he is doing, but there are others who can, many others. There always have been. We need more humanity, more care, more love. There are those who expect a political system to produce that, and others who expect the love to produce the system. My own faith is that the truth of the future lies between the two, and we shall behave humanly and a bit humanely, stumbling along, haphazardly generous and gallant, foolishly and meanly wise until the rape of our planet is seen to be the preposterous folly that it is.

For we are a marvel of creation. I think in particular of one of the most extraordinary women, dead now these five hundred years, Juliana of Norwich. She was caught up in the spirit and shown a thing that might lie in the palm of her hand and in the bigness of a nut. She was told it was the world. She was told of the strange and wonderful and awful things that would happen there. At the last, a voice told her that all things should be well and all manner of things should be well and all things should be very well.

Now we, if not in the spirit, have been caught up to see our earth, our mother, Gaia Mater, set like a jewel in space. We have no excuse now for supposing her riches inexhaustible nor the area we have to live on limitless because unbounded. We are the children of that great blue-white jewel. Through our mother we are part of the solar system and part, through that, of the whole universe. In the blazing poetry of the fact we are children of the stars.

I had better come down, I think. Churchill, Juliana of Norwich, let alone Ben Jonson and Shakespeare—Lord, what company we keep! Reputations grow and dwindle and the brightest of laurels fade. That very practical man, Julius Caesar—whom I always think of, for a reason you may guess at, as Field Marshal Lord Caesar—Julius Caesar is said to have worn a laurel wreath to conceal his baldness. While it may be proper to praise the idea of a laureate the man himself may very well remember what his laurels will hide—and that not only baldness. In a sentence, he must remember not to take himself with unbecoming seriousness. Fortunately, some spirit or other—I do not presume to put a name to it—ensured that I should remember my smallness in the scheme of things. The very day after I learned that I was the laureate for literature for 1983 I drove into a country town and parked my car where I should not. I only left the car for a few minutes, but when I came back there was a ticket taped to the window. A traffic warden, a lady of a minatory aspect, stood by the car. She pointed to a notice on the wall. 'Can't you read?' she said. Sheepishly I got into my car and drove very

Nobel Lecture

slowly round the corner. There on the pavement I saw two county policemen. I stopped opposite them and took my parking ticket out of its plastic envelope. They crossed the road to me. I asked if, as I had pressing business, I could go straight to the Town Hall and pay my fine on the spot. 'No, sir,' said the senior policeman, 'I'm afraid you can't do that.' He smiled the fond smile that such policemen reserve for those people who are clearly harmless, if a bit silly. He indicated a rectangle on the ticket that had the words 'name and address of sender' printed above it. 'You should write your name and address in that place,' he said. 'You make out a cheque for £10, making it payable to the Clerk to the Justices at *this* address written here. Then you write the same address on the outside of the envelope, stick a 16-penny stamp in the top right-hand corner of the envelope then post it. And may we congratulate you on winning the Nobel Prize for Literature.'